Full Figured 14:

Carl Weber Presents

Full Figured 14:

Carl Weber Presents

La Jill Hunt

And Latoya Chandler

www.urbanbooks.net

Urban Books, LLC
300 Farmingdale Road, NY-Route 109
Farmingdale, NY 11735

ISBN 13: 978-1-64556-102-6
ISBN 10: 1-64556-102-X

First Mass Market Printing October 2020
First Trade Paperback Printing October 2019
Printed in the United States of America

10 9 8 7 6 5 4 3 2 1

Distributed by Kensington Publishing Corp.
Submit Orders to:
Customer Service
400 Hahn Road
Westminster, MD 21157-4627
Phone: 1-800-733-3000
Fax: 1-800-659-2436

No Strings Attached

by

La Jill Hunt

Chapter One

Brooke

"Well, look who decided to grace us with her presence today."

I looked over at Helen Tolbert, the administrative assistant for my department, and gave her a smirk. "Well, I would be here more often if you'd quit sending me away for weeks at a time."

"Hey, I can't help it if you're the best corporate trainer in the entire company." She grinned at me. "And you are wearing that blouse, girl. Let me have it when you're done with it. Besides. you never wear the same thing twice."

I looked down at the belted yellow pantsuit I was wearing and smiled. "Now, what in the world would you do with this top, Miss Helen? It's about three sizes too big for you, and you know it. And I do wear a lot of things more than twice, ma'am."

The reality was that the shirt was probably more like five sizes too large for her, especially since it was a size twenty and Miss Helen had to be no bigger than a size four. But I appreciated the compliment. I prided myself on staying trendy. Just because I was a big girl didn't mean I couldn't be fashionable and fly. Some plus-sized women wouldn't dare wear the bright yellow ensemble I was rocking. Not me. I had taken one look at the overpriced suit and had known it would be a head turner, and I had instantly had to have it.

"Brooke, I keep telling you you'd be perfect for my nephew. He's smart, handsome, and he's a doctor. You're his type," Miss Helen told me for what had to be the hundredth time. Every time she saw me, she had to say something about her nephew.

"Thanks, Miss Helen, but I'm good," I told her.

"You have a new man in your life?" Her eyes widened, and her head tilted slightly.

"I'm not saying all that," I said. "But I'm not interested in dating."

"You've been saying that for years, young lady. You're too good looking and successful to be walking around here without a ring on your finger." Miss Helen shook her head.

She was a slightly older woman who put me in the mind of Louise on the old TV sitcom *The Jeffersons*. I really liked her, and not just because she handled the department travel arrangements and always looked out for me, making sure I always flew business class and stayed in the nicest hotels. She also made sure I got the inside scoop on the office happenings and all the gossip, which I appreciated.

I'd worked for Worldwide Holdings, a Fortune 500 company that owned several rental car companies, since graduating from college six years ago. In addition to providing me a moderate salary, a nice yearly bonus, and great benefits, they'd paid for both of my master's degrees, all of which I enjoyed. I even enjoyed all the traveling that I was required to do. But because I was out of my home office so much, I was sometimes blindsided by decisions that affected me, though I had not been consulted about them. Being buddy-buddy with Miss Helen sometimes prevented that from happening.

"Miss Helen, you've seen my schedule. Do you think I have time to date anyone? I'm gone three to six weeks at a time, what amounts to several months of the year," I said. "I'm sure your nephew is really nice, but I won't even get the chance to find out for myself, because I will be gone all the time."

"You'd make a perfect couple, Brooke. Trust me."

I wanted to ask Miss Helen why, if her nephew was so great, he was still single after all this time, but I didn't want to run the risk of starting that conversation. Besides, I knew there was probably a pile of intercompany mail piled on my desk for me to handle, along with the other endless tasks I had to take care of on the day I returned to the office.

"I'll talk to you later, Miss Helen," I said and then waved before I walked away from her desk and down the hallway. I opened the door to my small office, and just as I had suspected, I was welcomed by a pile of folders and mail on top of my desk. I placed my messenger bag on one of the small chairs that faced my desk, and immediately reached for the gallon jug of water under my desk and filled my aromatherapy diffuser. I always felt the need to air out and Zen my work space as part of my morning routine.

Tap. Tap. Tap.

"Good morning," said a male voice.

I turned around to see Brandon, my boss, standing in my doorway.

"Good morning to you."

"What's good, Brooke?" he asked as he strolled inside. "I see you 'bout to Badu-ify it up in here." He shook his head at me as I put drops of essential oils in the water and turned the tiny machine on.

"*Badu-ify*? Is that even a word?" I laughed. "Don't hate because I'm trying to ignite positive vibes in here."

"Your positivity is enough to brighten any room." Brandon smiled. "You're looking good."

I stood back and stared at him. He was looking well put together, as usual, in his perfectly fitting slacks and crisp white shirt with the collar open. I didn't even have to look down at his shoes, which I already knew were stylish and expensive, the only kind he wore. His handsome face was clean shaven, and his haircut fresh. His deep-set eyes were damn near as perfect as his smooth reddish-brown skin and white teeth. He was good looking, and he knew it, but not in an arrogant way. He was an all-around nice guy that everyone liked, including me . . . most of the time. But we had a history, and he had a tendency to try to use that to his advantage.

"What do you want, Brandon?" I asked, my bullshit meter suddenly alerting me.

"What? I can't give you a compliment?" he asked innocently.

"You can. But what do you want?" I repeated.

Brandon turned around and closed the door, letting me know that whatever he was about to tell me was going to make me either super happy or super pissed, both of which would cause a reaction that he didn't want the rest of the office to hear. He pulled the empty chair closer to my desk and sat down.

"Oh, I *know* this is about to be some BS." I shook my head and waited for him to speak.

"Okay, Brooke. Check it," he said. "I know you just got back, but—"

"No. Hell no. Absolutely not, Brandon," I told him before he could even finish his sentence.

"Wait. Just listen for a sec."

"No, I'm not listening. Come on, Brandon. I'm not scheduled to go anywhere else for a month. You promised me if I took this last training class, I was good for a minute. Now here you go," I snapped.

"I know, I know. But this isn't even for a full training. It's just a week in Denver," he explained.

"Denver? Oh, hell no. Send someone else, because I'm not going," I told him.

"Brooke, come on. I don't have anyone else to send."

"Send Holly's ass. She never has to carry her ass anywhere. She stays here and does what? She damn sure doesn't train, because I have to do the in-house classes here too, for some odd reason," I said, referring to my young blond coworker, whose only job responsibilities seemed to be putting up colorful bulletin boards in the office, planning potlucks for staff birthdays, and making sure everyone pulled a name for the Christmas gift exchange every year.

"Come on, Brooke," Brandon pleaded.

"Come on what? Why can't she go?" I asked. "If it's not for a full training, then you go, Brandon. You've done it plenty of times to do a short run."

"I can't go this time."

"And why not?" I peered at him.

His eyes went from mine down to the humming diffuser, then back up to meet mine. "Brooke, I need you in Denver. I'll have Helen book your flight for tomorrow."

"Oh, now you are really tripping. Today is Wednesday, and today is my first day back in the office. And you think I'm leaving tomorrow? You are really tripping, Brandon." I sucked my teeth at him. Anyone else in my position might be a little hesitant to talk to their boss in the manner in which I was speaking, but I'd known Brandon since before we'd both become employees at Worldwide.

"I gave you Monday and Tuesday off. I always give you a couple of days off when you come back after a full training assignment, Brooke, and you know I wouldn't be asking you to do this if I didn't have to," Brandon said. "I tell you what. Let's compromise. You can leave Saturday night and be ready to go on Monday. It is just a basic cross-training between billing and claims and is mainly for managers."

"If it's management training, then why the hell aren't you handling it?"

"Because I have something important to do next week and can't leave."

"Listen, I don't care what chick you got plans with. You gonna either have to take her with you or find someone else to go, because . . ."

"It's not a chick."

"Then why the hell can't you go?"

Brandon inhaled. He lowered his voice when he said, "I have to be here for the board meeting."

My eyes narrowed. "For what? Why would you need to meet with them?"

Again, Brandon's eyes dropped, confirming that there was something he wasn't telling me. But I was determined to find out whatever he had going on.

"Brandon," I said with a warning tone.

"Okay, but you can't say anything," he said.

"About what?" I waited for his answer.

"I'm being considered for an associate vice president spot."

"What AVP spot? There isn't an AVP spot available." I knew this to be true, because checking the company job vacancies web page was something I did religiously. Not only did this give me a heads-up about areas to which I may be sent to train new hires, but it also enabled me to see if there was another job that piqued my interest, not that I was looking for one. Besides, if there was a position available and Brandon was interviewing for it, Miss Helen would tell me, and she hadn't mentioned anything at all for quite some time. Oddly enough, she hadn't even mentioned the possibility that I would be going to Denver, so she probably didn't know about that either.

"It's not available, because it's being created, and I've already been approached to fill it," Brandon told me.

I pulled my chair out from under the desk and sat in it. I mentally spoke to myself as if I was speaking to one of my students. I told myself to think before speaking and to make sure I asked the right questions, to get all the answers I needed. Brandon was smart and educated, and he was well respected by everyone in the company, from the regional director to the janitor. He also knew how to play the corporate game very well. But he was fair, and he was a great manager, even to me. The fact that he was to be promoted came as no surprise to me. The fact that he was to be appointed a vice president was what was shocking.

"What position is this exactly?" I asked.

"AVP of diversity and inclusion. In light of recent events, the company is trying to identify measures to ensure we are meeting the needs of all members of society when it comes to—"

"They're trying to fix the racist and sexist bullshit now that we've been put on blast on social media. Call it what it is, Brandon. Both you and I know what the deal is. Certain locations were denying black and Latino customers the opportunity to rent certain cars. Plain and simple, they were profiling, and although it's not illegal, it's bad business, period," I said matter-of-factly.

"Well, that's another way of putting it." He shrugged.

"So, they're bringing in you, the token black man, to save face." I shrugged.

"Hold up. Don't act like I'm not deserving of this opportunity. I bust my ass around here the same way you do, and you know it," he said.

"You're right, and I'm sorry. This is actually a good look for you, Brandon. Congrats." I paused for a moment to think. "But the real question is, Once you're promoted, who gets your job?" I asked, suddenly realizing this meant that I would finally be getting the chance I'd been waiting for.

Brandon's eyes met mine, and he gave me a half smile, instead of the grin I was expecting. "All right, so . . ."

"You're kidding, right?" I threw my hands up in frustration.

"You know yours was the first name I said," he told me.

"And?"

"It's kinda like this. If you're promoted to management, then that means—"

"That means that y'all won't have anyone to send all around the damn country, doing everyone else's job. That's what that means." I sat back and fought back tears of anger, which were now threatening to fall.

"You know you're the best corporate trainer we have, Brooke. That goes without saying."

"Which is why I deserve this," I snapped.

"You do, but right now, we have too many upcoming . . ."

"The crazy part is that one of the main reasons you're even being promoted is that I help make you look good. You promised me that once you got a regional position, you were going to make sure I got your spot. And now here you are, telling me this bullshit." I shook my head in disbelief.

"Brooke, I know you're pissed right now, but I promise I'm gonna make this right. I just need for you to go to Denver and let me get through this process." Brandon sounded sincere, but I was too angry to accept what he was saying.

"Man, you just told me that they wouldn't even consider me. Why should I continue bending over backward for something that ain't gonna happen?" I asked. "Basically, what you're saying is I'm overqualified for the job I've been bending over backward to get. Ain't that some shit?"

"That's not what I'm saying at all." Brandon stood up and leaned across my desk, nearly knocked over my diffuser as he put his hands on my shoulders. He stared at me intensely and said, "I promised you when I got this job that I had your back, and I meant that. We go back a long time, even before working here, and you know when it's all said and done, we're friends. You're right.

You've gone above and beyond and helped me get this department to be the best. I told you what they said when I mentioned you, but now we know where their head is. Now we just have to make them see otherwise. If I don't know nothing else, I know how to play this game and win."

The sincerity in his eyes and the wisdom of what he was saying caused me to relax in my seat. Brandon had always kept it real with me, and I really didn't have a reason not to trust him. I inhaled the scent of rosemary and sandalwood from my diffuser and closed my eyes, then opened them. "I'm taking the rest of the week off. As a matter of fact, I'm leaving the office as soon as I finish my report and clear my desk. Oh, and this is comp time and doesn't come out of my vacation bank. I have something to do Friday and Saturday night, just so you know."

"My girl." Brandon smiled at me. "And I got you on all of that, and I'll make sure you fly out Sunday morning."

"You'd better," I told him.

"So, what you got going for this weekend?" He raised an eyebrow and sat back down in the chair, then put his hands behind his head.

"None of your business," I said. My cell phone, which was lying on my desk, began ringing, and the picture of my best friend appeared on the screen. I answered the call. "Hey, Em."

"What's up? How's your first day back?" Emory asked. We'd worked together at Worldwide Holdings for nearly six years, and she'd become more like a sister than a coworker. Emory was the one person I could confide in without having to worry about judgement, no matter what the situation was. She was also one of the few people in the office whose shoe collection could compete with mine.

"Girl." I sighed.

"That bad, huh?" She laughed.

"Hey, Em!" Brandon yelled out.

"Hey, Bran," Emory yelled, so loud that I held the phone from my ear.

"Don't speak to him," I told her. "We're not friends with him right now."

"That's not true, Em. Don't listen to her," Brandon yelled.

"So, I guess you're working through lunch." Emory laughed.

"As a matter of fact, I'm leaving for the day in a little while. I can meet you wherever." I glanced over at Brandon, making sure he understood that I meant what I had said earlier.

"Uh, okay. Is something wrong?" Emory replied. "Is he tripping again about what happened last time?"

The "last time" that Emory was referring to was an incident that had occurred six months ago, when Brandon and I had both attended a weeklong training conference in San Francisco. One night, we drank too much at the hotel bar, and I ended up in his hotel room. It wasn't the first time we'd had sex—we'd done so a couple of times during grad school—but I assured him that it would be the last. As much as I enjoyed it, I'd learned a long time ago that sleeping with a coworker brought a lot of drama along with it, and I didn't do drama. There was also the fact that he was now my boss. He had attempted a time or two since then and would occasionally flirt, but he had finally accepted that it wouldn't be happening again, and we continued to have a great working relationship.

"Nope, not at all. But I'll tell you later. Text me where you wanna meet and what time," I told her, then hung up.

"Well, I guess I'll get out of here so you can finish up. I'll make sure Holly gets the materials sent out to the Denver office, so you'll have everything you need for the week." He stood up.

"Please don't have Holly do me any favors," I said sarcastically. "She's already so busy."

"Funny. Thanks again, Brooke. I really appreciate you. Enjoy your time off doing whatever it is you're gonna do." He shrugged.

"Thanks, Brandon. I will," I said. "But trust me when I say this. If I get shit on with this promotion thing, Holly will have plenty of stuff to do around here."

"Understood," Brandon said. And just before he walked out of my office, he added, "I'd been looking forward to seeing you this week in the office. Lord knows you stay looking beautiful."

"Bye, Brandon." I couldn't help smiling as he closed the door behind him.

Chapter Two

Brittany

"Ms. Newman, we need you down here in D-thirty-six ASAP," the voice announced through the walkie-talkie attached to my hip. I looked at my watch. It was after two o'clock, and I was trying to leave on time for a change. I had already had a long day and had addressed the pile of paperwork on my desk that I'd needed to get through.

I pushed the button on the side of the walkie-talkie and, not trying to hide the irritation in my voice, asked, "What's the problem?"

"It's Marlena again. She's having a meltdown and threatening to take her clothes off," was the response.

I exhaled loudly and stood up, then stretched before I took the long walk up the flight of stairs and down the corridor to get to the recreation room, hoping to arrive before thirteen-year-old Marlena got naked in front of everyone, as she'd done several times before. As I moved as quickly as possible, I promised myself for the hundredth time that I was going to start going to the gym or at least walking in the evenings. I knew I was lying to myself, because by the time I usually left work, it was too late, and I was too tired to do anything other than go home, take a shower, eat, and go to bed.

"Where is she?" I asked when I got to the recreation room.

"Right over there, Ms. Newman. I told her you were coming down here," Crystal, one of the rec aides, announced loudly.

I looked over to where she was pointing, and there was Marlena, singing and rolling on the floor, barefoot and wearing only her white uniform shirt and flowered underwear. I was slightly grateful that most of her body was still covered.

"Marlena!"

The sound of my voice yelling her name caused her to stop rolling, and she slowly sat up, turned around, and looked at me. Her eyes were wide, and she looked shocked that I was in the room, even though she'd been warned.

"I told you." Crystal nodded and folded her arms.

"She sure did," said another one of the aides.

"I love it. I love it. I love it," Marlena said, and then she went back to singing loudly. But instead of rolling around, she began rocking back and forth.

The room erupted in laughter.

I looked around at the other students, who were watching and pointing. "Ms. Crystal, you all take the other students out of here while I handle this, please," I said.

"Where you want us to take them?" Crystal asked. "It's too late to go outside. And the other classrooms on this floor are either locked or have students."

"Take them down to the gymnasium," I told her. "It's open."

"But I thought Mr. McGee told us to wait here until the buses come," Crystal said, having to yell over Marlena and her laughing audience.

Before I could stop myself, I turned and snapped, "I don't care what Mr. McGee said. Get these students out of here."

"Yes, ma'am. Come on, everyone. Line up," Crystal said in a not too pleasant voice. I didn't care. I was too busy making my way over to Marlena, who was now pulling at the bottom of her shirt.

"Get your tail up and put your pants on. Now!" I said through clenched teeth.

At first, she didn't move and just stared at me as she continued singing. Then I grabbed her by the shoulder, and she stopped. "Ouch."

"You heard what I told you to do. Why are you in here acting a fool, Marlena? I told you the next time you felt the need to be a stripper in this building, you were getting put out. So, now let's go." I frowned as I looked around for her clothes. I spotted one sock under a nearby table and her brown shoes across the room. I still didn't see her pants anywhere. "Find those pants, so we can get to Mr. McGee's office and call your mother."

"I don't wanna get put out," Marlena whined. She was a pretty girl with bright eyes and a small dimple. Her hair, which her mother kept cut short, because Marlena would pull it out when she got angry, was standing on top of her head.

"I don't care what you want to do."

"I'm sorry," she pleaded.

"I don't wanna hear that. You weren't sorry when you were in here disrobing, were you?" I said, grabbing her sock and shoes and still looking for her pants.

"I told Ms. Crystal I was hot and needed some water," Marlena tried to explain.

I turned back around and said, "So, because she wouldn't let you get some water, you decided to do this? It's fifteen minutes until the buses come. You couldn't stop and get water in the hallway on the way to the bus?"

Marlena looked at me as if I'd just announced a way to end world hunger. "Oh."

"Oh, nothing. Find your pants and let's go." I sighed. "The buses are going to be outside in a minute."

"Ms. Newman, I'm gonna be good, I promise. I don't want no days," she pleaded again.

"Marlena, you said that last time."

"I know. But this time, I promise." She hopped up and reached behind the small bookshelf that she had been crawling in front of. Seconds later, her pants and her other sock were in her hand, and she pulled them on. She rubbed her hand through her hair and innocently asked, "Can I just go wait in your office, Ms. Newman? Please?"

If I had told anyone that moments before she had been acting like a wild banshee, they wouldn't have believed me. She looked like a normal ninth grader waiting to go home for the day. But I knew better. I'd been a social worker at the high school for almost four years, and prior to that, a special education teacher, but I'd never dealt with a student more challenging than Marlena. Although she was smart and funny, she was a handful, and I was one of the few people in the building that could handle her, which was why when she got out of control, I was the first point of contact. She responded well to me, like most of the other students with behavioral and emotional problems. I was kind and patient with them, but I was stern. They knew I did not play.

"Get up, put your shoes on, and let's go," I told her. "You have thirty seconds, and I mean it."

Just then Mr. McGee, the school principal, walked into the recreation room. "Ms. Newman, everything okay in here?" he asked. "I heard Marlena was having a moment."

I looked at him, thinking how convenient it was for him to arrive right when I had the situation handled. He had the same walkie-talkie that I did, and I knew he had heard them call me. There wasn't that much perfect timing in the world.

"She was, but she's getting herself together, and we were just about on our way to the office to see you. Right, Marlena?" I said.

"Yes," Marlena whined. "But I don't want no days."

"Come on. Let's go discuss it," I said with a smile, to make her feel a little more at ease and hopefully move a little faster. Honestly, it was up to Mr. McGee whether or not she got suspended. But considering that the last time she decided to undress, he had sent her home for two days, it was probably inevitable that she was going to get the unwanted vacation. But I was tired, and the sooner we got to his office, the sooner I could get back to my workload and go home.

"Okay." She sighed and slipped her feet into her shoes.

We followed Mr. McGee out the door and headed to his office.

"Let's take the elevator," he suggested. "We'll get there a little quicker."

We climbed on the elevator, which was only for staff and handicapped students, and he pressed the number for the bottom floor. Marlena stood in the corner, a sad look on her face. As soon as the elevator started moving, there was a jerk, and then it stopped.

"What in the world?" Mr. McGee said, looking around.

"Ugh. We're stuck," I groaned.

"What? We're stuck? We're stuck?" Marlena gasped and crouched on the floor.

"Calm down," I said softly.

"I can't believe this." Mr. McGee began pressing all the buttons on the panel. I could see that he was just as agitated as Marlena.

"What are you doing?" I asked him. "Why are you pressing all of those?"

"I'm trying to get us out of here. We can't be stuck," he said, his voice an octave higher than normal.

"Press the emergency button. Maintenance will hear it," I commanded.

"I did," he yelled.

Marlena began yelling. "We're stuck, Ms. Newman. We're stuck in here."

"Calm down, Marlena," I said, trying to remain as relaxed as possible.

"We need to get out of here." Beads of sweat were forming on Mr. McGee's forehead, and he loosened his tie. He took out his cell phone, examined it, and said, "I don't have any service to call anyone."

"We need to get out. We need to get out now!" Marlena jumped up and shouted. Her hands grabbed the metal bar at the back of the elevator, and she swayed back and forth, causing the small car to rock a little.

"Marlena! *Stop it*!" I commanded. She slowly eased back onto the floor. My heart began racing. I had to do something. I reached for my walkie-talkie and said into it, "This is Ms. Newman. We are stuck in the staff elevator. Can someone call maintenance and get us out of here ASAP?"

"Ten-four, Ms. Newman. We're on it," someone responded.

I turned to Marlena and said, "See? They're coming. We'll be out of here in a minute. Okay?"

"Yes, ma'am." She nodded, tears forming in her eyes.

I leaned beside her and closed my eyes. My blood pressure was already up, and this situation wasn't helping at all. All I wanted to do was leave work on time for a change. And here I was, stuck in a death trap with a scary-ass boss and a freaked-out student.

Moments later, there was a jerk, and we began descending. When we stopped, the elevator doors opened. I was relieved.

"Everybody okay?" one of the maintenance men asked.

"We're fine, Chuck. No worries." Mr. McGee shook his hand as he stepped off the elevator.

I reached down and helped Marlena to her feet. "See, I told you we would be okay."

She stood, and after we stepped off, she gave me a big hug. "Thanks, Ms. Newman. I love you."

"I know you do, sweetie." I rubbed the top of her head.

"Mr. McGee was scared, huh?" she asked, and we both glanced over at him as he talked with the maintenance man.

I nodded and whispered, "Yeah, he was."

We both laughed, and she said, "But you weren't. You made sure we were safe. You knew it, huh? Right then, you knew it. How?"

The bell rang, and students came swarming into the hallway from their classrooms. I looked at Marlena and said, "Go ahead, so you don't miss your bus."

"Huh?" She looked confused.

"We're gonna have a better day tomorrow, right? Promise me." I stared into her face. "If you don't, I'm gonna make sure you get so many days, you won't come back until after spring break."

"I promise, Ms. Newman." Marlena hugged me again and then took off down the hallway.

"Marlena, walk!" I yelled behind her.

"Why did you do that?" Mr. McGee's voice came over my shoulder. "You just let her go home?"

I turned to see the look of irritation on his face. "I figured she'd had enough drama for the day. Being in that elevator was punishment enough. She'll be fine the rest of the week."

"And next week?" he asked.

"I can't really say, Mr. McGee, but my grandmother used to say that sometimes it takes only one moment for your entire life to change. Maybe that elevator was her moment."

"Well, just so you know, if it wasn't, the next time she clowns, she's getting ten days," he said and walked off.

By the time I finished work, fought traffic, and made it home, it was after seven o'clock. I went straight into my bedroom, took off my clothes, and just before jumping into a hot shower, I ordered a pizza and some wings for dinner. I was standing in the shower and allowing the water to remove the stress of my day when I heard my name being called.

"Britt, where you at?" called Duane, my boyfriend. He was nearly yelling.

"I'm in the shower," I yelled back.

Grabbing my scented body gel, I hurried and finished washing up. I stepped out of the shower and wrapped my favorite robe around my body without bothering to dry off. Maybe seeing my damp body would be a turn-on for him. They said sex was a stress reliever, and I needed some relief badly. When I opened the door, Duane was sitting on the edge of my bed, flipping through the TV channels.

"Babe, don't sit on the bed with your work clothes on."

"I'm on the foot. Don't nobody lay their head down here. Damn. I just got here. Don't start tripping already," Duane groaned, his eyes still on the television.

"I'm not tripping. All I'm saying is—"

"You ain't cook?" he interrupted.

"No. I got home late," I said. "I texted you before I left school, and traffic was horrible."

"You complaining about me sitting on the bed in my work gear, but your clothes you wore to work are tossed on the bed. What's the difference?" he asked.

"The difference is I work in a school building and you work outside," I said as I looked for a pair of sweatpants and an oversize T-shirt to wear to bed, because clearly sex wasn't happening. I was tired, irritated, and Duane was being an asshole, something he was being more and more frequently these days.

At that moment the doorbell rang.

"Who the hell is that?" Duane frowned and stood up.

"It's probably the pizza I ordered," I told him, slipping my shirt over my head.

"Pizza? Damn. That's what I had for lunch. I don't want no pizza." The way he said it put me in the mind of Marlena complaining earlier.

I inhaled and reminded myself not to allow the frustrations of my job to spill over into my home. "I didn't know. I ordered wings too, though, if you want."

"What I want is a home-cooked meal. Man, Britt, you used to cook all the time, but now you barely even cut on the stove." Duane shook his head at me.

The doorbell rang again, and I went to answer the door. The pizza and wings had arrived. I thanked the driver and took the food. I was on my way to the kitchen with it when Duane came out of the bedroom and headed toward the front door.

"Where are you going?" I asked.

"I don't want no pizza, I told you. And I don't want no wings, either. I'm 'bout to go by my sister's crib and get a plate, and then I'm going home," he said.

I stopped and stared at him. "Really, Duane?"

"Yeah. I'll hit you up later. I had a long day at work, and I'm tired and hungry. I'm not in the mood to argue." He reached for the door handle.

I wanted to tell him that he wasn't the only one who had had a long day, and that I was just as tired as he was and had no intentions of arguing. I wanted to ask him why he had had such a short fuse and had been so irritated with me lately, but instead, I said, "I understand. I'm gonna eat and go to bed myself."

Duane barely brushed his lips across my cheek and walked out the door without saying anything else.

I went into the kitchen, and after putting one slice of the pie and two wings on a paper plate, I went back into my bedroom and got into bed. I looked at the clothes that I'd taken off earlier, now neatly folded and in a pile on the edge of my bed, and thought about Duane's comment. Had I overreacted when I came out of the bathroom and saw him sitting on the side of my bed in his dirty work clothes? Maybe I should've waited until he got here and asked him what he wanted for dinner before I ordered food. Had I been inconsiderate? My already bad day had gotten worse, and now I was crying. I needed to vent. I needed to talk.

I needed my sister.

Chapter Three

Brooke

My phone rang. I picked it up off the bar, and seeing that it was my sister calling, I answered. "Hello."

"Hey. Are you busy?" Brittany asked. I could tell by the sound of her voice that something was wrong.

"Pouring a glass of wine. What's going on?" I said, picking up my glass and heading over to the sofa.

"I don't know. Today at work was just . . . exhausting, I guess," Brittany told me. "I had a student take her clothes off, and then we got stuck in the elevator."

"I understand. And what else happened?" I knew there was more to this than her just having a bad day at work. My sister dealt with bad kids all the time, and when emergency situations went down, she was in her element. Not saying that what she did was easy, because that would be far from the truth. But my instincts were telling me that something else was bothering her.

"Duane was in a bad mood. He's been in a bad mood a lot lately, Brooke. It's like I can't do anything right. I know he's under a lot of pressure at work, but so am I, and he doesn't seem to understand that," Brittany explained.

I knew I had to choose my words carefully. My sister had a tendency to become quite defensive when it came to her man. Despite her nonstop roller coaster of a relationship with Duane, she seemed to think he was the greatest thing in the world. I wasn't impressed. I had learned a long time ago that Brittany loved being in love. She was rarely single.

"Have you told him how you feel?" I asked, knowing that she probably hadn't. My twin was also very nonconfrontational when she was in a relationship. She constantly read books on dating, love, and relationships, and she believed in doing whatever it took to be the best possible mate. The problem was her boyfriends didn't have that same energy when it came to her. Hence, she was often left feeling frustrated, depleted, doubtful and, when things ended, lonely.

"No. I haven't really had a chance. Tonight he walked out before I could really say anything." Brittany went on to tell me everything that had transpired between her and Duane prior to her calling me. I fought the urge to interrupt. Finally, she asked, "Am I tripping?"

I took a long swallow of my drink before answering her. "No, Britt, you're not tripping. Why do you always immediately think that you're doing something wrong?"

"Because I'm trying to see my situation from all sides, not just mine."

"I get that, but it seems like you're the only one doing that right now. You're always the one giving and trying and doing. Hell, you sent him a text and told him you were working late. He shoulda been the one asking if you wanted *him* to pick something up for dinner. He's a grown-ass man, not your child. And that's your bed, not his, and if you don't want him dirtying it up, that's your right," I told her. "You know what you need to do?"

"What? Call and ask him to come back over so we can talk?"

Instead of tossing my phone across the room, like I felt like doing, I took another gulp of wine and said, "No, Brittany. You don't need to call his ass. You need to give him a chance to miss you. Don't talk to him or text him for a couple of days. Show him how important you are by removing your presence."

"You think?" Brittany asked.

"I know," I told her. "Trust me on this. Treat him the same way he's been treating you and see what happens."

"Yeah. You're right. That's what I need to do," Brittany murmured. "Thanks, Sissy."

"Anytime." I laughed, hoping my advice hadn't fallen on deaf ears, as it had done in the past.

"Where are you this week?"

"Believe it or not, I'm actually home. Well, at least until Sunday I am." As soon as the words escaped my mouth, I regretted saying them. I knew what Brittany was about to say next.

Right on cue, she asked, "What? You're home? Does Mom know?"

"She does not," I answered. "And you don't need to tell her."

"I won't," Brittany said.

"I mean it, Britt," I said firmly. "I was gonna tell her, but when I went to work this morning, I found out I have to go back out Sunday morning. I don't have time to drive down and see her this week, and you know she would be mad if she knew I was home and didn't stop in. So, if she doesn't know I'm here, she won't have a reason to be upset about me not coming to see her. So don't say anything."

My sister was much closer to my mother than I was. Mainly because they were very similar in everything, from the way they dressed to the way they thought. They were both mild mannered, modest, and what I considered overly accommodating to others. My mother was a stay-at-home wife and mother who doted on my father and catered to his every need, but she also had been the same way to us while we were growing up. Brittany adored her. I was more like my dad, who worked hard as an insurance agent and took great care of our family.

"I'm not going to say anything. I promise. But—"

"No buts," I interrupted, stopping her before she could offer a rebuttal. "My schedule is full, and I can't make a three-hour drive just to have to turn around and come right back. I have to get everything done in two days that I thought I was going to have time to do over the next few weeks," I told her. "Hair, nails, feet, brows. My car has to be detailed, and I haven't had a massage in ages."

"And you think all of that's more important than seeing your mother, who you haven't seen in ages? I mean, I'm just saying," Brittany said.

"As long as you don't say anything to her . . ." I got up and went to pour myself more wine. Noticing the time on the microwave, I said, "Listen, I gotta go. Remember what I told you. Give Duane a chance to miss you. Don't even think about him anymore tonight. Stop being so pressed. You are the prize, not him, and if he doesn't appreciate that, then let his ass go and find someone who does."

"I'm not going to say anything. And you act like finding a new guy is as simple as walking down the street." Brittany sighed.

"It is. I've met guys while walking down the street."
I laughed. "Love you. Talk to you later. And do *not* say
anything to Mom."

"Love you too," I barely heard her say before I ended
the call.

An hour later, I was standing on the thirteenth floor
of the Downtown Westin, knocking on a door. When it
opened, there was Mitch, a pharmaceutical rep that I'd
met a few months earlier, looking even more handsome
than I remembered. The way he smiled at me let me
know that he was just as excited as I was about what
the night had in store for us. The last time we'd hooked
up had been monumental, and when he'd sent me the
random text telling me he was in town for a few days and
inviting me over to have a drink, I'd accepted.

"I was starting to wonder if you were going to show."

"Do you think I would stand you up?" I winked.

"Don't act like it ain't hit or miss with you."

He opened the door wider, and I entered the room. I
glanced into the bathroom area and saw a few toiletries
on the sink. A few suits were in the closet, along with a
pair of dress shoes and Nike running shoes. I stepped
farther into the room and saw an open briefcase, a laptop,
and some papers lying out on the bed. A discarded pizza
box was on the dresser; and an empty bottle of beer, on
the nightstand. It was clear that he'd been working when
I arrived. I put my wristlet, keys, and phone on top of the
television.

"You really thought I wasn't going to show, huh?" I
laughed.

"Yeah, but I'm glad you did." He looked me up and down as he wrapped his arms around my body, and then he pulled me to him. He went to kiss me, but I tilted my head, and instead of his lips meeting mine, they ended up on my neck. Kissing was something I didn't do, especially with men that were what I considered "run-ins," like Mitch. Those whom I would "run into" when I felt like it. Unlike Brittany, I wasn't trying to be "booed up" or tied down. I enjoyed my freedom and the flexibility of my life. I lived life on my terms and played by my own rules, and whoever couldn't deal with it wasn't my problem.

"You gonna clear the bed?" I moaned. As much as I enjoyed Mitch sucking on my collarbone, I was ready to get down to business.

"Oh, yeah." Mitch released me and went to put the items away. "I was waiting to order a bottle of wine from room service when you got here. Or we can just go down to the bar and grab a drink, then come back up."

"I'm fine," I said and slipped my shirt over my head, exposing the black lace bra holding my triple D breasts in place.

"You damn right you are." Mitch's eyes widened, and he tossed the papers he was holding onto the floor. He went to reach for me, but I held my hand up to stop him. We stared at one another as I slowly slipped out of my short black skirt. His gaze traveled from my lace panties to the black leather boots I kept on, and he whispered, "I swear you are sexy as fuck."

I placed my hands on my thick hips and shrugged. "I know."

Again, Mitch reached for me; this time there was no stopping him. He pushed me onto the bed, and I slipped off my bra and caressed my nipples as I watched him take off his clothes. He had a nice build, not athletic, but he wasn't pudgy, either. By the time he took off his sweatpants, I was moist and ready, and judging by the bulge in his boxer briefs, he was too. He stepped out of them and the sight of his hardened manhood made me even hornier than I already was. He eased on top of me, cupped my breasts, and took each one into his mouth. My back arched, and I opened my legs wider, grinding against him so he could feel my wetness. His hands found their way between my thighs, and he teased my clitoris briefly before putting his fingers into me, causing me to gasp. As incredible as his fingers felt, I wanted something else.

"Where's the condom?" I whispered.

"Wait. Not yet," he said. "I want to taste you."

I slid up a bit and looked down at him. "No. Just get the rubber and come on."

He exhaled and got up. A few moments later, he returned, gold wrapper in hand, and said, "Happy?"

"Not yet," I said, taking the condom from him and opening it. I seductively slid it on his thick penis, then pulled him back on top of me. He maneuvered himself and, in one swift motion, plunged into my welcoming canal. His grip tightened around my leather-bound legs, and the spikes of my heels dug into his chest, which seemed to be a turn-on for him. I closed my eyes and enjoyed the rhythm of his stroke game.

"This shit is incredible," he said as his hands slid down and pushed my thighs open wider.

"Is that all you got?" I asked him, wrapping my legs around his waist and meeting his thrusts. "Harder. Faster."

Mitch did as I commanded, and tried his best not to climax, but the pulsation of my inner walls was no match for him. "Oh shit."

"Yeah, that's it," I said, my hands holding on to his shoulders. "Yesss."

We came together, our bodies hot and sticky from sweat.

He rolled over and panted. "Damn. That was even better than last time."

"I'm glad you enjoyed it." I sat up and patted his chest before standing.

"Where are you going?" Mitch frowned at me.

"Home," I answered, locating my bra and panties, which were on the floor near the foot of the bed.

"Man, don't leave. You just got here."

"You know I'm not doing that." I laughed as I put my panties on.

"Just stay for a little while," he pleaded.

"No can do. I gotta go. But I really enjoyed myself." I snapped my bra and twisted it around my back.

"Enough to come back tomorrow?" He raised an eyebrow.

"I don't know about that," I said, pulling on my skirt and shirt.

"I guess we'll link up next time we're both in the same area, huh?"

"Text me and see." I leaned over and pressed my nose against his forehead. I grabbed my items off the television and waved before walking out the door.

When I got back to my luxury condo, I took a long, hot bubble bath, and when I climbed into my comfortable bed, I was sore, satisfied, and smiling. It had been a great night.

Chapter Four

Brittany

I tried my best to take my sister's advice and put Duane out of my mind, but I couldn't. The following day, he didn't reach out to me, and I didn't reach out to him. I was so busy at work that I didn't have time to think about him, but when I got home, I realized it. Then I got worried. It wasn't that I was pressed; it was more like I was concerned. I watched a little television, then tossed and turned for a couple of hours, hoping he would call or send me a good night text, but he didn't, and my worry turned to anger. I thought about my mother and all the relationship experts who said never to go to bed angry at your mate. So I reached out to him.

When he didn't answer my call, I sent a simple "Good night, baby" text and waited for his response. I was tired and unable to keep my eyes open and fell asleep. I kept waking every so often and checking my phone, but there were only a few notifications from Facebook and Instagram, none of which were from Duane. It was clear that he wasn't as concerned about my having a good night as I was about him.

"Maybe he was asleep," I said to my friend Kyra, whom I called on the way to work the next morning. She was usually a little more supportive of and optimistic about my relationship than my sister.

"Maybe he was. But if that's the case, then he should've responded when he woke up," Kyra replied, not giving me the supportive answer I was hoping for. "Stop making excuses for him. He's the one in the wrong, not you. Duane's a nice guy and all, but you spoil him and let him get away with way too much."

"I'm not making excuses, Kyra." I sighed as I pulled onto the interstate and eased my Camry into the bumper-to-bumper traffic, which was sure to make me late. "Damn it. The traffic is horrible."

"It always is. People can't drive, especially in the rain," Kyra commented. "I've been sitting in the same spot for, like, fifteen minutes."

I turned my windshield wipers to a faster speed and leaned my head against the window. "I swear, I'm ready for this day to be over already."

"Your day will get better, Britt. Come on, it's almost the weekend, and we're going to paint night," Kyra said, sounding so cheerful that instead of making me feel better, she irritated me. I'd been so excited when we finally got tickets to the popular "Trap and Paint" event, but now I didn't even want to go.

"Yeah." I sighed.

"Brittany, you can't flake on me. We been planning this for months. I know you're in your feelings, but you're gonna have to perk up."

I was just about to respond when my phone beeped with another call. For a second, I became excited, thinking it might be Duane. I looked at the caller ID and saw that it was my mother.

"Kyra, let me call you back. It's my mom."

"Tell her I said hello. Call me later. And I'm with Brooke. Don't even stress about Duane," Kyra said. "Bye."

I clicked over and greeted my mother. "Hey, Ma."

"Hey, Britt. Happy Friday," she said, sounding pleasant.

"Come on. Go," I yelled to the car in front of me.

"Who are you yelling at?" Mama asked.

"Traffic," I said.

"Well, I'm sure your yelling isn't gonna make the folks drive any faster." She laughed. "They can't hear you."

She was right, and I knew she was trying to be funny, but I didn't see any humor in it. I remained quiet.

"Britt, you okay?" she asked.

"I'm fine, Ma. I'm just running late. And it's raining, and I'm irritated," I told her.

"Well, take a deep breath and think positive thoughts and say positive things."

"Thanks, Ma."

"Well, maybe this will make you feel better. I've decided what I want to do for my birthday," Mama said excitedly.

"What's that, Ma?" I asked.

"A girls' day at the spa and then a photo shoot. Doesn't that sound like fun?"

A day at the spa didn't sound too bad. But taking pictures with my mother and sister was the last thing I wanted to do. When we were younger, it was easier, because Mama would dress Brooke and me alike, and all we had to do was pose and smile. Even then, my sister seemed to outshine me: her eyes seemed slightly brighter, and her smile bigger. People swore they couldn't see the differences between us, but I would stare at each and every photograph and see them. When we became teenagers, we were allowed to pick our own family-photo outfits, as long as they were in the same color scheme. Of course, Brooke's outfit was always more fashionable, and she stood out. She always seemed to be in the spotlight, and I had no desire to compete. Brooke loved pictures; it was obvious if you looked at her selfie-filled social media pages. But I doubted that a color-coordinated photo shoot with our mother was something she was interested in now.

"Did you tell Brooke this?" I asked.

"Not yet. I haven't talked to her in over a week. Have you spoken to her?"

"Uh, just through text," I lied.

"She's probably halfway across the country, in a different time zone. Hopefully, I can catch up with her this weekend," Mama said. "Oh, and I was thinking that maybe you and Duane may want to take some pictures at the same time. I know y'all were talking about getting engaged, so it would be perfect timing."

"I don't think so, Mama," I told her.

"Why not? Oh, Lord, what's happened now?" she asked.

"We're just not seeing eye to eye right now, that's all. But we'll be fine. I think I need a break . . ."

"A *break*? Brittany, if y'all aren't seeing eye to eye, the last thing you need is a break. You need to talk," Mama said. "That's y'all's problem. You keep taking these breaks."

"But—"

"But nothing," she interrupted.

I listened to my mother go on and on about how important communication was in a healthy relationship. She was talking so much that I didn't have time to explain

that it was hard to talk to a person who didn't want to talk back. Honestly, talking was something Duane and I really hadn't done in a few weeks. Recently, when he hadn't been fussing about something I did or didn't do, he'd been on his phone or glued to the television screen. Even our sex life had become mundane, and I had been the one to initiate sex when it happened. Hell, I'd actually been doing everything: cooking, doing the laundry, texting, calling.

"I'll call you later, Ma," I finally said and then hung up. My state of mind was becoming more agitated by the minute, and my already bad day became even worse when I finally arrived at work.

"What are you doing here?" Mr. McGee said when I walked into the building twenty minutes late and dripping wet due to my malfunctioning umbrella.

"What do you mean?" I asked, confused by his question.

"You're supposed to be at the central office this morning for a district meeting. I told them you would be there because Mrs. Cook and I wouldn't be able to make it." He frowned.

"You didn't mention it to me, and neither did she," I replied, wondering why neither he nor the assistant principal had said anything.

"She said she sent you an email."

"She didn't," I told him.

"Are you sure? That's not like her." His response gave me the impression that he didn't believe me.

"I'm positive, Mr. McGee. No one said anything to me about a meeting at the central office," I insisted.

At that very moment one of the teachers walked up. "Ms. Newman, I'm glad to see you," she said.

"Good morning," I mumbled.

"We need you over on the A hallway please. Dennis is having a meltdown and is refusing to go into the classroom. Can you come and check on him?" she said.

"Uh, give me a moment . . . ," I replied.

"She'll be right there," Mr. McGee told her. Then he turned and faced me. "Go and take care of the student, and then get downtown as soon as possible. I'll call them and let them know you're on your way. Oh, and don't forget we have a parent meeting this afternoon, at two thirty."

"What par—" I began, but he turned and walked off.

The teacher stood there and looked at me. "You want me to take your stuff to your office while you go handle Dennis?"

"No, I don't," I said. Then I added, "I'm not going to handle him."

"Huh?"

"Find someone else. Call the guidance counselor, one of the behavior techs, or Mrs. Cook. Better yet, get Mr. McGee. Because all of them are equipped to handle this situation. I'm not the only one. And guess what? I'm not going to. As a matter of fact, I'm not even going to be here today. I'm leaving," I announced.

"Leaving for the meeting?" she asked, as if she wanted to clarify matters.

"Nope. Leaving and not coming back," I told her and turned to walk back out the same door through which I'd entered.

"Wait, Ms. Newman. You're not coming back for the day or, like, uh, forever?"

I paused and then said, "I don't know."

It wasn't a lie. In that moment, I wasn't sure what I was going to do other than get into my car and get the hell away from everyone.

I went home and sent a quick email to Mr. McGee, letting him know that I had gotten sick and wouldn't be back for the remainder of the day. I made sure I copied Mrs. Cook. Then I packed an overnight bag, grabbed some snacks and a bottle of water, and hit the road. My first instinct was to make the two-hour drive to my parents' house, but recalling the conversation with my mom earlier, I changed my mind. Instead, I went in the totally opposite direction, praying I wasn't going to get cussed out.

Sometime later, Brooke's voice came through the intercom in the entryway of her building. "Can I help you?"

I pressed the button and spoke into the silver box. "Brooke, it's me. Let me in."

"Britt? What the hell? Are you at my building?" she asked.

"Yeah. Hurry up. I have to pee," I told her. The drive to her house had taken a little longer than I had anticipated, especially since I hadn't stopped at all. I'd been afraid that if I did, I would've turned around and gone back home. A last-minute, unplanned road trip wasn't something I had ever done.

"What are you doing there? I'm not even home," she said. "Thomas, the doorman, isn't there?"

"No, I don't see him. Where are you?" I hadn't thought to call to make sure she'd be home, and I had forgotten that she mentioned all the beautification errands she planned to do.

"I'm at the hair salon. Hold on. I'll buzz you in. Do you even know what floor my apartment is on?"

I tried to remember. "Um, six?" I'd been to her house only three times in the past two years. I was surprised I'd remembered how to get to her fancy apartment building without using GPS. But I had spotted the huge glass building from the interstate and had found it after I exited.

"Seven," she said, correcting me. "When you get off the elevator, go to the left, and my apartment is seven-fifteen. Text me when you get there and I'll unlock the door from my phone."

"You can do that?" I asked, trying not to sound impressed.

"Yes, Britt. When you hear the buzzer in a few, hurry and pull open the glass door. Text me when you get to my door. Seventh floor. Seven-fifteen."

I did exactly what Brooke had told me to do. Moments after stepping off the mirrored elevator and walking down the long, carpeted corridor, I arrived in front of her door and sent her a text. Seconds later, I heard a click, turned the knob, and walked into her massive apartment. Once inside, I put my cell in my purse, tossed the purse on the dining-room table, and put my small overnight bag underneath it. I made a beeline for the bathroom, stepping over Amazon boxes and shopping bags from various stores. Brooke was a shopaholic. Even her bathroom counter held more beauty and makeup products than she needed.

After washing my hands, I ventured back out to the living-room area, which was separated from the dining room by a bar. The bar held several bottles of wine, more boxes, and a Bluetooth speaker. Despite the clutter of online purchases, Brooke's living-room area still looked better than an IKEA showroom, with its grey sectional and yellow pillows. An entertainment center spanned one of the walls and held various awards and certificates and a huge television. I sat down on the sectional and picked up the remote on the coffee table. I turned on the TV, got comfortable, and before I knew it, I had fallen asleep.

"Well, thanks for telling me you got in safely."

Startled, I sat up and turned to see Brooke walking through the front door. "Huh? Oh, my bad. I told you I had to pee. I went to the bathroom, then went to sleep."

"Hey, Britt." Brooke's best friend walked in behind her. She was cute, petite, and just as fashion forward as my sister. The two of them reminded me of me and Kyra, only we were way less dramatic and way more laid back. But the genuine friendship and connection they had with one another was recognizable.

"Hey, Emory." I waved and stretched. "What time is it?"

"It's almost six. I've been calling and texting you," Brooke told me.

"Oh wow. I didn't even hear my phone." I retrieved it from my purse and saw that I had several missed calls from her and one from Mr. McGee. There was nothing from Duane. "I can't believe I fell asleep."

"I can't believe you're at my house." Brooke walked over and flopped down on the sofa beside me. "I guess you and Duane broke up, huh?"

"No, we didn't. Why would you say something like that?" I gasped.

Brooke ran her fingers through her perfectly layered bob. "Because the last time I talked to you, he was tripping. And now you're here."

"That doesn't mean we broke up," I said.

"Maybe she's taking your advice and getting ghost for a few days." Emory shrugged as she picked up one of the multiple shopping bags in the living-room area and took out a box of shoes. "Oh, these are *cute*. When did you get these?"

"Um, a couple of months ago, I think. Aren't they adorable? And they were on sale for, like, two hundred bucks," Brooke told her.

Two hundred dollars. I couldn't fathom spending that much money on a pair of shoes, especially ones that I would barely wear. But that was how Brooke was. If she saw something she liked—shoes, men, jobs—she went after it without a care in the world. She was fearless. Even if I had an extra two hundred dollars, I would save it, just in case an emergency came up and I needed it. Or I happened to get married, whichever came first.

"And you didn't get me a pair? Heffa, you could've at least called and shown them to me. I would've put the money in your account." Emory fondled the shoes as if they were fragile pieces of glass.

"They didn't have your size. I asked. Otherwise, you know I would've hooked you up. I think I'm gonna wear them tonight with this." Brooke got up and grabbed one of the boxes on the floor, opened it, and took out a sexy black jumpsuit.

Emory nodded. "That is hot."

"What's going on tonight?" I asked them.

"Nothing. We're just going out. You should come with us," Emory said.

"She's not going to do that." Brooke laughed.

"Why not?" Emory looked at me for an answer.

I turned to Brooke and said, "Yeah. Why not?"

"Because you'd rather just lie here on my couch and do Netflix and chill while waiting on Duane to call or text you, that's why." Brooke laughed.

I hated that she was right. All I wanted to do was relax on her comfortable sofa, order Chinese food, and watch Hallmark movies. I also hoped that I would hear from Duane.

"She does not. She did not drive all the way here to be cooped up in the house all weekend. Come on, Britt. It'll be fun," Emory said.

"How long are you staying?" Brooke asked.

"Just tonight. I'm going to Trap and Paint tomorrow night with Kyra," I told her.

"That sounds like fun," Brooke said. "Well, if you want to hang out with us, you need to get changed. We're about to pre-game and head out in a little while."

"Uh, what is the dress code?" I looked down at the polo shirt with the school crest embroidered on the collar and the khaki pants I was wearing, and thought about the two pairs of jeans and the sweatshirts in my bag. I knew none of my attire would suffice for anywhere these two were going.

"It's an after-work event, but it's at a rooftop bar, so casual but chic," Emory answered.

Brooke looked at me and said, "Let me guess. You don't have anything to wear."

"Not really." I shrugged. As fun as the event sounded, I knew there was no way I could go. "But you guys go ahead. I'll be fine."

The two of them looked at one another, then back at me. Brooke walked over, grabbed my arm, and pulled me off the sofa, and Emory clapped like a five-year-old who'd just been told she was getting a pony for her birthday.

"This is going to be fun. I'll pour us some drinks," Emory announced.

"What's going on? What's going to be fun?" I whined.

"Shut up and come on." Brooke continued pulling me by the arm.

"We're giving you a makeover," Emory squealed.

Chapter Five

Brooke

"There. How does that look? Too much pink?" I asked Emory as I inspected my work.

"Um, it looks good. Maybe blend it a little bit on the top." Emory pointed, and I picked up the small brush and made the small adjustment to my sister's face. It was kind of weird applying makeup on a face that looked so similar to mine. Like looking into a mirror, but slightly different.

"Don't put too much on, Brooke. You know I don't wear a lot of makeup," Brittany told me.

"Shut up and let me do this. You don't wear *any* make-up. That's your problem. I've always told you that you need to start jazzing yourself up a bit. I ain't saying you gotta do all of this." I dramatically pointed to myself. "But you are beautiful. Show it off."

"That's not me." She shook her head and gave me a hard look.

I continued applying the makeup without saying anything else. If I did, we would end up in an argument. The same argument that we'd had for decades. Time and time again, I'd tried to help Brittany step up her fashion game, but she had sworn that I was trying to make her like me and that just because we were identical didn't mean she couldn't have her own identity. So I had let her. If she wanted to be a wallflower instead of a beautiful rose, that was on her. But there was no way I was going to let her step out with my best friend and me looking like a widowed librarian with three cats at home. If she was going out with us, she had to look the part.

"Okay. That's perfect." Emory smiled.

I stood back and admired my handiwork. "Yep, it is. Now Em is gonna do something to your hair right quick, and I'm gonna find you something cute to wear."

"Let me look right quick." Brittany went to turn toward the mirror, but I stopped her. "No, you see it when we're finished. Now stay put," I said.

"Okay, let's see . . . We got a flatiron, a big-barreled curling iron, an InStyler, gel, spritz, mousse. Oh, do you have any bobby pins?" Emory said.

"In the drawer over there." I pointed, then went into my bedroom to find something decent for Brooke to put on. In addition to looking alike, we were the same size. I foraged through my oversize walk-in closet for something subtle yet sexy that she wouldn't balk at when she saw it. I was just about to give up the search when I spotted a sheer white kimono blouse with a plunging neckline that I'd never worn. I grabbed it, along with a pair of high-waisted, animal-print denim jeggings and high-heeled black boots. I damn near thought about wearing the outfit myself. *Perfect*, I thought.

"All right. How's it going?" I called as I walked back into the bathroom. Then I took a good look at Brittany. Emory had done just as amazing a job on Brittany's hair as I had done on her face. Instead of the tight bun she normally wore, her hair was now a mass of flowing curls. "Yes, Em! You did that."

"Thanks. It was easy, and you know how I do."

"Can I look now?" Brooke asked.

"Not yet. Here. Put this outfit on." I handed her the clothes and the boots.

"That's cute." Emory nodded her approval.

"I can't wear those." Brooke pointed at the boots. "The heels are too high."

"They're the shortest heels I own, so you're gonna have to make them work. You damn sure can't wear those Hush Puppies you have on." I looked down at the sensible brown shoes she was wearing.

"I walk a lot at work," Brittany said in her defense.

"So do I." I sighed. "That's no excuse."

"Ah, but Brandon likes to see you in heels," Emory noted, then laughed.

I nodded. "Yes, he does, and he knows he can look but he can't touch."

Emory said, "And don't act like you don't want Brandon to touch you, again. If I recall, you said his touch was the bomb."

"Wait. Brandon? Brooke, you're sleeping with your boss?" Brittany gasped and put her hand on her chest.

"Calm down. I'm not sleeping with him," I told her, trying not to laugh at her reaction.

"Not anymore, she isn't," Emory volunteered. "But she has."

"Em, stop. And for the record, when I did sleep with him, we weren't even coworkers. And that was years ago, and it wasn't that serious. We hooked up only twice," I explained. "Now, go get dressed."

"Trust me, if Brandon had his way, it would be way more than that, though," Emory observed, continuing to share information that didn't need to be shared. Brittany already thought I had no scruples, and I damn sure didn't need her to think any less of me. Or my mother, whom Brittany would probably waste no time telling.

"Well, that ain't happening," I said.

"Hey, maybe if you let it happen, you'd definitely be getting promoted," Emory teased. "I don't know why you don't just give in, anyway. Brandon is fine, smart, successful, and he likes you, and you know it."

"Oh, I'm getting promoted, and I won't be doing that, and you know it." I laughed.

"If you've already slept with him, and you think he's fine, smart, and successful, and he likes you, then what's the big deal?" Brittany asked. "You don't like him? Or was he whack in bed?"

"Don't get me wrong. Brandon is a nice guy and all, and he wasn't no slouch in bed, either. But one, Daddy always told me you never shit where you eat, and two, I ain't feeling him like that," I said.

"You never feel *anyone*," Brittany said. She shook her head and gave me one of her judgmental looks.

"Oh, she feels them. And they definitely feel her. Just not like that," Emory remarked.

"Don't you want to find someone special one day? Don't you want to be in love, Brooke?" Brittany asked.

Emory folded her arms and said, "This should be good."

I thought about Brittany's question and then said, "I don't know. I like my life and the freedom I have, and I don't need anyone complicating things for me."

"You just haven't met the right person yet. That's all," Brittany declared. She rearranged the clothes and the boots she was holding and then stood up.

"I've met plenty of men, trust me. That's not the problem." I laughed. "And I'm going to meet plenty more. I have friends, and they serve their purpose, and I'm good with that for right now."

"One of these days you're going to meet a dude and have a moment. It's going to be nothing like you've ever felt before, and in an instant, your life is gonna change. Don't say I didn't tell you," Brittany said. She smiled at me before she walked out of the bathroom and into the guest bedroom.

When she was gone, Emory and I laughed as we went back into the living room. I loved my sister, but she was so naive that it was comical at times. Back in that bathroom it had taken me every ounce of self-control I could muster not to point out that she'd driven all the way to my house, unannounced, because she was disappointed in a dude, a dude whom she swore she had fallen in love with a year ago. He'd turned out to be just as flaky as all the rest of them. I didn't have time for emotional roller coasters. I was too busy taking flights to catch feelings. When it came to men, I was the one in control, and I never allowed myself to get caught up.

"She's adorable," Emory said, pouring both of us a drink. "I can't believe you're twins."

"I can't believe we're even related." I shook my head. "Have a moment? Hell, I had a *moment* the other night with Mitch, and trust me, it was a good-ass moment."

"You're horrible, Brooke. I swear."

"I'm not horrible. I'm just real. Now let's go get dressed, so we can get the hell outta here. Who knows? I might meet someone new to have a moment with."

***

"This shirt keeps coming open. Do you have a safety pin?" Brittany whispered as we got off the elevator on the top floor of the Skyline Westin and headed toward the Sky Bar located on the roof of the hotel. It was crowded, and a line had formed.

I turned around and said, "It's a low-cut shirt, Brittany. It's supposed to be open. Stop closing it up. It shows off your cleavage."

"I feel naked," she said, putting her arms across her chest.

"Girl, you look amazing. Shit, your outfit is flyer than mine. We really should've switched." I laughed.

She looked down at the stiletto sandals on my feet and said, "There's no way."

"Come on. Let's get in here and grab a booth with a view before they're all gone." I took her by the arm and guided her alongside me toward the front of the line.

"Wait. The line starts back there," she said.

"Line? Girl, we don't stand in line," Emory told her. "We have memberships."

We continued to the front of the line, smiling as we walked past the well-dressed patrons who had to wait, and when we got to the glass door of the club, Emory and I flashed the black VIP membership cards that we'd each shelled out 250 bucks for. They really were a bit pricey, especially since I was in town only a few times a year to use mine. But I enjoyed having the ability to use the perks when I wanted to, including not having to stand in a long-ass line and being guaranteed VIP seating.

"What's up, Ms. Brooke?" Kedrick, the bouncer, greeted. "Nice to see you and Ms. Em tonight."

"Hey, Kedrick." I smiled and gave him a wink. Suddenly, he did a double take, and I said, "Kedrick, this is my twin sister, Brittany."

"Damn. I thought I was tripping for a sec. You beautiful ladies look exactly alike. My goodness."

"Thank you," I said, looking at Brittany and admiring my handiwork. In her outfit and makeup, you really couldn't tell us apart.

"Enjoy yourselves, ladies, and it's nice to meet you, Miss Brittany." Kedrick gave Brittany a look that was borderline sexual, and she began blushing.

"Bye, Kedrick," I said and motioned for Brittany to follow me.

We maneuvered our way through the crowded bar and arrived at the designated VIP area, which was located a bit above the bar area. There was one empty booth that I considered prime real estate, as it was close enough that you could see the dance floor but still far enough away that you didn't have to worry about being bothered too much by unwanted patrons. I grabbed the booth.

"What can I get you, ladies?" a waitress asked as soon as we sat down.

I bobbed my head to the music and said, "Three vodka and cranberries."

Brittany balked. "Uh, I was just gonna get wine."

"Oh my God, Britt. Live a little, please. You need something stronger than damn wine to take the edge off." I exhaled.

"Fine." She sat back and adjusted her shirt.

I was beginning to think that inviting her out was a bad idea. This was the last night I had to kick back and enjoy myself before having to pack up and catch a red-eye flight, and I didn't need her messing up my vibe. The waitress returned with our drinks, and I handed one to my twin.

"To a good-ass night." I raised my glass.

Emory lifted her glass, and we both waited for Brittany to follow suit. She hesitated and finally lifted her glass, clinked it against ours, and took a sip.

"It's strong." She frowned.

"It's good. Now relax and have a good time. Please," I said.

"Oh damn, Brooke. There's Omar." Emory nodded toward the bar. "I haven't seen him in a while."

"That is him. Looking fine as hell with his whorish ass." I laughed.

"Pot meet kettle." Emory giggled.

I nodded. "You're right."

The waitress came back over with another round of drinks. "Compliments of the gentleman at the bar."

"Looks like he spotted us before we spotted him," I said, and I waved at Omar, a well-known playboy and a guy that Emory used to date. He nodded back at us. I glanced over at Emory and asked, "Well, what are you going to do?"

"I guess the polite thing would be to go over and thank him, huh?" she said.

"It would," I agreed. "Besides, we haven't done a walk-through. Come on, Britt."

"We're leaving?" Brittany asked.

"No, we're not leaving. We're mingling," I told her.

"I'd rather not. You guys go ahead. I'll wait here and watch your drinks," Brittany offered.

"Well, we were going to take our drinks with us, but fine. We'll be right back." I sighed.

Emory and I walked through the crowd again, making small talk with people we knew and pausing to check out the packed dance floor. We made our way over to the bar to thank Omar for the drinks, and within minutes, Emory was mesmerized by his smooth talk and flirtatious smile. I glanced over my shoulder at our booth to check on Brittany. She was still sitting in the booth, her face down, her eyes on her phone.

I leaned over and told Emory, "I'll be back," then headed back to the booth. "What are you doing?"

Brittany quickly put the phone away and said, "Nothing. I mean, chilling."

I sat close to her and faced her. "Brittany, listen to me. I'm not gonna let you sit here and wait for a phone call that ain't coming from a jerk who doesn't realize how amazing you are. Look around. There are hundreds of men in here to choose from. Pick one."

"You don't understand." Brittany shook her head. "I can't."

"Can't what?"

"Do that," she answered.

"Why not?" I frowned.

"It's not that simple. Well, not for me."

"We have the same damn face, Brittany, and almost the same body. Although my boobs are perkier. But still, you sound crazy," I said.

"It's different, and you know it. It's never been easy for me, like it is for you," she replied. "Guys just gravitate to you, but not to me. They always have. I sat here and saw five or six guys stop and talk to you. No one has even looked in my direction."

"Because you're sitting here looking like you lost your best friend and would rather be playing *Candy Crush* on your phone," I snapped.

"That's true." Brittany went to pull at the shirt.

"And stop pulling my damn shirt. It's made to be revealing. Listen, you are beautiful and amazing. I'm not saying you'll find a new love up in here, but if you relax and forget about everything else you got going on for tonight, like Duane, your job, and everything else, I guarantee you will have a good-ass time. Just listen to me for once." I reached across the table and offered her what was left of my drink. "Here. Take it to the head."

Brittany shook her head. "I already had one."

"Have another one and another one, and another one after that," I said.

She took the drink out of my hand and drank it.

When she was done, I said, "Now bring your ass. We hitting the dance floor."

Chapter Six

Brittany

The music was pumping, drinks were flowing, the dance floor was jumping, and I was having a blast. When Brooke had initially pulled me through the crowd and onto the dance floor with her, I had swayed back and forth to be polite. But then someone had grabbed my hand and spun me around. I'd come face-to-face with a cute guy, who was now smiling at me. I loosened up a bit. I hadn't danced with a guy in a long time. Duane didn't like crowds, so we didn't go to clubs, and dancing wasn't his thing. I felt a little awkward until I heard Brooke's voice hyping me up.

"Yesss, sis! You betta handle him, BB!" she yelled, calling me something I hadn't heard in a while. She was older than I was by eight minutes, and she used to referred to me as Baby Brittany, or BB for short. Instead of causing me to cringe, as hearing that nickname had done so many times while I was growing up, it energized me for some reason.

I didn't know what *handling* him meant, but I put a little more effort into my moves, and judging by the look on my partner's face, he was enjoying what I was doing. We danced for a little while longer, until I felt perspiration on my forehead.

"Okay. I need a break," I told the guy. The dance floor was even more packed than when we had first started, and I could barely move.

He looked slightly disappointed. "I hope I get another dance before the night is over."

"I think I can do that." I winked, and he smiled.

I went to look for my sister, who was nowhere to be found. Despite my efforts to carefully navigate my way back to the booth, I was pushed slightly from behind, and I collided into someone. I quickly said, "Excuse me. I'm so sorry."

"No you aren't."

I swallowed hard as I gazed into the eyes of the person that had spoken. For a second, I was speechless. He had to be one of the best-looking men I'd ever laid eyes on. I knew he had to think I was crazy, because the only word I could mutter was, "Huh?"

"You aren't *sorry*. You are beautiful." His compliment left me even more flustered as his confident smile revealed the most perfect teeth. For a second, I wondered if he had worn braces as a kid. I continued staring as he said, "But I appreciate your apology, and I'm willing to let you make it up to me."

By now I was fascinated by what he meant. I finally gathered myself together enough to acknowledge that he was speaking to me. "And how's that?"

"Let me buy you a drink."

Again, I became lost in his gaze and slowly nodded. "Sure."

He gently placed his hand on my elbow and guided me over to the end of the crammed bar. I was finally able to take my eyes off his face and notice that he was well dressed in a pair of nice jeans, a button-down shirt, and a blazer.

As we patiently waited for the bartender to acknowledge us, he leaned over and asked, "So, what would you like?" The scent of his cologne added to his magnetic persona. I didn't even mind his invasion of my personal space.

"Vodka and cranberry," I answered.

He ordered our drinks, and after we were served and he paid, he spotted a nearby empty table, and we headed over before someone else claimed it. As soon as we sat down, I felt the vibration of my phone in my pocket. My first thought was that it was Duane. Had he somehow sensed that I was out having drinks with another man? I checked the Apple Watch on my arm and saw that it wasn't a call or a text from Duane, but a text message from Brooke.

Where the hell are you? it read.

I took out my phone and typed my response. Having a drink with someone in the corner near the bar.

Really? Everything okay?

I glanced up and saw that my companion was looking at me, and I realized I was being rude. "Yeah, I'm here with my sister and her friend. They were just checking on me."

"Oh, okay. Let them know you're in good hands." He grinned.

My phone vibrated again with another message. Is he fine? An eye emoji followed the question.

I couldn't help laughing as I typed, "As hell!" and then sent the text. I put my phone away and picked up my drink and took a sip.

"So, beautiful lady, what's your name?"

"You can call me BB," I said, now eager to embrace the nickname as my alter ego.

"BB, huh? Okay, then you can call me T," he said.

He made small talk, most of which I really wasn't paying much attention to, since I was so focused on how sexy his lips were. But I did pick up on the fact that he was a guest at the hotel and was thinking about relocating to the area. I told him I was also visiting.

"I guess your bumping into me was fate, huh?" he said.

I nodded. "I guess so."

We ordered another round of drinks, and he eased closer to me. His eyes fell on my visible cleavage, which I no longer tried to hide. The attraction between us was undeniable. A familiar Usher song began playing, and when he asked me if I wanted to dance, I didn't hesitate to accept. This time when he guided me through the crowd, his hand wasn't on my elbow. It was on my waist, and he remained close behind me. When we arrived on the dance floor, he held me closer than necessary, and I responded by pressing my body against his. His eyes didn't leave mine, and his hands moved to my lower back, damn near touched my ass. I couldn't tell if it was the alcohol or the overall vibe of the club at the moment, but I felt hot and sensuous. T was turning me on. I wrapped my arms around his neck, and we continued dancing.

He leaned over and whispered in my ear, "I would love for you to come to my room for a nightcap."

When I didn't respond right away, he released me slightly and our eyes met. By now we weren't moving at all, just standing in place as the music continued.

"A nightcap? That's all?" I blinked. I was breathing so hard that my chest was rising and falling fast. It wasn't that I was out of breath from dancing. It was just that the intensity of this moment was that strong.

"That's all." He nodded, then added, "Unless you want something else."

"Gimme a moment," I said.

He shrugged. "I'll be over by our table."

"I'll be right back." I turned and quickly made my way back over to the booth, in search of Brooke. When I got there, she and Emory and three guys were laughing and talking.

Brooke beamed when she saw me. "Well, look who finally came up for air." She looked over my shoulder. "Where is Mr. Someone?"

"Wow. You weren't lying when you said your twin was here," one of the guys shouted. "How you doing, sweetheart? I'm Omar."

"Calm down, eager beaver. It ain't happening," Emory told him. "Move, so she can sit down."

"Oh, my bad." Omar went to stand, but I shook my head.

"No, it's fine. You can stay," I told him.

"Britt, you okay?" Brooke asked.

"Uh, yeah. I need to ask y'all something right quick, though. In private," I said, not wanting to discuss the issue at hand in front of mixed company.

"We'll be right back," Brooke told the three guys as she and Emory got up from their seats.

We headed to the ladies' room, but when we got there, it was too crowded, so instead, we went to the main entrance to exit the club.

"Leaving so soon?" Kendrick asked.

"Nope. We'll be right back," Emory told him. We left the club, walked down the hallway, and sat on a bench near the elevators.

"What's going on?" Brooke asked.

"He wants to take me for a nightcap," I said.

"Okay?" Brooke said, sounding like she was waiting for me to say something else.

"Like, leave with him," I added.

"And?" Again, Brooke sounded like she expected there to be more to the matter.

"And go have a nightcap," I told her.

"I still don't understand the problem. Do you wanna go?" she replied.

"Yeah, I think so," I said, confirming out loud what I'd been thinking in my head. I nodded and smiled. "Yeah, I do."

"Then go," she and Emory said at the same time.

I hesitated. "But . . ."

"Okay, let's start with this. Are you drunk?" Brooke said.

"No, I'm not drunk. I'm a little tipsy, but no, definitely not drunk," I answered.

"Clearly, you like him, or we wouldn't be having this conversation," Emory interjected. "So, next question. Is he married?"

"No. I don't think so." I shook my head.

"Did you ask, or did you at least check for a ring?" Brooke asked.

"Hell, he wouldn't tell the truth if he was, and you know married dudes don't wear rings to the club," Emory said.

"True." Brooke shrugged. "But are you feeling him like that to the point that you wanna go?"

I thought about the way my body felt when T's hands were on me, and the intensity of his stare, which made me hot in places I hadn't felt in a long time. "I'm definitely feeling him."

Brooke looked exasperated now. "Then what's the problem?"

I exhaled and said, "All I know about this man is his name is T, he's from out of town, and he's a guest at the hotel."

"And you're feeling him," Emory reminded me.

"Okay, that too," I agreed.

"Then you don't need to know anything else." Brooke tossed her hands up in the air. "Brittany, listen, this isn't a love connection. It's a hookup. That's it. If you're trying to figure out if this dude has the potential to be Mr. Right, then don't. But if all you want now is to go and have a 'nightcap,' then by all means, go handle your business."

"Simple as that?" I asked.

"Yes, simple as that. There is a difference between love and lust. Just because you wanna get it in with somebody does not obligate you to wanna have to be in a relationship with them. I get it. That's not what Mom says, but it's true. So, either you say, 'Fuck it. I'm 'bout to go with this dude and enjoy the rest of my night, and when it's done, it's done.' Or you say, 'No. I'm good,' and you bring your ass back to my crib. Either way, it's up to you. There's no right or wrong answer. And please don't bring up anyone else, because they aren't even a part of this equation."

I knew she was referring to Duane, and she was right. I hadn't heard from him in days, and I'd had a good time ever since I stopped thinking about him.

"You're right! I'm going." I stood up and pulled my shirt open a little more.

"I am? You are?" Brooke said. She and Emory looked surprised as hell.

"Yep."

"Good for you," Emory exclaimed, then jumped up and gave me a hug.

"All right. It's your choice. Here's the thing. One, keep your location on and text me whatever room number you're in and let me know you're okay. Two, take this." Brooke reached into her clutch, took out a condom, and handed it to me.

"You carry these all the time?" I asked.

"Hey, I never know when I'll get lucky. I stay safe." She laughed. "One more thing. This guy T, you make sure you tell him you're down, but whatever happens, no strings attached."

"No strings attached," I repeated. "Wait, how am I gonna get home?"

"You can have him bring you to my building, but don't bring him upstairs, or call an Uber," Brooke replied as she stood up.

"Or Lyft," Emory volunteered. "Or call me. I'll come scoop."

"All right. I got it," I told them.

"Our little BB is all grown up," Brooke said and gave me a hug.

"Shut up," I told her.

"Remember, Britt, it's a hookup, not a love connection. No strings attached," Brooke stated as we walked past Kendrick, who held the door open for us to go back inside.

I gave them both one final hug, and they headed back toward the VIP section while I went back to find T. Other people were now sitting at the table where we'd sat earlier. I scanned the bar area to see if he was there, but he wasn't. I checked the dance floor and walked around the entire club, hoping I would find him. But to my disappointment, he was gone.

Chapter Seven

Brooke

"I'm worried about your sister," my mom said.

I sat up in my chair and adjusted my AirPods so I could hear better. My mom had sent me a text message telling me to call and saying it was urgent. Thinking something had happened to my dad, I had tried not to panic as I called her back immediately. "Why? What's wrong?"

"I don't know. She's acting like she's distracted or something's on her mind. I keep asking what's wrong, but she says nothing. Do you have Duane's number?"

"What? No. Why do you need his number?" I relaxed and tried not to sound irritated. Here I had been thinking it was an emergency, and it wasn't. As usual, my mother was overreacting about nothing.

"I figured I'd call and talk to him to see if he knows."

"Mama, you do know they broke up, right?" I said.

"No, they're on a break. She told me."

"Same thing."

"I think there's just been a misunderstanding and it'll work itself out. I told her that they've both invested too much time and effort in their relationship to just toss it in the trash. Duane is a nice guy, and he has a good job. She deserves someone like him," Mama told me.

I wanted to point out to my mother that Brittany and Duane had gone through more breakups than I could count, but I didn't want to risk starting an argument.

"She'll meet someone else," I said.

"Why would she need to do that when she has Duane? I swear, Brooke, I don't know why you are so detached. Where did you get that from? Certainly it didn't come from me or your daddy. You just act so cold when it comes to dating. You need to work on that. I was watching Iyanla the other night, and there was this girl . . ."

Tap, tap, tap.

"Mama, I have to go. Someone just walked into my office. I'll call you later," I said and then ended the call.

"Am I interrupting?" Emory asked as she stood in the doorway of my office.

"Yes, thank God." I exhaled dramatically.

"Everything good with Mom?" She walked in and sat down.

"Yeah. She's just digging for information about my sister, that's all," I said. "Being nosy and overstepping boundaries. You know how she does that."

"Oh Lord. How is Britt? Has she recovered yet?" Emory asked.

I exhaled and shook my head as I thought about my poor sister, who had been getting on my nerves since the night at the Sky Bar. "I'm starting to regret letting her hang with us. She's really being extra about it."

"Awww, she's just disappointed, that's all," Emory said sympathetically. "She really wanted to go with that dude."

"Girl, the way she's been acting, you woulda thought she missed the chance to hook up with Michael B. Jordan or somebody. All she keeps saying is she really felt something and has to find him. I keep explaining that what she was feeling was tipsy and horny, that's all."

"You are so mean." Emory laughed.

"I'm not. I'm honest. The problem is she doesn't go out enough. If she did, she would see there are hundreds of guys like him out there." I smirked. "Who knows? This may be a blessing in disguise. If she's acting like this and didn't even hook up with him, imagine if she had. She'd be stalking his ass."

"Stop it." Emory was laughing so hard that she was crying, which made me laugh.

"That's my sister, and I love her, but she can't hang out with me anymore. That was the last time." I shook my head.

"At least she didn't have to be carried out because she was too drunk to walk, like my sister did," Emory reminded me.

"Oh, God, yes," I said, recalling the last time we let Emory's sister hang out with us.

"How was the Denver office?" Emory asked.

"Cold and boring," I told her as I flipped through the files on my desk.

"Oh, so same as here." She laughed. "I thought you had decided to stay for a minute."

"Hell no. We missed a few days of training because of the damn weather, and we had to make it up. And then I caught hell tryin'a catch a flight out to get home," I said. "What's been going on around here?"

"Same ole same. I did hear that Holly was getting a new position, though."

"What?" I said a little louder than expected. I'd spoken with Brandon—who was conveniently out of the office for the rest of the week—several times while I was gone. He'd assured me that although his interview with the board of trustees had gone well, everything was still under wraps and he didn't have any updates. Now I wondered if he'd been lying. "What position?"

"I don't know. Apparently, some position that hasn't been posted yet," Emory said. "I figured you would know. Brandon hasn't mentioned it to you? Normally, y'all are the first to know everything."

"He hasn't said anything to me." I shook my head and reached for my diffuser, then turned it on. I needed something to calm my nerves.

"I'm sure we'll hear something soon. You know folks can't keep quiet about nothing around here. It's crazy how I've been waiting forever for a different position over in accounting, but somehow the 'good' jobs over there are never posted but always magically get filled."

"True," I said, thinking about the job Brandon was just offered, which no one knew about.

"I'm really thinking about going back to school to finish my MBA. I have only a couple more classes and I'll be done."

"I think that's a great idea, Emory. Go for it," I said, encouraging her. Emory was one of the smartest people I knew. She was a math genius and could troubleshoot computers like a pro. She had been with the company longer than I had and was my go-to person when I needed information on company processes that I couldn't find anywhere else.

"What's crazy is this chick named Kelly, who's been here for, like, only four months, got some job over in the business service department that we didn't even know was open. She doesn't know shit about what she's supposed to be doing, and keeps IM'ing me a million questions. But she has an MFA in creative writing, and they consider that advanced education and put her in a cubicle on the fourth floor. A-freaking-mazing, huh?"

"Damn." I shook my head.

"Anyway, so what's the deal for tonight? We hanging around for Wine Down Wednesday at the Sky Bar after work?" she asked, changing the subject.

"Sounds like a plan," I said.

"Well, let me get back upstairs before I'm fired. Not all of us have the luxury of being buddy-buddy with our boss like you."

My cell phone rang just then, and I saw it was Brittany. "She must know we were talking about her."

"Tell her I said hi," Emory said before she walked out.

"Hey, Britt," I said.

"Hey, what do you have going on this weekend?" Brittany asked.

"Uh, I don't know yet," I told her, prepared to say no before she even suggested we go visit my mother. "But I'm not driving anywhere, so don't ask."

"I wasn't going to ask you to drive anywhere. I was thinking about driving to see you," she said.

"You were?" I asked.

"Yeah. I want to hang out with you and Emory."

"I don't know. It's not like we hang out every weekend, Brittany," I said, not mentioning the fact that we were, in fact, going out after work. I knew what she was trying to do, though, so before she even got started, I let her know. "Look, Britt, you don't have to drive all the way here to go out and have a good time. There are plenty of bars and clubs in your area. Just pick one and go."

"I don't know," she said.

"Know what? There's nothing to know. You don't need me and Emory to have a good time. I'm sure Kyra would go with you if you invited her. Didn't you say y'all had a blast at Trap Karaoke?"

"Yeah, we did have fun."

"Okay. Then you'd probably have fun somewhere else too."

"But I don't know if it would be the same, though, you know, because I was hoping to possibly run into the same people that I ran into last time I went . . ."

"Brittany, you're really tripping. The chances of running into the same people are slim to none. I have a membership and run into the same folks only every now and then on the same night. Jeez, Britt, let it go. You're acting like this dude is the last man on earth. He's not. Get out and you'll see there are plenty more, I promise. Oh, and don't think I ain't noticed you took that damn outfit I let you *borrow*. I thought you said the boots were too high for you to walk in, heffa." I laughed.

"Oh, I accidentally put them in my bag. I can always bring them back this weekend. Then we can go back to the Sky Bar," Brittany offered.

"No, Britt, I don't want you to bring them back. I want you to keep them. As a matter of fact, put that same outfit on and go out somewhere with Kyra and maybe even meet another dude." I paused, then reminded her, "Just remember, if you decided to go home with him, use the condom I gave you, and no strings attached,"

"Fine. I will remember." Brittany sighed. "But, Brooke, I doubt if I'll meet someone like him. He was just . . . I don't know . . . magnetic. I felt something."

"You felt tipsy and horny." I giggled. "Trust me, I've been there."

"If you say so."

"I do, and I can't wait to hear about how much fun you guys had," I told her. "I gotta go. Love you, Britt."

"Love you too."

After work, Emory and I were back at the Sky Bar, this time seated at the bar, enjoying glasses of two-dollar Chardonnay and fried calamari. The atmosphere on Wednesdays was more laid back than it was on Fridays, and the crowd was thinner. There was no need for VIP seating. I really preferred the vibe on Wine Down Wednesday but rarely had the chance to enjoy it, because of my travel schedule. There was a different caliber of guys that came out. Friday nights were for those "on the prowl" for the weekend, whereas Wednesdays mainly attracted a more professional crowd looking for a midweek chill spot to have a drink and enjoy conversation.

"Omar says he's 'bout to roll through and buy a round," Emory said, reading the text she'd just gotten.

"He coming by himself, or is he bringing that cutie from the other night?" I asked.

"Should I ask?" Emory laughed.

"You should." I nodded. "I haven't had fun in a minute."

"Uh, didn't you just have fun before you left for Denver?" She raised an eyebrow at me.

"That was weeks ago." I pretended to be offended by her accusation. "And if I recall, you had some fun of your own with Omar recently. Which is why he's so willing to come and hang out tonight."

"You might have a point," Emory said.

As I laughed, I suddenly felt the presence of someone behind me. I slowly turned, and then I looked up and into a pair of deep-set, dark chestnut eyes.

"Damn. I've been looking for you," he said, his baritone voice so deep that it caused the hair on my neck to stand. "I forgot to give you something the other night."

He was standing so close to me that I wondered if he could hear my heart, which was beating rapidly. I slowly released the breath I hadn't realized I'd been holding, and said, "What?"

"This." He leaned down, cupped my face in his hands, and before I could stop him, his lips met mine. At first, I was too shocked to move, and then instinctively, my mouth opened and became captivated by our kiss. It was warm, inviting, and sensual, as if our tongues were made for one another. In that moment, everything around me stopped and everyone disappeared. Nothing else mattered except tasting him, and even though I had no idea who he was, I wanted and needed more. My arms encircled his neck, and he held me closer.

"Brooke. Brooke?" I could hear Emory calling my name, but she sounded like she was somewhere far in the distance.

After what seemed like an eternity, our lips finally parted.

Again, Emory called my name. "Brooke!"

"Yeah?" I said, still breathless from the kiss with the stranger, whom I was still staring at.

"What the hell?" she whispered. "Who is this?"

"This? Oh, this is . . ." I blinked, realizing I didn't have a name to give her.

"Taurus," he said with a grin.

"Taurus," I repeated.

"Okay, Taurus." Emory pushed me to the side a little to get the attention of both of us. "I'm Emory, Brooke's best friend."

"Nice to meet you, Brooke's best friend," Taurus said, his eyes never leaving mine. "Can I buy you ladies a drink?"

I nodded. "Definitely," I said, deciding then and there that it didn't matter whether Omar and his friends showed up or not. I knew exactly whom I would be leaving with.

Chapter Eight

Brittany

"You're kidding, right?"

"No, I'm not."

"So you mean I got dressed for nothing?" Kyra whined and flopped down onto my sofa.

"I'm sorry. It's not my fault, I swear." I sighed and pointed to the box of folders on the floor. "I have to have the data pulled for all those files and a full report ready and on his desk in the morning."

"That's insane. He just told you today." Kyra shook her head in disbelief.

"I know, but I've gotta get it done. I'm already on thin ice after leaving the other week and going to Brooke's instead of to the meeting at the central office."

"But you sent an email saying you were sick, so why is he tripping?" Kyra asked.

"Because he's an asshole, that's why." I reached for my laptop.

"That's a lot of work, Britt. Is there anything I can do to help?"

I glanced over at her. She was looking unusually cute in a belted, one-shoulder jumpsuit and peep-toe heels. "No, I got it. You look so nice. You should still go."

"I'm not going without you. The only reason I was going was that you wanted to go," Kyra said, slipping out of her shoes.

Hearing her say that made me feel even worse. I didn't know what I'd been thinking when I suggested that she and I go out on a weeknight, anyway. I called myself being daring and taking Brook's advice after I heard a commercial on the radio inviting people out for a night of great music and drink specials. It had sounded fun, and I had immediately thought about that night at the Sky Bar. The night I met *him*. I'd played the night over and over in my head. The moment I bumped into him, the scent of his cologne, the feel of his hands on my hips. But most of all, I'd thought about the way he looked at me. I'd never had anyone look at me with such desire. It had been enthralling. And even though he was long gone, I felt the need to find him, despite what Brooke had said.

"Is that your phone?" Kenya asked.

I jumped up and located my vibrating phone on the desk, in the corner. To my surprise, it was Duane. I answered. "Hello."

"Hey, Britt. How are you?"

"Hey, Duane. I'm good," I told him. Kyra looked just as shocked to hear me say his name.

"I'm a'ight. What's going on?" Duane said.

"Uh, nothing really," I answered.

"You sure?"

"Yeah. Why?" I wondered why he was concerned about how I was doing after he had ignored me for weeks.

"I spoke with your mom earlier and—"

"My mom? How? Why?" I was even more confused.

"Oh, she called me, and we had a nice conversation. She was worried about you . . . well, actually, more so about us." He said it as if having a conversation with my mom about our relationship was as normal as brushing his teeth in the morning.

"So, because you had a conversation with my mom about us, you decided to call me?"

"What?" Kyra whispered loudly.

"Well, yeah, I did. I wanted to make sure you were good," he said.

I began to wonder what my mother had told him to make him suddenly decide to call me. How had she even got his number?

"I'm fine, Duane. I don't know what my mom called you for, because I haven't said anything to her about you, other than we were on a break. So I'm sorry if she made you worry."

"No, it's fine. I've been meaning to call you, anyway. I mean, I'd really like to come over tonight and see you. You know, talk face-to-face."

"Tonight's not a good night, Duane. I'm sorry. I'm busy," I told him. "As a matter of fact, I have to go, because I have company right now, and I'm being rude."

Kyra covered her mouth to stifle her giggles.

"Company? Oh, for real? It's like that?" From the sound of his voice, I could tell that my statement had caught him off guard.

"Yeah. I'll speak with you another time. Thanks for checking on me," I said just before I hung up.

"What in the entire hell was that about?" Kyra squealed.

I shrugged. "I don't know. He said my mom called him to talk about me and us."

"I'm not even talking about that. I'm talking about your sudden indifference. A couple of days ago you were moping because he wouldn't call or text you back, and now he wants to come over and you say no?" Kyra waited impatiently for my response.

"I guess I'm not pressed anymore. Like, I didn't even get excited when I saw his name on my phone," I told her.

"So, are you saying you're done with him for good, Brittany?"

I paused, and then I nodded. "I am."

"Wow. I can't believe this. You always said Duane was your soul mate and you knew that's who you're supposed to be with. What happened?"

"You know what happened," I told her. "The Sky Bar."

"By Sky Bar, I hope you mean you went out with your sister and had fun for a change." Kyra gave me a warning look. "This better not be about that dude you danced with again."

"First of all, I danced with two dudes. And don't act like that. What I will say is that I have never felt with Duane what I felt with that guy the other night. It was surreal." I sighed.

"You met a guy in the club, and he invited you to hook up, Brittany. Chances are, he probably hooked up with someone else, which is why he was gone. It's what guys do all the time in the club. I really think you're romanticizing what happened. It was not that special." Kyra shook her head.

"You don't understand," I told her.

"I understand that you can be kinda dramatic when it comes to love, or finding love. And I'm not saying that in a bad way," she said.

"I can't tell." I rolled my eyes at her.

"But real talk, the way you handled Duane was absolutely perfect. Hell, the way he's treated you the past few weeks, he'd better be glad you answered the phone."

"I still can't believe my mother, though."

"You think she called him? He may be lying."

I knew Duane wasn't lying about my mother calling him. As crazy as it sounded, it was something she'd do. She liked Duane, and more importantly, she liked me *with* Duane.

"He's not lying. She called him," I said. Then I instructed Siri to call Mom.

She didn't pick up, but like clockwork, she called me back the following morning, as I was on my way to work.

"Mama, did you call Duane to talk about me?" I asked when she called.

"Well, good morning to you too, Brittany," she said.

"Good morning, Mama. Did you call Duane to tell him you were concerned about me because we broke up?"

"Well, I called to see how he was doing, and he happened to ask about you. So, I told him I had some concerns." She sounded just as nonchalant about her and Duane's conversation as he had.

"But why, Mama? You've never called him while we were dating, so why the sudden need to talk to him now?"

"Because I am concerned, Brittany. I'm concerned about both of you. You've been acting distant and won't talk to me these days," she said.

"Mama, I talk to you at least three times a week. What are you talking about?"

"No, we talk on the phone, and I ask you questions, which you avoid answering. That's not talking."

"Because you ask me questions I don't have the answers for. I don't know what Duane's doing or how he's feeling. And the reason I don't know is that for two weeks straight, I called and texted Duane, and he never responded. He ignored me," I told her. "I listened to you telling me to give it time and pray and we would work out, because we were meant to be."

"You are. And that's why he called you last night. Did y'all talk?" she said, disregarding everything I had said about Duane ignoring me for two weeks.

"Yeah, but not for long. I had company and had to go."

"Company? What kind of company?"

"Just a friend, that's all."

"What friend, Brittany? And whoever he was, he should not have been more of a priority than Duane," she asserted. "And furthermore, you don't know them well enough for them to be coming over to your house at night. That's not something you'd do. That's more like Brooke, and you are nothing like her."

"Lord, Mama, don't start. There's nothing wrong with Brooke," I replied, coming to my sister's defense. "And calm down. It was Kyra."

"Oh." She sounded relieved.

"But you should know that even though Duane called, that doesn't mean we're getting back together."

"I thought you loved Duane. And from what he told me yesterday, he loves you too."

"I don't know what I'm feeling right now. As a matter of fact, I'm thinking about seeing someone else I met," I told her.

"Who?"

"Just a guy," I said. "Like I said, I'm thinking about it, that's all. "

"Well, that's your choice, Brittany. But I know how much you loved Duane, despite how you're feeling right now. And he was good for you. You were good for each other."

"Even so, you shouldn't have called him," I told her.

"Well, whoever this guy is, I hope he's worth jeopardizing what you have with Duane. You deserve to be happy. That's why I called him. Because I know he makes you happy," she explained. "Now, if that makes me a bad mother, then so be it."

"I understand, Mama. Just please don't call him again."

When our call ended, I thought about what she had said. Not so long ago, Duane had been everything I wanted. But when his job had become stressful, he'd taken it out on me. It wasn't fair. We had hardly ever gone out, except to dinner and an occasional movie, and I hadn't realized what I'd been missing until I hung out with Brooke. That night I had had fun, had looked beautiful, been treated like a queen, and had met a man who made me feel amazing, and Duane had been the farthest thing from my mind.

Chapter Nine

Brooke

I had fucked up. I had really fucked up. Now it was six o'clock in the morning, and I was sitting in my parking garage, wondering what I was going to do. What started out as one of the best nights of my life had turned into one nightmare of a morning.

Taurus had bought Emory and me more drinks, and then Omar and a couple of his friends had shown up at the bar. More drinks and appetizers had been ordered, and we'd laughed, talked shit, and had a great time. Taurus had never left my side, and even though we'd been with a group of people, we'd somehow seemed to feel like we were the only two people in the room. He would lean close and say something to me, and when we laughed, our eyes would meet and our stare would linger. I kept trying to figure out where we'd met before, but I couldn't. I told myself it had probably been one of the few nights when I'd been too wasted or distracted by someone else at the moment. Because if we'd met when I was sober, I damn sure would've remembered.

After a while, he leaned over and whispered, "You ready to get out of here?"

I nodded and whispered back, "Damn right."

We said our goodbyes, and I gave Emory the signal that I'd text her and to let her know I was good.

When we got on the elevator, he said, "I just moved into a new place not far from here. Napoleon Place. You heard of it?"

"I have." I nodded. "I was considering moving there when they were first built last year. Nice."

"So, do you wanna follow me? Or you can just leave your car, and we can get it later," he said. "It's up to you."

"I can follow," I told him. "I valeted my truck. Are you parked in the garage?"

"No. I'm on valet as well."

Hearing that he used the hotel valet service was just as impressive to me as hearing he lived in a luxury condominium comparable to the one in which I lived. He was handsome, well dressed, funny, and he had a couple of dollars; he was definitely turning me on more and more. Plus, he was a damn good kisser.

As we waited for our vehicles, he said, "You're gonna follow me, right!"

"Yes, I am." I was confused by his question.

"You sure? You betta not disappear on me!" He ran his finger along my neck and caressed my collarbone. My desire quickened, and I was glad his condo was less than ten minutes away, because I was ready to see if he was the real deal.

"I'll be right behind you," I said. They couldn't bring our cars fast enough. As I trailed him to his place, I called Emory to give her a quick update on where I was headed.

"Napoleon Place? What?" She sounded impressed.

"Yeah. He says he just moved in."

"I like him. He seems really cool, and you guys seemed to be having a lot of fun tonight. Like you've known each other for years," Emory said.

"I know. That's crazy, huh? I'm trying to rack my brain and figure out where we met. But at this point, it don't even matter. That brother is fine."

"That kiss, girl. I ain't never seen you react like that, Brooke. For a second, it was like you were caught up," Emory teased.

I thought about the kiss, which had left me breathless, and quickly changed the subject. "Are you still with Omar?"

"No, but we're supposed to hook up this weekend. We'll see if that happens. You know how he is. But you go ahead and get it in, bestie. Make sure you keep your location on."

"I will," I told her.

"Oh, and I know this dude is fine and a good kisser and all, but don't forget NSA!"

"NSA!" I replied as we arrived at Taurus's gated community. He entered the code that opened the iron gates, and I quickly drove behind him before they closed. A few minutes later, he pulled into a driveway and pointed for me to park beside him. I jumped out of my car and followed him.

"You kept your promise," he said as he unlocked his front door and held it open for me.

"I did," I said, stepping inside after he clicked on a light. I looked around and saw that the only thing in the great room of the condo was a large television mounted over the fireplace and few boxes sitting along the wall.

"I haven't really gotten settled in yet. I'm going to look at furniture this weekend. But you can . . ."

Before he said anything else, I grabbed his hand and pulled him down the hallway toward what I hoped was his bedroom. I was horny as hell, and the last thing I wanted to talk about was his lack of decor in his nice-ass condo. I had come there for one thing and one thing only. We reached a slightly open door at the end of the hall. He pushed the door all the way open, and we stepped into a huge bedroom that held more boxes, a large dresser, and a king-size bed with a small nightstand beside it. He took my phone, keys, and purse from me and placed them on the dresser, then turned me toward him. He went to kiss me again, but I moved away.

"What's wrong?" He frowned.

"Nothing. I just wanna make something clear, so we're on the same page," I told him.

"Wait. Are you married?" His eyes widened.

"No," I answered. "Are you?"

"No, I'm not."

"Cool. But I need for you to know that if we do this, it's no strings attached. I'm not looking for anything special other than what we're about to do, and the only thing I'm thinking about is right here and right now. Understand?"

A wide grin spread across Taurus's face, and he pulled me toward him. "Oh yeah, I definitely understand."

We didn't waste any time undressing one another and climbing into the large bed. His body was toned and athletic, and I enjoyed the feel of his muscular chest as I ran my fingers across it. He was just as eager to enjoy me as I was him. He touched and caressed every inch of my curves, and by the time he took out a condom and slipped it on, I was more than ready for him to enter. The sex was hot, satisfying, and left both of us breathless. But there was something different about it, about him. Afterward, he held me close and nuzzled my neck. I went to get up, but he held me tighter.

"Don't go yet. I need you a little longer," he said.

"I'm not spending the night, Taurus. I told you what this was," I reminded him.

"Just chill for a little while longer, that's all." He stared at me, and even in the darkened room, I could see the longing in his eyes.

"Fine. Ten more minutes." I laid my head back on his chest, and he kissed the top of my head and snuggled closer. He tipped my head up, and then he did exactly what I didn't want him to do: he kissed me. The kiss was soft, wet, and just as gratifying as the sex we'd had moments before.

"You feel so damn good. I'm glad I found you," he whispered, then fell into a deep slumber.

I closed my eyes for what I thought would be a few minutes. When I opened them, I checked my watch and had to blink a couple of times to make sure I was seeing the time correctly. It was after five o'clock in the morning. I'd done the unthinkable and spent the night. I eased out of bed and searched for my clothes. Taurus rolled over, and I watched him reach for me. Then he sat up.

"What time is it?" he asked.

"Later than I thought," I told him.

"You're leaving?" he asked as he squinted in the darkness. The slivers of light from the streetlight outside provided just enough illumination for me to admire his handsome face.

"Yeah, I have to get ready for work."

"Damn, well, at least let me walk you out." He placed his feet on the floor, and before I could stop him, he was out of the bed and hugging me from behind.

"You don't have to. I can see myself out." I wiggled my way out of his arms.

"I know you can, but I want to," he told me. "I can't believe you were gonna just slip out without saying anything. I mean, can't I at least get your number before you go?"

I turned around and faced him. He grinned slightly and thought for a second. He was cute, fun, and he was definitely a good time in and out of bed. I decided that I wouldn't mind hooking up with him again, if the opportunity presented itself.

"Fine." I exhaled and shook my head.

"Wow. Don't act so excited to give it to me. What? Don't tell me you're gonna call Emory and give me a BDR."

The laugh I'd been trying to suppress escaped. "What? Why would I do that? You know that's a myth, right? Women don't talk like that."

"You're shitting me. Oh, y'all talk, probably more than men do. And before you leave, I need to make sure you're good." He folded his arms across his naked chest. I tried not to lower my eyes to his manhood but couldn't help it. "Hey, eyes up here, missy."

I blushed, having been caught. "No, I'm not giving you a Bad Dick Report."

"Does that mean I'm getting a Good Dick Report?"

"No, that's not what that means," I told him. "Where is your phone?"

He reached toward the nightstand and grabbed his phone, unlocked it with his fingerprint, and handed it to me. I entered my phone number and handed it back to him. A few seconds later, my phone buzzed. I walked over to the dresser and saw a text from a strange number.

"You're texting me right now? Really?"

"What? Don't act like you don't want my number too," he said. "Especially since you're gonna give me a good report to your friends."

"Just remember what I said earlier. I'm not looking for anything special. It is what it is," I said.

"I know. No strings attached. I get it," he said, reaching into a drawer and taking out a pair of basketball shorts, which he slipped on.

He walked me to my truck, and I gave him a hug.

"I did have a good time," I told him.

"I did too. And I meant what I said. I'm really glad I ran into you again. Last night was definitely worth your disappearing that night and missing our nightcap." He hugged me again.

In that moment, everything became clear and made sense. The reason he'd been acting so familiar and comfortable. The sudden kiss he'd given me. The way we'd instantly vibed. It was him. Taurus was the guy, and he thought I was Brittany.

My heart raced, and I swallowed hard. "Taurus, I—"

He interrupted me before I could finish. "I know. You have to go. Can you please let me know you made it home safely, though, Brooke?" The way he looked at me when he said my name sent a chill down my spine.

Tell him. Tell him who you are, I screamed in my head. My mouth opened, but nothing came out.

He kissed my forehead, and I jumped in my truck. As I backed out of his driveway, he waved at me. I put my truck in drive and didn't look back. While I was driving home, my mind was a myriad of emotions. I arrived at my building and pulled into my assigned parking space. As tears streamed down my face, I realized I didn't even remember driving home, because I'd been so zoned out. My phone buzzed, and I jumped. I glanced down and saw that it was a text message from Emory.

How was it? she asked.

I stared at the message, not knowing how to respond. I got out of the truck and went inside. After taking off my clothes, I climbed in the shower and stood under the water for what seemed like forever, trying to get my mind together. I couldn't believe I'd run into the man my sister had been talking nonstop about for the past few weeks. Not only that, but I'd also slept with him. But the worst part about the entire situation was that I had totally enjoyed it. After showering, I got dressed and sat on the side of my bed.

My phone buzzed again with another message from Emory. Well, damn, it must've gone well, because you're home and you haven't responded. You good?

She was still tracking me. I picked up my phone and typed several words. Yeah, I'm fine.

She texted back immediately. Can't wait to hear the deets. Lunch date?

The "deets," as she called them, were the last thing I wanted to think about. But maybe telling someone what had happened would help me feel better. To be honest, there was only one person in the world I trusted enough to tell about this situation without having to worry about being judged or criticized for my actions, and that was my best friend.

"What? Are you serious? How?" Emory's jaw dropped, and she was just as shocked to hear what had happened as I was to realize it.

"I don't know," I said as I sat across the table from her. We were seated at Jake's, a local barbecue spot not far from the office. Normally, my food would be almost gone by now, but I had only picked at the ribs, baked beans, macaroni and cheese, and corn bread on my plate. I couldn't eat. I was too distracted and had been all day. "At least now I know why he felt so comfortable with me. He thought I was Britt."

"What did he say when you told him?" Emory asked.

I looked up at her, then back down at my food. I didn't say a word.

"Brooke, you didn't tell him? He doesn't know?"

"What was I supposed to say? 'Hey, I know you think I'm the girl you met last month at the bar, but I'm not. I'm her sister'?"

"Uh, yeah." Emory nodded.

"I know, and you're probably right."

"Probably?"

"You're not making me feel any better about this situation, Emory. Damn it. I already feel bad enough," I whined and sat back in my seat.

"I'm not trying to make you feel bad. It was an inno-cent case of mistaken identity. It could've happened to anyone. You both were kind of tipsy, and that was partly to blame." Emory shrugged. "Blame it on the alcohol."

"Now you're trying to be funny." I gave her an expres-sionless stare to let her know I wasn't amused.

"What did Britt say when you told her?"

Again, I looked down at my plate.

"You didn't tell her, either?" Emory groaned.

"When did I have time to tell her? This shit just happened this morning, Emory. I've been at work all morning," I said.

"Well, when are you going to tell her? You *are* going to tell her, right?"

"I don't know. I mean, do I really need to tell either one of them?" I said.

"What?"

"Okay, what if I just never see him again? I can block his number, and then I'll just never see him again. Simple as that. Pretend last night never happened," I said, suddenly feeling like a genius.

"That won't work." Emory shook her head.

"Why not? I've had one-night stands before. That's all last night was for me. A forgettable one-night stand."

"I think it was way more than that."

I understood what Emory was saying, and deep down, I knew she was right. But I somehow convinced myself that what had happened the night before was some magical sexual escapade that I'd imagined. When I got back to my office, I blocked Taurus's number from my phone. I couldn't bring myself to delete it. And I went on with my life as if nothing had happened. For the next few days, I forced myself not to think about him and the way I had felt when he kissed me in the club. How he had made me laugh throughout the night and the next morning. And most of all, how, as I was lying beside him, listening to his light snoring as I drifted off to sleep, I had never felt safer. I also avoided Brittany's calls and texts by telling her I was swamped at work and unable to talk. I didn't go out at all over the weekend, even though Emory pleaded for me to hang out. My plan was going the way I had hoped, and by Sunday, I thought I had pulled it off. Then that afternoon I got a voicemail from a strange number.

"Hey, Brooke. It's Taurus. This is actually my new house number. I've been trying to reach out to you for a couple of days, but you haven't responded. I hope everything is okay, and I hope I didn't do anything wrong. I thought we had a great time, and I was looking forward to getting to know you. Maybe I was wrong. Anyway, let me know if you'd like to meet up. If not, it's cool. Take care."

For a split second, I considered calling him back. We had had a great time, but as much I wanted to see him and hang out again, I knew it was wrong. I listened to the message one more time before hitting DELETE and adding his house number to my blocked call list.

Chapter Ten

Brittany

"Ms. Newman, guess what?" Marlena said after bursting into my office, unannounced. I looked up from my computer, and before I could respond, she said, "I'ma get to go on the class trip next Friday."

"You are?" I realized I sounded more surprised than supportive, and so I quickly changed my tone. "That's great, Marlena."

"Yep, I haven't had any behavior incidents, so Mrs. Cunningham said I could go with everyone else. Are you proud of me?" She beamed with pride.

"I am." I nodded. "I'm very proud of you."

Just then Ms. Crystal entered through the same door that Marlena had come through moments before. "Marlena, you're in trouble. I told you, you did not have permission to leave the classroom."

"But I needed to see Ms. Newman, and she said anytime I need to see her, her door is always open." Marlena looked over at me and added, "Isn't that what you said?"

"That's what I said, but—" I began, but I was interrupted.

"You didn't have permission. I'm writing you up," Ms. Crystal told her, disregarding the fact that I hadn't finished speaking.

"You can't. You can't write me up." Marlena began to panic.

"I can, and I will," Ms. Crystal said, reaching for Marlena.

"Hold on a sec, Ms. Crystal," I said.

"Nah! Fuck that!" Marlena yelled and snatched away from her.

Ms. Crystal reached for the walkie-talkie on her hip and put it to her mouth. "We need security down in Ms. Newman's office, please."

"Why you do that? I ain't even do nothing!" Marlena screamed.

"Marlena, calm down," I said. "Ms. Crystal, she's fine."

"She's getting written up for leaving the class without permission and for using profanity too. You're getting some days, Marlena," Ms. Crystal said with a smug look.

A few seconds later, one of the security guards walked in, and Ms. Crystal said, "Marlena needs to be escorted down to Mr. McGee's office."

"I don't need to go to the office. I ain't do nothing. Ms. Newman, tell them I ain't do nothing!" Marlena pleaded, her eyes filling with tears.

"Wait. Hold on." I stood up.

The security guard looked from Marlena to me, then to Ms. Crystal, as if he was wondering what he should do.

"Let's all just take a moment," I said.

"Ms. Newman, I'm writing her up, and that's final," Ms. Crystal said. She looked at the security guard and told him, "Tell Mr. McGee I'll send the referral ASAP." Then she walked out of my office.

"Man, this some bullshit." Marlena folded her arms.

"Marlena," I snapped.

"That's enough, young lady," the guard said. "Let's go."

I knew that Marlena was not going to leave without a fight, so I immediately walked over to her in an effort to diffuse the situation. I then reached for my desk, grabbed a Kleenex, handed it to her, and said, "Here. Straighten your face up."

She took it from me and wiped the tears that were streaming down her face and sniffed. "All I wanted to do was tell you I kept my promise, so you could be proud of me, that's all."

I looked at her and said, "I *am* proud of you. You did a great job. But you still disobeyed."

"I'm sorry," she said.

"You don't have to apologize to me. You need to apologize to Ms. Crystal," I told her.

"Okay." She nodded. "Is she still gonna give me an incident report?"

"I don't know. I'll go talk to her and see. Sit," I said. Then I told the guard, "Wait here for a second, until I come back. Don't take her anywhere yet."

"No problem, Ms. Newman." He nodded.

Marlena relaxed and sat down in one of the chairs in my office. I hurried down the hallway to see if I could reason with Ms. Crystal. I was just about to turn the corner when I heard her talking to someone. I peeked and saw that it was an assistant in another classroom.

"Now, you know I was waiting for her bad ass to do something so I could write her up. As soon as she walked out of the classroom, I wanted to shout for joy. I was already pissed that Mrs. Cunningham told her she could go on the damn field trip in the first place. Ain't nobody gonna be dealing with Marlena's bad ass in public. It's bad enough we gotta deal with her ass in school."

"Girl, she is a handful. I'm glad she ain't in none of my classes. But you know Ms. Newman gonna figure out a way for her to go," the other assistant said.

"Ain't nobody thinking about her fat ass, either. She needs to be worried about keeping her job, because word on the street is that her contract ain't being renewed. Even Mr. McGee commented the other day that we would be getting a new social worker next year, and I'm glad. All she does is make excuses for us to keep these badass kids here in school," Ms. Crystal said. "With her big ass gone, Marlena and a whole lot of other problem kids will be gone. Thank God."

I stepped around the corner and stared at the two of them for a second. They were so busy laughing that they didn't notice me at first. Then the assistant looked up, and when she saw that I was standing there, she immediately stopped. Ms. Crystal, whose back was to me, slowly turned around, and the smile faded from her face. No one said anything. We just stared at one another until I finally turned around and walked back to my office.

"You can take her back to class," I told the guard when I went back inside. "If anyone has a problem with her coming back, tell them to come talk to me directly."

"For real?" Marlena said excitedly.

"Yes, but you betta not get into any more trouble, and I mean it this time. And next time you want to come and talk to me, you get permission. Better yet, I'll come and check on you."

"Thank you, Ms. Newman," she said, jumping up and hugging me.

"A'ight, Marlena. Let's go," the guard told her. He looked at me and said, "I'm glad you looked out, Ms. Newman. She may get out of pocket sometimes, but she's a good kid at heart. You're 'bout the only one around here who looks out for some of these kids. We need more people like you, for real."

"Thanks." I gave him a semi-smile as I recalled what I'd just overheard in the hallway.

I spent the remainder of the afternoon trying to work, but I was too distracted. First, I was expecting Ms. Crystal to walk in at any moment, but she didn't. I was also bothered by fact that she had said my contract was not going to be renewed, and wondered if there was any truth to that statement. As soon as the school day ended, I went to Mr. McGee's office. His secretary told me he was in the middle of a conference call and then had another meeting scheduled, and I told her I'd wait. It took almost an hour, but she finally told me I could go into his office.

"Ms. Newman," he said, barely looking up from his desk. "Is this about the Marlena incident I was told about earlier?"

"No, Mr. McGee. It's about something else. It's been brought to my attention that my contract isn't being re-newed for the upcoming school year. Is that true?" I said.

He glanced up and seemed surprised by my question. "And who, might I ask, brought that to your attention?"

"I'd rather not say, but I would like to confirm if it's true," I told him.

"Well, I'm not at liberty to confirm or deny that infor-mation at this time, Ms. Newman. The budget and con-tract renewals won't come out for another week or so." He sat back in his chair and removed his wire-rimmed glasses, then placed his hand against his chin. I could tell by his avoidance of the issue that there was some truth to what Ms. Crystal had said.

"I'm sure you had to make the staff recommendations when you submitted the budget, Mr. McGee. Was my name included?" I stared back at him.

"I'm not really sure. But I will say this. Had you shown up at the central office for the meeting last month, like other social workers from the school district did, you would know. There were several who were interested in working at this school. But you were sick, remember?" He raised an eyebrow at me.

I realized that this conversation was pointless. I turned and walked out without saying anything else. I was tired, frustrated, and it was taking everything not to become overwhelmed. I damn near sprinted to my car, and after enduring almost an hour of traffic, I finally arrived home. My head was pounding. I popped three Motrin and did something I rarely did. I took a nap.

When I woke up, the sun had set and I was still agitated. I dialed Brooke's number, but as usual, she didn't answer. I was disappointed, but I knew she was going through her own work struggles and was unavailable. We hadn't really talked in over a week, but the last time we chatted, it had been brief, and she had told me that she was waiting to hear about a possible upcoming promotion, which she wanted, and that she had a lot on her plate. Kyra was at work, so I couldn't talk long to her. And I needed to vent freely, talk without having to censor my words, so I opted not to call my mother. By now, my stomach was rumbling. I got up and decided to go get something to eat from one of the Mexican restaurants not far from my house.

"Dining alone?" the hostess asked when I stepped inside the restaurant.

"I'm actually ordering takeout," I told her.

"No problem. Let me know when you're ready," she said, passing me a glossy menu.

I was scanning the items when I heard a familiar laugh from across the room. I looked up and saw that it was Duane, who was sitting across the table from another woman. His eyes met mine, and for the second time that day, I hated the fact that I walked up on a situation that I had not expected.

"You ready?" the hostess asked.

"No. I'm sorry. I've changed my mind," I said, handing her the menu. I walked back out the door as fast as possible.

"Britt! Britt, hold on," Duane called after me.

I unlocked my car door and climbed in. Before I could close the door, he was standing there, holding it.

"Move, Duane," I told him.

"Wait. Let me holla at you for a sec," he pleaded.

"There's nothing you need to holla at me about, Duane. Go back in and holla at whoever that chick is," I snapped.

"Don't be like this. It ain't like what you think."

"It don't matter what I think. You don't owe me an explanation."

"But I wanna give you one. That's a friend of Denisha's. She wanted to get something to eat right quick. That's all," he told me.

"I told you I don't care."

"But I do."

"And?" I frowned.

"Why are you tripping like this? I mean, aren't you the one who had company the other night, when I wanted to come through and talk? Now you're acting upset because I'm out eating with a coworker?"

"A coworker? I thought she was a friend of Denisha's, Duane?" I gave a sarcastic laugh.

"I mean, she is. She's Denisha's friend, and she works with me. She just started, as a matter of fact," Duane muttered.

"Please move, Duane," I told him.

"Britt, come on."

"Bye, Duane," I said.

"So that's it?" he asked.

I looked into the face that I once couldn't get enough of, at the person that I had thought would make me happy, and at the man I had once hoped I would marry, and I realized that I no longer felt the same. I'd spent the past two years of my life doing any and everything I thought was necessary for him to be satisfied with me, and deep down, I didn't want to be with him now. It wasn't sadness I felt. It was regret.

"That's it," I said.

He slowly backed away, enough for me to close my door. Then he walked away.

I felt an entirely new sense of urgency to talk to someone, so I called Brooke and prayed she'd answer. When she didn't, I sent her a text asking her to call me back ASAP because it was important. Duane and I were officially over, and not only did I want to move on, but I also wanted to move.

Chapter Eleven

Brooke

"Everything okay?"

I glanced over and nodded. "Everything's fine."

"You sure?"

"Yes."

I stared at my watch and read the text that I'd just received, then quickly dismissed it, promising myself that I would reach out after I got home. I'd been telling myself that for over a week now, and I still hadn't done it. I couldn't. Not yet, anyway, and now definitely wasn't the right time to do so. Not while I was with him. But I knew I had to tell her, and I had to tell him. I just didn't know how. I wasn't sure how either one of them would react, and the truth was that none of this had been planned. It had just happened. Despite my blocking his number and staying away from the Sky Bar for two weeks in a row, somehow, it had still happened.

A few days prior, I had been out enjoying one of my all-time favorite Saturday morning pastimes: shopping at Target. I had been wanting one of those filtered water pitchers for a while but had never picked one up. Luckily, when I read through the ad paper, I saw they had them on sale, and I hurried over to the aisle, only to find the shelf empty. Then I looked up and saw that there was a pitcher at the very top. I struggled to reach it. Just as I was about to give up, a hand reached up and grabbed it, then passed it to me.

"Thanks," I began, turning around, then stopped speaking before I could finish my statement. My eyes widened, and I was both stunned and pleasantly surprised to see Taurus beside me.

"Don't mention it," he said, then grabbed the basket behind him and walked away.

"Taurus, wait," I said.

He paused, then turned and looked at me. "Yeah? What's up?"

"I mean, damn. I wanted to at least say hi." I smiled at him. He was looking just as handsome in a pair of sweatpants and a T-shirt displaying a motivational slogan and a Nike swish. His hair looked like it had just been cut, and the full beard he had had the last time I saw him was now a trimmed goatee.

"Oh." He shrugged and gave me a nonchalant stare.

"Oh? That's it? I mean, how are you doing?" I asked.

"I'm good." He went to turn away again.

"Well, it was nice seeing you," I told him.

He didn't say anything else as he walked off down the aisle. I couldn't believe he was tripping. I mean, I knew I'd blocked him, even though I had hated to do so, but I'd also told him that it was no strings attached. Despite me having to force myself not to think about him constantly and having images of that night in bed flash in my mind randomly, I figured not being able to reach me would be no big deal to him. I felt bad, and my feelings were kind of hurt by his reaction to seeing me. Then I thought about why I'd blocked him, and reminded myself that it didn't matter, anyway.

I shopped around a little more and was walking down one of the main aisles near the home decor when I heard my name being called.

"Yo, Brooke."

"Yeah?" I answered. I looked over, and Taurus was standing near the towels.

"Which one of these do you like better?" He held up two shower curtains, both of which were brightly colored and had a floral pattern and looked horrible.

I pushed my cart over to get a closer look. Then I gave him a half smile and said, "Honestly, neither."

"Damn. That's what I was thinking too." He sighed, putting them both back on the hook.

"I mean, this one is okay," I said, pointing to what I thought was a nicer shower curtain.

"Yeah, I thought about that one. But it's dark gray. I was trying to get something with a little more color."

"I mean, you can add color with your accent towels. I mean, it's gray, so any other color will work. My living room is gray, but my accent color is yellow."

"That sounds dope." He nodded, then took out his phone. "This is the furniture I'm thinking about getting today." He handed me the phone.

I looked down at a picture of a living-room set, which looked as horrible as the shower curtains he had just been contemplating. The sofa, love seat, and chair on the screen looked like something more suitable for a college dorm than an upscale condominium. "You did say thinking about, right? Please tell me you didn't buy this."

"Not yet. I'm heading over there when I leave here. The salesman is giving me a good deal on it," Taurus said with pride.

"Is he lowering the price from two hundred dollars to one fifty?"

"Oh, you got jokes, huh?" He smirked. "Nah, it costs more than that. And what's wrong with it?"

"Other than looking cheap and plastic?" I handed him back his phone.

"It just looks like that in the pic. It looks nicer in person." He put his phone in his pocket.

"Where is this furniture coming from? Best For Less?" I laughed, and then I saw that he wasn't amused.

"My coworker said it was the best place to go, and they have free delivery," he replied.

"Your coworker lied," I said.

"Well, you have somewhere better?" he asked.

I paused and said, "Yeah, I do."

"Well, show me."

"Okay. I can pull up the directions right now, and you can go check it out." I went to take my phone out of my purse.

"Nah. I want you to take me wherever it is. You can help me pick out something else. That's if it's better than the deal I already got," he said in a daring tone.

I looked at him, contemplating what I should do. I had nothing else planned for the remainder of the day and didn't mind helping him out. And Lord knows, from the looks of his current selections, he could use all the help he could get. I told myself there would be no harm in shopping for furniture with him. It was like a good deed for the day.

"Fine," I said. "Grab that shower curtain, though."

"Bet." He smiled. "Oh, and let me get some yellow towels to go with it."

Hours later, we had found not only the perfect living room set for him but also decor for his kitchen, bathrooms, and bedroom. We'd gone everywhere, from a local furniture store to IKEA, Pier 1 Imports, and TJ Maxx. The furniture he'd originally picked out may have been cheap, but he'd had no problem spending a pretty penny on everything I'd suggested.

"I think that's about everything I need," he said as he put the last of his purchases into the backseat of his car. His trunk was already full, and nothing else could fit back there. The sun was setting. The sky was an array of pinks, and the temperature had dropped slightly.

"I believe it is," I said. "I'm glad you were able to get everything, though. Your place is going to be really nice once your furniture arrives and you put everything together."

"Yeah. I appreciate all your help today. You've really got an eye for stuff like this. But then again, I'm not surprised. Look at how fly you are," he told me.

I looked down at the simple outfit I was wearing, which consisted of a white T-shirt, jeans, and a pair of Ugg boots, and looked at him like he was crazy. "Um, this isn't what I'd consider fly."

"Look at your earrings, your necklace, and your purse. It's a well put-together outfit, and you're sexy as hell in it." He winked.

"Thanks," I said, trying not to blush. "Well, it's been fun."

"It has been. And now I'm starving. How about I buy you dinner?"

"You don't have to do that," I told him.

"I know I don't have to, but I want to. It's the least I can do to repay you for helping me out," he said. "Besides, you owe me for lying to me."

My heart began racing. How did he know? How did he find out? Was that why his initial reaction to seeing me had been so cold?

"I . . . listen . . ."

"Yeah, look at you stuttering. I knew you gave me a BDR." He smirked.

"What?" I frowned.

"Isn't that why you blocked me? Or have you just been ignoring me since that night? I mean, you coulda just said you weren't feeling me. I'm a grown-ass man. I can handle it." He leaned against his car and waited for my response.

"Taurus, I did not give you a BDR. Your D was fine." I sighed.

"I know it was," he murmured.

"Whatever." I gave him a hard side-eye.

"So, what's the problem? What's up with you?"

I looked down and said, "There isn't a problem. It's just a little complicated."

This is it. Now's your chance to come clean and tell him. Do it now.

"Complicated how, Brooke? Are you married?"

"No." I looked at him like he'd asked me the most absurd question in the world.

"You have a boyfriend, huh?"

"No." I shook my head.

"A girlfriend?"

Again, I gave him another hard side-eye. "Hell no."

He threw his hands up and said, "I had to ask. Well, if it's none of those, then why is it complicated?"

Answer him. Explain to him that Brittany was the one he met first and that you're not her. Tell him. I opened my mouth, but nothing came out.

"Okay. Since you seem to be stumped, I'm just gonna put it out there that I had a damn good time the other night. Did you?"

"I did," I answered.

"I had a damn good time today too." He shrugged.

"I did too," I said.

"And I'd just like to point out that we didn't have sex today." He raised an eyebrow at me.

"Point taken." I laughed.

"See? It ain't complicated. Now, let's go eat," he said. "You lead, and I'll follow."

Now we were sitting at a table in one of his favorite restaurants, and I had just dismissed that text I received. Dinner was just as fun as the day had been. So much so that he invited me back to his house. As much as I wanted to go, I declined. Hanging out and shopping was one thing, but I knew what would happen if I went home with him. To my surprise, he didn't protest, although he did make me promise to unblock him, which I did. I even dialed his number to prove it and was tickled when the name Strings appeared on the screen of his phone.

"Really?" I gasped.

"Hell, you blocked me. That's even worse."

When he called me later that night, I answered, and we talked until we both were damn near asleep. All that week we spoke on the phone. Our phone conversations were just as enjoyable as the ones we'd had in person. Taurus was not only handsome and humorous but also well educated and intelligent, and I learned that he enjoyed world traveling as much as I did. We both planned on visiting Greece and Ghana by the end of the year. Talking to him each night became the highlight of my day, and we would also text one another throughout the day. In the middle of the week, he asked me out to dinner, but I declined and reminded him that I wasn't looking for anything and that it was still no strings attached, despite us going out to eat after shopping.

At the end of the week, his furniture was scheduled to be delivered, and he asked if I would come over and help him set his place up. I reluctantly agreed, convincing myself that it would be for only an hour or two, and then I'd leave.

We feng shuied his living room and arranged everything he had purchased during our shopping adventure. Once we were done, I looked around. It looked amazing, and had I not done the decorating myself, I would've thought a professional decorator had done it.

"Damn. This looks amazing," he told me. "Man, I never woulda thought it would look this cool."

"I told you." I smiled. "And look at the valance you said you didn't need. Makes a difference, doesn't it?"

"It does. And you were right."

"Well, I guess I'll be going," I told him.

"You can't leave yet." He frowned as he turned to look at me.

"Why not? You said it looks amazing. We're done."

"We're not done. I was gonna make you dinner."

"You don't have to do that," I said, suddenly nervous. I was torn: I knew I should be making my way out the door, but I didn't want to leave.

"Come on. You know you want to try my culinary skills." He stepped closer to me.

Between the way he was looking at me and the intoxicating smell of his cologne, I knew I wouldn't be leaving anytime soon. *There's no harm in having dinner*, I told myself. *I can leave after I eat. Then, before I go, I'll just tell him the truth.*

The steaks, baked potatoes, and grilled asparagus went perfectly with the bottle of Cabernet I'd brought him as a housewarming gift. During one of our dinner conversations, we talked about our visits to France, and he mentioned that Cabernet was his favorite wine. After dinner I helped him clean the kitchen, and then he suggested we watch a movie on his new sofa. He poured more wine, popped a bowl of popcorn, and sat beside me. By the end of the movie, we were cuddling under one of the throws I'd insisted he buy, and I was enjoying the feel of his chest as I laid my head on it, his fingers gently playing in my hair. When the movie ended, neither one of us moved for a while. It was as if we wanted to enjoy the closeness of the moment for as long as possible.

"Brooke," he finally said.

"Yeah?" I looked up at him.

"You wanna watch something else?"

"No. It's late. I need to go." I sat up.

"It's not that late," he said, pulling me into his arms. "Stay a while longer. I really don't want you to leave."

"Taurus, I really can't stay." I shook my head. "And actually, I need to tell you something. Well, you remember that night at the Sky Bar, when you walked over and kissed me?" I said.

"Yeah. Like this?" He cupped my chin, and before I could say another word, he kissed me just as quickly and passionately as he'd done the first time. I became so caught up in the taste of his mouth, the sensation of his tongue, and the energy in the oral exchange that nothing I had to say even mattered anymore.

His hands went from my face to my blouse, which he slowly unbuttoned. As it slipped off my shoulders, his mouth moved to my neck. I tugged at his shirt and pulled it over his head and rubbed my fingers along his nipples. He stood up and pulled me to my feet, and I followed him into his bedroom, where we continued to undress one another before climbing into his bed. Unlike the last time we were together, our sexual exchange was prefaced by foreplay, something I almost always avoided when I was with someone. Normally, sex for me was a simple act to bring gratification and satisfy a physical need. But with Taurus, I needed and wanted more than simple. I wanted intimacy and arousal.

My body yearned for his touch, which was both gentle and firm, as his hands made their way all over. I couldn't get enough of his kisses, which I'd pushed away before. And as his lips tasted every inch of my voluptuousness, I didn't deny him the opportunity to press my thick thighs open and explore my now-dripping center. I closed my eyes and gripped his headboard as he sucked, teased, and pleasured me with his mouth. My legs tensed as I felt myself begin to rupture from deep within, and I reached for his head and begged him to stop, but he refused and continued. Unable to hold back my climax any longer, I screamed his name as I released over and over again, like a river bursting through a dam. Taurus eventually rolled over, and I was able to compose myself.

"Damn," I whispered.

"Oh yeah." He laughed.

"That's funny?" I asked, rolling onto my side.

"I wouldn't say funny, but it was quite entertaining. I enjoyed it, and clearly, so did you." He grinned.

I wiped the sides of his mouth, still glistening from my juices, and said, "You think you're cute, huh? Okay, bet."

"What does that mean?" He peered at me.

"You'll see."

I eased myself in between his legs, where his manhood stood at full attention, welcoming me. I fondled his hardness, caressed his impressive shaft. I was becoming turned on by just touching it, and I could see that he was too. I kissed the tip slightly as I licked it.

"Brooke, what are you doing?" Taurus groaned and tried to sit up.

I pushed him back down and said, "Haven't you heard of reciprocity?"

Once I'd returned the favor, we immediately went into a marathon session that left us both exhausted. I'd been with a few men, but I'd never felt the level of comfort and pleasure I felt afterward with Taurus. We joked with one another about the sounds and the faces we made, then chatted about random topics until both of us drifted off to sleep. I slept until the vibration of my watch woke me up a little while later. It was a text from my sister. The calmness and comfort I'd felt earlier was now replaced with guilt and regret.

"I really have to go. I have to be at work in the morning, and so do you," I said as I got up.

"We can always carpool," he suggested.

"We don't even work near each other." I sighed as I gathered my clothes.

"For you, I'd make an exception."

"That's nice and noble of you, but I don't think so." I quickly got dressed, and he finally got up.

"Thank you again for everything. My condo and I appreciate you," he said as he walked me to my truck.

"No problem. I'm glad I could assist," I said, then turned and faced him. I took a slow deep breath, preparing myself for what I was about to say. "Um, Taurus . . ."

"Wait. I already know what you're gonna say." He put his arms around my shoulders. "I get it. No strings attached. You don't have to remind me. But, Brooke, I really, really enjoy talking to you and hanging out with you."

"But . . ."

"But let me finish." He put his fingers on my lips. "All I'm asking is for you to give me the chance to take you out on a proper date this weekend. One date. That's it. I promise you that's all I want."

I swallowed hard and nodded. "One date. That's it."

And then I'll tell him. No matter what.

The following morning, I was sitting at my desk, reminiscing about the night before and smiling at the thought of going on a date with Taurus, when Brandon knocked on my door.

"Well, look at you glowing," he said.

"Yes, I am. It's Friday, it's payday, and I'm looking forward to my weekend," I told him.

"You sure that's all it is?"

"What do you want, Brandon? I hope you're coming in here to tell me some good news," I snapped at him. It had been weeks, and he hadn't given me any update on his transitioning to his AVP position or my being promoted.

"Depends on how you respond to what I'm about to say." He sat down.

"Oh, damn. Here we go with the bullshit," I said, reaching for my diffuser and turning it on.

"Stop it." He shook his head. "But I will tell you whatever you have planned for the weekend is gonna have to wait. Your plans just changed."

"Oh no," I told him. "I looked at the training schedule, and there are no new hires for another month and a half. I checked in with all the trainers this week and made sure no one was sick or had vacation. I don't know what you think you're about to spring on me, but the answer is no."

"Fine. I'll call Delores and tell her you can't make the IT Systems Conference this weekend."

"I don't have to attend that. That's only for . . ." Realizing what he was saying, I gasped, "Wait, management? Am I—"

"Shhh," Brandon hissed, then jumped up and closed the door. "No, you are not. Not yet. But I've been adamant about them giving you my position, and I think they're finally listening. During the conference call this morning, they asked if you'd be in attendance." He walked back over and sat down.

"What did you tell them? I hope you said yes," I gasped.

"Why do you think I'm in here?" He gave me a knowing look. "Flight leaves at three."

"Three?" I squealed.

"Three, Brooke. You'd better have your ass there on time. This is your chance to show and prove." He stood up. "I believe in you, and I told you I had you. I meant it."

"Thanks, Brandon. I mean it. I will be on time," I said, excited about what was happening.

"And, Brooke, this is still under wraps. Don't go running your mouth," he told me just before he walked out the door.

I turned off my diffuser and desk computer and grabbed my training bag, making sure my work laptop and all the accessories were inside. I had to make sure I was prepared. The IT Systems Conference was one of the company's most important events. It was where managers from each department met with developers and other technical resources in and outside the company. It was also a major networking opportunity for anyone who attended.

I was headed home to pack when Emory called.

"Hey, girl. I came to see if you wanted to meet up for lunch, but you were already gone. Is everything okay?" she said.

"Yeah, everything's fine."

"Well, are you coming back? I needed to talk to you about something."

"Actually, I'm not. I'm gone until Monday," I told her.

"Well, you wanna get some drinks later? We haven't hung out in forever. I miss you, friend." She laughed.

"I miss you too. But I can't hang tonight." I sighed.

"What? Why not? Come on, Brooke. You've been acting weird the past few days. You got something going on with somebody. I know you. You haven't wanted to hang out. We haven't even had our reality chitchats. Who is it?"

My best friend knew me better than anyone, including my twin sister. But there was no way I could tell her why I'd been MIA or whom I'd been with. I knew the first question she'd have for me would be if I'd told Taurus that essentially I wasn't who he thought I was. Her next question would be if I'd told Brittany about Taurus, and I didn't want to deal with her reaction once I admitted that the answer to both of those questions was no. What

I was doing was wrong on so many levels, but it felt right, for some reason. And I knew that despite how much I enjoyed spending time with Taurus, Emory would have a lot to say about it, which I didn't want to hear.

"It's no one, really. I've just been doing me, and you know how I am," I told her.

"Yes, I do. Which is why I'm asking. Fine. You don't have to tell me now. You can tell me later at the club. There's a guest deejay at the Casbah, and I'm trying to go," Emory said.

"I can't, Em," I said. "I'm flying out this afternoon, and I'll be gone for the weekend. But I promise we can hang when I get back."

"What? Where the hell are you going? Why am I just now hearing about this?" she whined.

"It's a last-minute trip. I literally just found out about it," I said. My phone beeped, and I saw that it was Taurus. "Listen, I gotta take this call. I'll text you later tonight and fill you in."

Fine," she said. "Be safe and don't forget I need to talk to you about something."

"I won't," I said and clicked over. "Hey there."

"Hey, you. How's your Friday?"

"It's actually quite interesting so far," I said. "I have good news, and I have bad news."

"Gimme the bad news," he said.

"I can't go on a date this weekend," I said.

"What? This better be some damn good news," he said teasingly.

I filled him in about Brandon and the conference I was headed to. He was supportive and happy for me.

"That's good stuff right there. I'm glad your boss finally came through for you. I'm sure this waiting game has been a little stressful."

"It has been. But I'm disappointed about our date. Now you see why I told you I can't really be involved with anyone. My job requires me to travel often and at the last minute." I sighed.

"Listen, I get it. It's no big deal, and we can go on our date when your schedule permits. I hope you do have a great trip, though. I'm happy for you." Taurus sounded sincere. I realized I really was disappointed that we wouldn't be going on our date.

"I mean, I can FaceTime you if you'd like," I suggested.

"Look at you. I've progressed from being blocked and having a BDR to being offered FaceTime calls," he taunted me. "Admit it. You like me."

"Don't flatter yourself. I just feel bad because I'm the only friend you seem to have in the area, and now I'm leaving. I don't want you to be all sad, that's all," I replied. "I'll talk to you later."

I ended the call and thought to myself, *He's right. I do like him.*

Chapter Twelve

Brittany

Once I'd finally comprehended my decision that I wanted to move, somehow I seemed to feel a lot lighter. It was as if the weight of the world had been lifted off my shoulders. I contacted a Realtor and immediately put my house on the market and began gathering boxes to pack. I also made it a point to begin leaving work on time and being unavailable to handle situations that weren't part of my job responsibilities.

"Ms. Newman, can you please come to Hallway B? We have a student refusing to go into the classroom."

I picked up the walkie-talkie, which I now kept on my desk instead of my hip, and said, "I'm in the middle of a webinar right now and can't leave my office. Someone else is going to have to handle it."

I knew the staff was probably having a field day talking about my new unwillingness to take on the behavior issues throughout the day as I had been, but I didn't care. I had two more months of school, and then I was done. I also had plenty of sick days and accrued vacation to use before my departure. I checked the time and saw that it was almost noon. I decided to take a chance and reach out to Brooke once again, hoping she'd answer instead of sending me a brief text message apologizing.

Here I was, making plans to relocate, and I still hadn't talked to her about it. I also hadn't mentioned it to my mother. I hoped that Brooke would help me break the news to her.

"Hello."

I was shocked to hear her voice on the other end of the line. I quickly paused the webinar and said, "Damn. You answered. I don't believe it."

"Funny," she said. "What's going on, Britt?"

"Oh my goodness, where do I begin?" I said. "I have so much to tell you."

"Well, you'd better make it quick. I have a flight to catch, and I gotta leave in a few. You got ten minutes, so talk fast."

"Where are you going now? I thought you said after the last trip you'd be home for a few. Did you get the promotion you've been working for?" I asked.

"If all goes well on this trip, I will," she told me.

"That's great. Well, I did want to let you know that I put my house on the market," I said.

"You what? Why did you do that? Please don't tell me this has anything to do with Duane or God forbid, anyone else," she moaned.

I'd expected her to be a little more excited, but I figured her attitude would be better once I explained my reasons. "No, not really. Well, partly . . . but mainly, because I need a change. Now is the perfect time. I found out my contract at the school isn't being renewed. And Duane and I are finally done."

"Y'all have been done before, remember? And can't you find another school within your district?" Brooke said. "You're really selling your house? You love that house."

"I know, but I can get another one," I told her as I stared at the picture on my desk of Duane and me standing in front of my house. I quickly laid it down.

"Well, where are you moving to? Back home with Mom and Dad?"

"Definitely not," I said. After taking a deep breath, I added, "I was thinking I'd come and stay with you for a little while."

The phone got quiet, and I thought that I'd lost my cell signal, until I heard Brooke clearing her throat. "Me, Britt? You want to come here?"

"Yes, Brooke, with you. What's wrong?" I said. "You have an extra bedroom, and you're hardly ever home. I have money saved, and I'm sure it won't take me that long to find another job in my field. I can pay half of your rent and the utilities."

"Do you realize how much my rent is, Britt?" Her tone was condescending, and I could imagine her rolling her eyes as she said it.

"Well, the point is I can contribute," I said. "It's not like I'll be freeloading or mooching off of you."

"That's not what I'm saying."

"What are you saying, then? Tell me."

"I'm saying I'll have to think about it. I mean, I'm used to living alone, and I'm sure you are too, Britt," she told me.

"I know you're worried about your privacy, Brooke. I will make sure I'm not around when you have company. Jeez."

"Oh God, Britt. You're really tripping."

"I'm not. Well, how about I come and spend a few days and we do a trial run? I have some vacation days I gotta use up, anyway, and I can set up some interviews—"

"Let me get through this trip, and we can discuss it more when I get back. I promise," Brooke said.

"How long are you going to be gone?"

"A couple of days," she answered.

"Brooke, what about Mom's birthday?" I moaned.

"I know, and I feel horrible. I'm gonna try my best to make it back in time. You know how my job is, Britt. I can't help it. But I booked and paid for the appointment at the spa for Sunday afternoon, so you guys can still go if I'm not here. Oh, and if you pick out a gift, I'll pay for it, so say it's from both of us."

"She'd like it if all of us went, like we'd planned. Brooke, you promised."

"Listen, I have to go. My Uber is here, and I cannot miss this flight. We'll talk about your relocation plans when I get back. Tell Mom I'll call her when I can, and I'll text Dad. Love you," she said, then hung up.

I now took the frame that held the photo of her and me and turned it down on the desk as well. She was my sister, my twin sister. And had the tables been turned and she'd called me and asked to come and stay with me, I would've welcomed her with open arms. But then again, that was how Brooke was. In her own world, doing her own thing, caring only about her own happiness. But there was something else going on with her. Something was off. Not only had she been distant the past few weeks, but now she seemed like she didn't want to be bothered. And now I was tasked with telling our mother that Brooke wouldn't be home to celebrate her birthday. After deciding that there was no better time than the present to break the news, all of it, I picked up my cell phone and dialed her number.

"Well, to what do I owe the pleasure of this midday phone call?" she greeted me.

"Hey, Mom. Don't act like I don't call you during my lunch sometimes." I laughed.

"Well, I haven't talked to you much these days at all. I was starting to think you were acting like your sister. You know I don't hear from her unless I call, and usually, she doesn't answer. She stays busy."

"Yeah, speaking of her busy schedule, I just talked to her, and she's about to fly out again."

"Let me guess. She won't be coming for my birthday." My mother said it more like a statement than a question.

"She's gonna try, but either way, you and I are still gonna have our spa day, and we got you plenty of gifts, too," I replied. The part about the gifts was a little white lie, but although I hadn't picked anything out yet, I planned to over the weekend. And now that Brooke was footing the bill, my mother's gifts would be much nicer. "Like I said, we can still go to the spa. We just can't take the pictures."

"Humph," was her only response.

"I do have something else to tell you, though," I said, hoping she would be distracted by my news about her birthday.

"Really? What is it? Lemme guess. You and Duane are back together," she blurted out.

"No, Mom." I sighed. "Duane and I are not together, and we won't be getting back together. That ship has sailed and won't be making a return trip."

"Oh, Britt. I'm sorry, baby. I was hoping—"

"And you don't have to be sorry, Ma. I'm good. I'm glad we're over, and I'm looking forward to moving for-ward," I told her.

"Moving forward with someone new?"

"No, but I am moving. I'm selling my house, and when the school year ends, I'm leaving here."

"You're selling your house? Oh my. Well, I'll be glad to have some company around here. I thought when your father retired last year, he'd be home more, but he's always gone. I swear, he and your sister are more like twins than you two are." She laughed.

"No, Mom. I'm not moving home," I said.

"Well, where are you moving to, Brittany?"

"I was thinking of moving in with Brooke for a while, until I find a new place. I like it there," I said.

A voice came through the walkie-talkie just then. "Ms. Newman, we need you down in the cafeteria for a situation."

"Hold on, Ma," I said as I picked up the device and turned it off completely. If anyone asked why I'd done so, my answer would be that I was on my lunch break. "I'm back."

"What about your job, Brittany?"

"I'll find another one," I replied.

"And your sister said you could come and stay? That's surprising."

"Not exactly," I said. "She said she'd think about it when she got back into town."

"Well, what if she says no?"

I didn't have an answer to that question. I'd just assumed that Brooke would say okay and allow me to stay for a few months. I knew my sister well enough to know she would be a little reluctant, but I couldn't imagine her turning me away.

***

"Well, what if she does say no?" Kyra asked as she picked up the pile of clothes in the middle of my living-room floor and placed it in a plastic bin. She'd opted to spend her Friday night helping me go through my closets.

I opened the pizza box on the floor beside me and took out a slice. The cheese oozed as I bit into the pizza, and after chewing, I told her, "I honestly don't know, really. But I'm still moving. But believe it or not, my mom is actually supportive. She's helping me figure out my options, and she's going to help me talk to Brooke, I think."

"I thought she was Team Duane." Kyra grabbed her own slice of pizza.

"She is, but she's more Team Brittany right now. I think she's being sympathetic, especially since Brooke is acting funny," I said.

"What's up with that?" Kyra asked.

"I think she thinks I'm moving because I'm trying to find that dude I met at the bar." I leaned back against the sofa.

"Well . . ." Kyra shrugged.

"Kyra, that's not why I'm moving."

"You do kinda talk about him a lot."

"Because he was everything. You'd talk about him a lot, too, if you'd met him and felt what I felt," I told her. "But I'm not crazy. I'm not selling my house and going on some wild hunt for a stranger I met in the club."

"Not even a little bit?" Kyra twisted her lip and squinted.

The truth was that I still thought about T and had dreamed about him on more than one occasion. After all this time, I still couldn't shake the feeling that we'd connected somehow. I remembered his sexy smile and the way his eyes had lit up as he looked at me. The sensation that had gone through my body when he was pressed against me. It wasn't just physical; it was more than that. In the dreams I'd had, he reached for me, and I grabbed his hand just before slipping away.

"No, but somehow I get the feeling I'm going to see him again, Kyra. I can't explain it. It's like I know our paths will cross at some point," I told her.

"Girl, I hope you do. Whoever this brother is, he must be something else. In all the years I've known you, I've never seen you so adamant about a guy, not even Duane, and you were in love with his ass." She laughed.

"I may have been in love with him, but trust, Duane has never made me feel the way T did."

"Brittany, you are hilarious. I guess I'm thinking more like Brooke. Most of the time when a guy in the club makes you feel like that, it's because you're drunk and horny."

I shook my head and continued sorting through the clothes. I wasn't about to let Kyra or Brooke make me feel like I was imagining things. I'd been drunk before, and I'd been horny. Maybe not at the same time, but I knew how they felt. I hadn't lied when I said I was not moving so I could search for the sexy stranger, but the possibility of finding him was an added bonus.

Chapter Thirteen

Brooke

"You know I'm hella proud of you, right?" Brandon said as we stepped onto the hotel elevator.

"Really? You think I did okay?" I asked.

"You knocked it out of the park, Brooke. And when Jon Holmes, the director from the Southwest region, asked what you thought was the biggest obstacle the training departments are faced with, and you said, 'Inconsistency of leadership expectation,' I wanted to high-five your ass." He nudged me.

"I only said what you and I have been talking about forever." I smiled.

"And you confirmed exactly what I've been telling *them* forever. I'm telling you, they were eating it up," he said.

Brandon's vote of confidence gave me a much-needed boost of energy. True to his word, he had introduced me to each and every person we'd run into so far the weekend and he had also made sure that I was in the right place for the right conversations. He'd also given me the background information on key managers that he felt I needed to know. It amazed me that he was so knowledge-able about the company and was able to call everyone by name. I could hardly keep up, but I had so far. As much as I was enjoying the conference, it was exhausting, and after a full day of sessions, we still had the banquet to attend in a few hours.

"I hope so." I nodded, adjusting my bag on my shoulder as the small mirrored box we were riding in carried us up to the floor our rooms were on. My feet were killing me, and I was tempted to take off my cute yet uncomfortable heels, especially since we were the only two people on the elevator. Instead, I shifted my weight from one foot to the other as I gripped the polished brass bar to steady myself. We arrived at our floor with a jolt, and my body shifted into Brandon's.

"Hold on," he said, reaching his hand out and grasping my upper arm. "You okay?"

"Yeah." I gave him a half smile, slightly embarrassed. We stepped out of the elevator and into the hallway. "Well, thanks again, Brandon. I appreciate your looking out for me."

He stood in front of me and said, "Brooke, you don't have to thank me. You've earned this position, and I have no doubt you're going to get it. You proved that to me and everyone else the past three days."

"It's been only three days? Are you sure? It seems like it's been longer." I laughed. "Well, I'm gonna go and catch a quick nap before we have to be back downstairs."

Brandon took a step closer to me and gently rubbed my shoulder as he stared at me. "You know," he said, "we really don't have to go to the banquet. They won't miss us. We can have dinner in my room."

I immediately knew what he was suggesting, and simply said, "Come on now, Brandon. You know we can't go there again. It was one thing when you weren't my boss, but we both agreed a long time ago, that book is shut."

"In a few days, you won't be directly reporting to me, so technically, I won't be your boss. We can reopen it," he said with a seductive grin. "Admit it. We're good together at work and at play."

He was right. We were good together, both in the office and the times we were in the bedroom, and there was a time not so long ago that I'd contemplated hooking up with him again if the right opportunity presented itself. But now that it was standing right in front of me, I didn't want it. All I wanted to do was go into my hotel room, get undressed, lie across my bed, and FaceTime Taurus, the same way I'd done every night since I arrived at the conference.

"I feel you, Brandon, but I can't. You've been a great boss, an even better friend and, no doubt, once upon a time, a long time ago, a great lover. But that can't happen again." I sighed.

"Hey, it wasn't *that* long ago." He shrugged. "And I respect that. I guess I'll see you downstairs, at dinner."

"Of course." I nodded. He walked down the hallway to his room, and I headed to mine and used my key to go in. After tossing my bag down and kicking the painful heels off, I took off my suit blazer. I didn't even bother taking off anything else before I hopped onto the bed and dialed Taurus's number.

He answered on the first ring, letting me know that he was just as excited about talking to me as I was to him. "Well, how was today?"

"Today was great. Although I was a little sleepy, because someone wanted to talk me to death all night about how Will Smith deserves way more Oscars," I said. "But Brandon gave me my props and said I knocked it out of the park."

"I'm not surprised to hear that, and I'm sure you did," he said.

I noticed the shelves in the background on my phone's screen and asked, "Are you at Bed Bath & Beyond?"

"Uh, yeah. You like these?" He held up a pair of ugly blue sheets.

"Ew, no. And what thread count are those?" I looked closer at my phone.

"I don't know. I was just gonna grab some new ones, since they sent me a coupon. Because, you know, some-one seems to mess mine up sometimes," he whispered.

His hilarious comment caught me off guard, and I laughed hysterically, then told him, "That's because you don't listen to directions. When I say stop, it means stop."

"Nah. Once I start, ain't no stopping, boo. And the thread count on these is two hundred."

"Oh God, Taurus. Those are gonna tear up after you wash them twice, and they're probably stiff as hell," I said.

"You like stiff . . . Never mind." He laughed. "So, what thread count should I get?"

"Get Egyptian cotton, four hundred. Those should be good," I told him.

"Okay. What about these?" He held up a nicer burgun-dy set that I recognized.

"Those are fine. I actually have some like that," I said.

"Really? I wouldn't know, because I've never seen your bed," he said. "But you're the decorating expert, so I'll get them."

It was the first time he'd mentioned my place, and it dawned on me that I'd never invited him over. My apartment was my sanctuary, and I rarely, if ever, invited a man over. Not even Brandon. I didn't feel comfortable with anyone in my space. The only person who had the access code to even get into my place was Emory, and she used that only in case of emergency or when I needed her to go in. It was my safe haven, and I kept it guarded. That was also why I was skeptical about having Brittany come and stay. Well, there was also the fact that I hadn't mentioned Taurus to her, either. But even if I wasn't dealing with my current conundrum, I would still be just as hesitant. I loved my sister, but living with her wasn't something I wanted to do, unless it was absolutely necessary.

"I'm not an expert," I said, tucking my feet under the comforter.

"So, are you finished for the day?" Taurus asked.

"Well, we actually have a banquet to close the conference out in a little while, but Brandon says it's not a big deal if I don't go. So, I'm actually thinking about skipping out on it. I don't feel like getting dressed up, anyway."

"I don't believe that. You're always dressed up. You're probably dressed up now," he said. "Looking all fancy."

"I'm not dressed up. I have on a business suit, thank you." I laughed.

"It's probably dressy. Hold the phone out and let me see," he instructed.

"Fine." I stood up, walked over to the mirror, and held the phone out so he could get a good view of the white blouse and gray slacks I wore. "See? Simple business attire."

"Nice. And where's the lace?"

"What lace?" I asked, looking down at my outfit.

"The lace underneath."

"Taurus, I don't know what you're talking about." I smirked.

"You do. Now, show me the fancy lace." He winked.

"Oh, you mean this?" I opened my blouse just enough for him to see a hint of the black lace bra I was wearing.

"I knew it," he said. "Come on. Show me some more."

"Aren't you in the store?" I whispered.

"Nobody can see you but me, girl." He kissed his teeth and made a face at me. I unbuttoned another button and opened my shirt a bit more, revealing my cleavage. He licked his lips as he continued to watch. "Ah yeah."

"You're such a perv." I giggled.

"Nah, if I was a perv, I would be telling you to take it all off," he said.

I was about to respond when there was a knock at my door. I told Taurus to hold on before I put my phone on the bed and walked over to see who it was. I looked through the peephole and saw Brandon standing there and smiling.

"Brandon, what's up?" I asked him as I opened the door.

"You did it," he announced as he stepped inside my room.

"Wait, what do you mean? Do not play with me, Brandon." I tried not to get excited.

"Well, when you declined my invitation to join me in my room, I went back downstairs to the bar, and Gregg and a few others were there. They didn't waste any time letting me know that I was right and you're the ideal person to replace me when I move up," he announced. "Congratulations, you will soon be the new manager of training, education and development."

"Oh my God!" I exclaimed. Then I squealed and threw my arms around Brandon's neck.

"I'm happy for you. Damn happy," he said when I released him. I saw that he was staring at my partially open blouse. "Now, you sure you don't wanna go and celebrate?"

"I'm sure," I said, pulling my blouse closed. "When do I start?"

"Well, the official announcement will be made at the midyear office meeting next month, along with some other changes. So, don't go moving into my office just yet," he said. "And you still have to train your replacement."

"It's not gonna be Holly, Brandon," I told him.

"We'll talk about it this week. In the meantime, I'm going to find some trouble to get into around here." Brandon turned to exit.

"You know you're a high-level exec now, Brandon. Please remember that before you get into trouble you can't get out of," I said.

"Point taken." He waved as he walked out.

When he was gone, I squealed once again. All my hard work and sacrifice, not to mention patience, had paid off, and I'd landed the management position I wanted.

"Uh, hello?" said a faint voice.

I looked at the bed and saw Taurus's face still on my phone. "Oh my God. I'm so sorry. That was Brandon, my boss, and he came to tell me—"

"I know, I know. Congratulations, Brooke," he said.

I could hardly contain my excitement. "I guess you heard all of that, huh?"

"I did. When you squealed at first, I thought something was wrong, and so did all the folks at the checkout."

"My bad," I said, apologizing.

"You good. Why didn't you wanna go celebrate with him, though? This is big news for both of you," Taurus said.

"Nah, I'm not celebrating with Brandon. I really think I'm gonna grab the next flight out and come on back," I told him.

"Tonight?"

"Yep," I said. "I believe I am. So, let me go and find a flight and an Uber, and I'll hit you up when I get to the airport."

I was on cloud nine as I pulled up my travel app on my phone, found a flight that I'd be able to make, and requested an Uber. I got packed in record time. I was heading to the hotel lobby when Brandon, who was standing outside the banquet he had said he wouldn't be going to, spotted me.

"You're leaving?" He glanced down at my suitcases and gave me strange look. "You . . . I . . . Uh, are you all right?"

"Yes, Brandon. Calm down. I'm fine," I told him, and he relaxed. "I decided to just head out when you said the banquet was no big deal."

"Oh, okay," he said. "Cool. I thought about leaving myself, honestly."

Gregg, our manager, walked over and asked, "Brooke, you're leaving us?"

"Yes, sir, I am. Tomorrow's my mom's birthday, and I was supposed to spend the weekend with her. So, I'm trying to do what I can to stay in her good graces," I told him.

Gregg nodded. "Say no more. I totally understand."

"I would like to say thank you so much for allowing me to attend the conference. It was truly an invaluable experience, and I learned a lot." I extended my hand, and he firmly grasped it.

"It was wonderful having you here with us. You made a big impression on some important folks, and I'm sure Brandon has already told you that you'll be getting a new title, and so will he." Gregg beamed.

I nodded. "He did mention something to that effect."

"You deserve it. Both of you. You make a great team, and I hate to see him go, but I have no doubt this will be a smooth transition for the two of you. You won't let me down." Gregg looked over at both of us like a proud father might.

"We definitely won't, Gregg," Brandon assured him.

"Well, gentlemen, my car is out front. I'll see both of you on Monday," I said.

"Make it Tuesday. The three of us will have a sit-down and discuss some things. Besides, you deserve an extra day off. You can spend it with your mom," Gregg said.

"See you Tuesday," I told him.

I made my way out of the hotel and climbed into the Suburban that was waiting. As soon as I boarded my flight and settled into my first-class seat, my phone vibrated. It was a call from Brittany.

"Talk fast," I said.

"Hey, what time are we supposed to be at the spa to-morrow?" she asked.

"Two thirty. The appointment is under her name," I told her.

"Are you going to make it back in time? You know she's already been complaining that her girls' weekend has been cut down to one day."

"I'll meet you guys there. And she'll be okay. After the spa we'll go somewhere nice for an early dinner, and y'all can be on your way back home before dusk," I said.

"All right. We'll leave here around noon, I guess," Brittany said.

"Cool. I gotta go," I told her and hung up so I could get adjusted in my seat. The plane took off soon after, and I was asleep before the flight attendants gave their presentation, and I remained asleep until we landed.

"Hey. What are you doing?" I said into the phone as I grabbed my two bags from the conveyor belt at the baggage claim.

"Braiding my sister's hair," Emory said.

"Damn. You're at her house, or is she at yours?" I asked.

"I'm at hers. I ain't have shit to do this weekend, so I drove out here. Why? What's up?"

"I needed a ride from the airport," I told her. "It's all good. I'll catch an Uber."

"Why didn't you say something earlier?" Emory asked.

"I decided to come back at the last minute. But I do have some news to share with you, though," I told her.

"Good news?"

"Great news," I said.

"I can't wait. I have something to talk to you about too," Emory said.

I felt someone staring at me, and I looked up. There was Taurus, smiling as he held a piece of paper with my name written across it and a rose. I blinked a few seconds to make sure I wasn't tripping.

"What are you doing here?" I asked as he walked toward me.

"I figured you'd need a ride. I'm here to pick you up." He kissed my cheek and placed the flower in my hand.

"Hello? Brooke? Are you there?" Emory's voice came through my AirPods.

"I'll call you back," I told her and hit the END CALL button.

"Are these the only bags you have?" he asked, reaching for my luggage.

"Yeah," I said, still shocked to see him. "How did you even know what time my flight was landing?"

He shrugged. "There weren't too many flights coming in from Fort Lauderdale, so I used deductive reasoning and hoped for the best."

"I don't know if I should be happy or afraid," I told him.

"Why? Don't you need a ride?"

"I mean, I do. But that's kinda stalkerish, don't you think? And what would have happened if I had had another dude waiting here for me? Did you even think about that?" I asked as we walked out of the airport.

"I did. But I figured the possibilities of that happening weren't that great, considering you really ain't looking for nothing special with anyone. Most dudes who ain't special don't do airport runs," he said. "And don't get it twisted. Just because I'm giving you a ride from the airport doesn't mean this is a thing. We still ain't attached, Strings."

We arrived at his car, and he opened the door for me. I climbed inside, then leaned over and opened his side while he put my bags in the trunk. I sniffed the rose and fastened my seat belt. I was still surprised. He'd shown up at the airport to pick me up without me even asking, with a damn flower and a name card. Had it been anyone else, I would've felt extremely uncomfortable. But because it was him, as much as I hated to admit it, I kind of liked it. I thought to myself, *This is totally not you. What are you doing, Brooke*? It was an unexpected gesture, and I was impressed. I was also something else.

"So, are you hungry?" he asked when he got inside the car. "Or are you tired and ready to go home?"

"I'm ready to go home, but I'm not tired. And I'm hungry, but not for food," I told him.

He grinned as I gave him my address, and he put it into the car's GPS system. We got to my apartment, and he carried my things up for me. For some reason, I was nervous as I opened my front door and we stepped inside.

"You can leave the bags right there," I said as I cut on the light.

"Wow. Your place is really nice," he told me as he looked around.

"Excuse that area over there. That's my shopping corner." I motioned toward the boxes and bags near the wall in the dining area.

He sat on the sofa, and I handed him the remote. "Here you go. Make yourself comfortable." Then I poured him a glass of wine, and handed it to him. "I'm going to take a shower. I'll be back out shortly."

He smirked, "Are you sure you don't want me to join you?"

As enticing as the thought of his body all soaped up and pressed against me in the shower was, I politely declined. "I don't know you well enough to share my good soap."

My shower left me smelling fresh, and I was ready to be satisfied, knowing Taurus would not disappoint. I lotioned my body down and wrapped myself in one of my silk robes, only to walk back into my living room and find him knocked out and snoring on my two-thousand-dollar sofa. I smiled and couldn't even be mad. After all, it was late, and I did take a long shower to ensure I was refreshed after my long flight. I gently nudged him and pulled him to his feet, then led him into my bedroom, where I had lit a few candles and Alexa was playing my "Gettin' It In" playlist to set the mood.

Taurus's lust-filled eyes went from the top of my head to my toes, and he whispered, "I swear to God, the first time I laid eyes on you, I thought you were the sexiest woman I'd ever seen."

I froze, my heart suddenly pounding from guilt at the thought of who it was he'd actually seen first. But when he leaned down and kissed me, the nervousness that had started to creep over me was erased. He pulled the belt on my robe and it opened, and then he brushed the robe off my shoulders, and it fell to the floor. In one swift motion he effortlessly lifted me and placed me on my bed. Then we did something that I'd never done before: had sex in my own bed. Before I fell asleep afterward with my head on his chest, I decided that everything in my life was damn near perfect.

That is, until the next morning, when there was a knock on my front door.

Chapter Fourteen

Brittany

"Who is it?"

I could tell Brooke had an attitude from the tone of her voice. I'd told my mother that we should've called before showing up unannounced and that we were supposed to just meet Brooke at the spa, but she had insisted she was our mother and didn't need permission to show up anywhere. When we'd arrived at the building, I was about to press the intercom and give Brooke a heads-up, but I didn't get the chance, because Brooke's doorman must've assumed I was her. He greeted us with a smile and graciously held the door open for us to come in.

"It's your mother," my mom answered a little too loud.

"Shhh, Ma. You don't have to yell. You're gonna wake her neighbors," I whispered.

"As much as they're paying to live up in here, these walls better be soundproof." She gave me a look that let me know that she didn't appreciate me suggesting that she tone it down a bit.

"Ma?" Brooke called from the other side of the door.

"Do you have another mother I don't know about? Open up," Ma told her.

"Uh, one second. Gimme a minute, and I'll, uh, be back in a sec," Brooke stammered. I could imagine her inside, trying to hurry and get rid of wineglasses, put away liquor bottles and that pile of shopping bags and boxes before opening the door.

"A sec? Girl, if you don't open this damn door . . . ," Ma warned.

"She's coming, Ma. She probably needs to put on some clothes right quick. It is still kinda early," I said as I tried not to laugh. This entire situation was becoming funnier by the minute. I had known it was going to be eventful when my mother woke up and announced that since my sister couldn't make the drive to come and celebrate her birthday, then she would make the drive to my sister instead.

"It's almost nine o'clock. It ain't early," Ma said.

There was a click, and the door slowly opened.

"Uh, surprise?" I shrugged.

"Hey, Ma. Happy birthday." Then she hugged our mother and gave me a look that let me know if she could wrap her fingers around my throat and squeeze, she would.

"Hey yourself, baby." Mama grinned and kissed her cheek.

"What are y'all doing here?" Brooke asked as she ushered us inside. She looked more confused than surprised. She was wearing a gorgeous silk kimono robe, and her hair was pulled on top of her head.

"What? I can't come and visit you?" Mama continued into the living-room area. "This is nice, Brooke."

"Thanks, Mama," Brooke said. Then she looked over at me and in a lowered voice said, "What the hell, Britt? You just gonna pop up on me like this?"

"She wanted to see you for her birthday, Brooke. What was I supposed to do?" I replied.

"Um, I'm glad you're here," Brooke said, loud enough now for Mama to hear. "Look, there's a really great restaurant down the street called Taylor's, and they have a great brunch. Y'all can, uh, go ahead over there, and I can come and meet you after I get dressed," she suggested, looking around nervously.

"We can wait. We ain't in no rush," Mama told her as she looked around the spacious apartment.

"Okay, well, they have fresh coffee downstairs, in the area near the lobby, and a really nice area where you guys can sit and relax," Brooke said.

"We're fine, Brooke. Why don't you show me around your place," Mama replied.

"There's really not much to see, Ma. This is pretty much it right here—the kitchen and dining room and the living area. I mean, it's just my bedroom and another bedroom, where I store stuff. Nothing special."

Mama looked at Brooke's shopping pile and said, "You got more stuff than this to store?"

"Oh, and the balcony. It's a nice morning." Brooke rushed over to the sliding-glass door to the balcony, which overlooked the pool area, and opened it. She pointed to the small cushioned love seat and said, "You guys are welcome to sit out here and enjoy the view."

I frowned at my sister and the strange way she was acting. Something was up.

"Mama, I could use some coffee. Why don't we go downstairs and get some and then come back up?" I said.

Brooke nodded and said, "Yes. Then we can decide how you want to spend your birthday, Ma. I'll be dressed by the time y'all come back."

"I'd rather stay here and meet whoever that is you've got hiding back there in that room." Mama smiled.

I looked over at Brooke, wondering if somehow my mother was right and that this was the reason my sister was acting so weird. One thing I knew about Brooke was that she never brought guys to her home. She was insanely private in that respect. If there was a man in her bedroom, I would be shocked.

"Mama, what are you talking about?" Brooke shook her head.

"Brooke Daniel Newman, please don't play with me. I know you better than anyone on this earth, despite the fact that we barely talk or see one another." Mama stared at Brooke.

"Mama, Brooke may do a lot of things, but she doesn't have company like that." I laughed.

"Then I should be able to go back and see the rest of your place, right?" Mama started walking toward the small hallway that led to both bedrooms.

"Mama, wait." Brooke stopped her.

"Yes?" Mama said as she turned back around.

"Don't go back there," Brooke told her. "Please."

"Oh shit," I said before I could stop myself. I couldn't believe that my sister really did have a guy in her bedroom. I felt even worse about our impromptu pop-up. The tension in the room became thick.

"Listen, I do have a guest. I wasn't expecting you or anyone else this morning. Had I known, I would've made other arrangements. Can you two please go and wait downstairs so he'll have the opportunity to leave?" Brooke pleaded.

"He doesn't have to leave. If he's here, then he must be someone special, because Brittany is right. You don't really have company like that," Mama told her. Then she yelled out, "Young man, whoever you are, please come out and introduce yourself."

Brooke shook her head anxiously. "Mama, now isn't the time for you to meet him."

"Wow, Brooke. I kinda agree with Mama about this. I wanna meet him too," I said, now just as curious as Mama was.

"Come on out, sir. We promise we won't bite," Mama yelled out again.

"Mama, please don't do this." Brooke now looked as if she wanted to cry. I'd never seen her so embarrassed. I wondered if it was because whoever she was hiding was someone much younger or maybe white or, even worse, ugly. Either way, I was ready to see who it was. A few seconds later, I heard the bedroom door open, and he walked out.

"How you doing, ma'am?"

I was still staring at the horrified look on Brooke's face, so I heard the voice before I saw who was talking. A chill went through me, and I thought I was imagining things as I looked from her over to him. I had to do a triple take to make sure my eyes weren't playing tricks on me. But no, I was seeing things clearly, and I had no doubt in my mind that the man I'd been thinking and dreaming about since the night we met was now standing in my sister's living room.

"I'm wonderful," Mama said. "And you are?"

"T?" My voice cracked as I tried to understand what was happening. I looked back over at Brooke, who was breathing so hard that I could see her chest moving up and down. Our eyes locked, and I could see the regret on her face.

"Britt," she said.

"You've gotta be kidding me! Him, Brooke? Him?" I gasped.

"What's wrong?" Mama asked.

"You really *are* a piece of work. You know that? Him? Out of all the men out here, you had to have *him*?" My voice was an octave higher, and I was damn near yelling. "I mean, I knew you were a slut, but I at least thought you had boundaries."

"Brittany Nicole, what is wrong with you?" Mama touched my shoulder, but I snatched it away.

"You don't have enough dudes around here to fuck, Brooke? Randoms at the club, guys you meet while traveling for work? Let's see . . . There's Mitch, Joe, DJ, Jonathan. Hell, Brandon, your boss. They aren't enough for you? You had to have him as part of your sexual rotation too?" I screamed as the tears of anger that had formed now began to fall. "And then, how many times did I ask you if you'd seen him again, and you told me no? So, not only are you a whore, but you're a liar too." My hands were shivering with rage, and it took everything inside of me not to grab Brooke by the throat and throw her to the floor.

"Can someone please tell me what's going on?" T said.

I turned and looked at him.

He stared at me for a split second, then frowned. "Whoa. Are y'all twins?"

Mama answered his question. "Yes, they are."

"Taurus, this is my sister, Brittany," Brooke told him. "She . . . she's the—"

I interrupted her and said, "You and I met one Friday night at the Sky Bar a little while back. We danced and talked, and you invited me for a nightcap. I told you I'd be right back, but then you left."

"Hold up. Wait a minute. *You're* the one that disappeared that night?" he said.

I nodded. "Yes, that was me."

T looked from me to Brooke, who now had the nerve to be crying, then back to me. "Man, this is crazy. So, how did—"

Brooke finally spoke. "A couple of weeks later, I was at the Sky Bar, and you came up to me and . . ."

"Kissed you," he said, completing her sentence, and they looked at one another.

"Wow," I said, shaking my head in disbelief.

"Yeah." Brooke nodded. "I didn't know at first, not until after we . . ."

"And you didn't say anything?" he muttered. The look of disgust he gave her made me feel slightly better, but I was still livid. "This whole time, you ain't say nothing?"

"I wanted to, I swear. I tried to," Brooke said.

"You damn sure ain't say nothing to me. That's for damn sure," I snapped.

"I know, and I'm sorry. I was going to." Brooke looked over at him and said, "I was going to tell both of you, I swear."

"But you didn't. You lied to me, and you kept lying! Now I see why you didn't want me to come and visit, and why you're so against me moving." I began getting angry all over again. "You've always been a narcissistic bitch who thought she was better than everyone else, Brooke, but this is low, even for you. I hate you!" I told her. Then I turned to Mama. "You can stay here if you want to, but I'm gone." I started for the door.

My mother spoke. "Brittany, calm down."

"Brittany, wait, please," Brooke called after me, but I kept going. Her apartment door slammed shut behind me.

I wiped my silent tears as I rode the elevator down, and by the time I made it to my car and climbed behind the wheel, I was crying uncontrollably. I was heartbroken. Despite our differences, Brooke had always had my back. She was the person I had thought I could trust with my life. But now I realized that the only thing she cared about was getting whatever she wanted from whomever she wanted. She was selfish and didn't give a damn about whom she hurt, including me. She had known all along how I felt about him, but none of that had mattered.

"Hey, are you okay?" I heard someone ask. I looked out my window and saw T standing beside my car. I opened my car door and stepped out.

"I'm fine." I sniffed.

"Man, I'm sorry this happened like this. You and her . . . I mean, y'all look just alike. I didn't know. I feel horrible." He sighed. "Really, I do."

I stared into his handsome face. Seeing the concern in his eyes was comforting, and I managed a half smile. "I appreciate that. But you don't have to apologize. This isn't your fault. She should've been honest with both of us."

"You're right," he told me as he looked me up and down. "I can't believe I didn't realize it wasn't you. I mean, y'all definitely look alike, that's for sure. Damn, twins. But, you look a little different from the way you looked that night."

Damn. He is fine.

Suddenly, I felt self-conscious and wished I'd put a little more time and effort into the outfit I selected this morning. The oversize T-shirt and leggings I was wearing made me feel underdressed, and I probably could've used a little lip gloss and curled my hair, which was tucked under a baseball cap. Not that the polo shirt, jeans, and running shoes he had on were anything fancy. But I wanted to look a little more appealing than I did. For weeks I'd thought about what I'd say if I ever saw him again, and now that he was in front of me, I seemed to be at a loss for words. I tried to remember the things I'd planned to say, but couldn't think of them.

"Listen, T," I told him, "I really was gonna leave with you that night. But you were gone. I looked for you and couldn't find you."

"I saw you walk out the door and thought you were leaving the club, so I left," he said. "If it's any consolation, I did go back to the Sky Bar to look for you."

"But you found Brooke instead." I shook my head.

"Yeah. I did." He looked down.

"So, now what?" I asked, hoping that he'd gather me in his arms and kiss me now that he knew it was me he had wanted originally and not Brooke. He had to feel the same connection I did when we met.

"Honestly, I really don't know," he said.

Chapter Fifteen

Brooke

I curled up on the end of my sofa and cried. I'd made some huge mistakes in my life, but this one had to be the biggest. Even though it hadn't been my intention, I'd managed to break my sister's heart and destroy the potential friendship I was developing with Taurus. I felt horrible, and even more so because this entire situation had unraveled in front of my mother, on her birthday.

"Lord, Brooke," she said as she sat next to me and rubbed my back.

"I'm sorry. I didn't mean for any of this to happen. I didn't mean to hurt anyone," I sobbed.

"I get that." Mama sat me up and passed me a Kleenex. "But it happened. What made you think you'd be able to keep this from both of them?"

I shook my head. "I wasn't going to. I was going to tell them, eventually. I was just waiting for the right time."

"Well, seems to me the right time would've been the moment you realized that young man . . . What's his name again?"

"Taurus."

"Taurus? Like the bull?"

"Yeah." I nodded.

"Is that his real name?" She frowned.

"Yeah."

"Why did his mama name him that? Is that his zodiac sign?"

"Yes, Ma," I told her.

"Oh, I guess it makes sense, then. Anyway, as soon as you realized Taurus was the man Brittany had been talking to you about, you should've told him."

"I know," I wailed.

"So, why didn't you?" Her eyes became small, and she added, "And be honest with yourself and with me."

I swallowed the lump that had formed in my throat, and I told her, "Because I liked him."

"You mean you liked *having sex* with him?"

"Oh God." I groaned and turned away, no longer wanting to continue the conversation.

"Come on now, Brooke. I'm trying to help you," she told me.

I stood up and said, "No, Ma. I mean, yes, but . . ."

"You *didn't* like having sex with him?"

"It is not about sex."

She gave me a side-eye and said, "Brooke."

"Okay, real talk. It started out that way. Initially, I thought it was gonna be a one-night thing. He came up and kissed me at the club, and it was on and popping."

"On and popping," Mama repeated and shook her head.

"But that's not all it is. He's different. I enjoy being around him. When we talk, it's effortless, and he makes me laugh. We have the same interests, and we're just so much alike," I explained. "I'm comfortable with him, and I don't have to try. He respects me and listens to me. He thinks I'm beautiful and sexy, and I know it not because he says it, but because of the way he looks at me.

He gets me. And as much as I hate to admit it, I honestly don't believe he's even compatible with Britt. Taurus enjoys a challenge, and that's really not her."

"Brooke, Brooke, Brooke." She stood up. "I guess I'll be going."

"You're leaving? But your birthday," I said, not wanting her to leave.

"Your sister's upset, and I need to go and check on her and make sure she's okay." She hugged me.

"I'm sorry, Ma. Let me go and talk to her. I'll fix this, I promise."

"No, I don't think now is the right time for the two of you to talk. Emotions are running high, and some things have already been said in anger. You both need some time to process all of this." Mama gave a deep sigh. I could see the worry on her face, which made me feel even worse. It was her birthday, and we were supposed to be celebrating at the spa. Instead, she was now in the middle of an unfathomable situation between my sister and me. We hugged once more, and she promised we would talk later.

When she was gone, I went into my bedroom. My eyes fell on the side of the bed where Taurus had been lying earlier. I picked up the pillow he'd slept on and inhaled the scent of his cologne.

Seconds after my mother had called for him to come out of the bedroom, I had begun to panic. Not only because I had known Brittany would be upset, but also because I hadn't known if he'd emerge shirtless and displaying signs of all we'd done in my bedroom the night before. Luckily, he'd walked out fully dressed, sneakers and all. And even though I knew it really didn't matter now, the fact that he'd had the presence of mind to think quickly and put on his clothes while I begged my mother and sister to leave was somehow the silver lining to the fucked-up cloud that I'd created. He'd apologized to my mother and walked out of my apartment soon after Brittany had stormed off, barely looking at me as he exited. I knew the chances of his coming back anytime soon were probably nonexistent, but I nevertheless considered calling or texting him. My ego wouldn't allow me to. Instead, I climbed in bed, still clutching the pillow, and cried myself to sleep.

When I woke up hours later, the first thing I did was reach for my phone, hoping that Taurus had reached out. He hadn't, but Emory had. I didn't waste any time calling her back.

"Are you back?" I whined.

"Yeah. What the hell is wrong with you?" she asked.

"Can you come over now? I need you," I told her.

"Sure. Wait, I thought you and your sister were having a spa day for your mom's birthday today."

"I'll explain when you get here. Oh, and, Em . . ."

"Yeah?"

"Bring tequila."

"Oh shit. I'm on my way," she said.

Thirty minutes later, I was sitting on the sofa and sobbing all over again while taking shots and telling her what had happened. She sat next to me and listened, her face mirroring a myriad of emotions as I talked. When I finally got to the end, her mouth gaped open.

"Say something," I pleaded with her.

"Lord, Brooke." She said the exact words that my mother had uttered earlier and then drank the shot she'd been holding since the moment I started talking.

"Say something other than that." I poured both of us another drink.

"I don't even know where to begin." She sighed. "I mean, first of all, you know your ass is dead wrong for a lot of things."

"I know. I was going to tell them, I was," I repeated for what seemed like the hundredth time.

"I ain't even talking about that right now. I'm talking about the fact that you hid this shit from me. For the past month I've been wondering what the hell was going on with you, and I was starting to think that I'd done something wrong. And now you're sitting here telling me this? Now, after the shit done hit the fan?" She shook her head. "All the shit we've been through over the years, and you didn't think you could tell me what was going on?"

It hadn't dawned on me that my actions since I had started hanging out with Taurus were having an adverse effect on my friendship with Emory. I had been so focused on strategically withholding the truth, in an effort to continue enjoying the time I spent with him. Every time I had thought about telling Emory, I had stopped myself, because I had known she would tell me that what I was doing was wrong, and I hadn't wanted to hear it. So I had blown her off the same way I'd been blowing everyone else off.

"I fucked up, and I owe you an apology. I knew you would call me on my bullshit, the same way you did when I first told you about Taurus, and I didn't want to deal with it. So, instead, I just avoided you." I knew there was no point in making any kind of excuses. Emory deserved better than that.

"I get it. I can't believe your mom and sis popped up, though. Like, I wish I coulda seen your face when you opened that damn door, Brooke." She snickered. "I know you were like, 'What the hell?'"

For the first time that day, I laughed. "Em, you know me. But I was too damn shook to even be mad. I tried my damnedest to get them to leave, but nothing worked. It was as if Mama could sense that someone was up in here, and she was not budging until she saw who it was. This is all your fault, though."

"My fault? How?" she asked.

"If your ass had been here to pick me up from the airport, I wouldn't have had to have Taurus take me home," I said matter-of-factly.

"Heffa, based on what you've been sitting here telling me about you and him, you would've still hopped in the car with his ass," she replied. "Man, this is crazy. So, wait, if Taurus picked you up from the airport, who were you out of town with? Someone else? And what was the great news you had to tell me?"

"Great news?" I frowned.

"When you called me about needing a ride, you said you had some great news to tell me."

With everything that had happened, I'd forgotten all about my being promoted. I hadn't even had the chance to tell my mother and sister.

"Oh shit, I forgot. Well, I was in Fort Lauderdale with Brandon," I said.

"Brandon? What? This is too much, Brooke." Emory gulped down another shot.

"It wasn't like that. We were at the IT Systems Conference. The one all the managers have to attend." I smiled.

"Wait, so that means . . ." A smile spread across her face.

"Hell yeah!" I nodded, and then we both began screaming and hugging one another.

"Oh my God, Brooke. That's so good. I'm so happy for you," she said.

"Yeah, I found out yesterday, while we were there. Brandon . . ." My voice faded, and the sadness that had momentarily vanished came back over me.

"Brandon what? What's wrong?" Emory frowned.

"When he came to my room to tell me about me being promoted, Taurus was on the phone. And today, when Brittany was going off, she pretty much announced that Brandon was one of the guys I'd slept with." I didn't bother wiping the tears that fell from my eyes.

"Oh, Brooke," Emory said. "I'm sure he doesn't think it was anything other than a business trip, which it was. And you can explain it to him when y'all talk this out."

"Man, I don't even know if that's gonna happen. He was just as hurt and confused when he left here as Brittany was. And I just let him walk out. I didn't try to stop him or go after him or anything. I just sat here crying while my Mama patted me on the back," I told her.

"Maybe you should try calling him," she suggested.

I shook my head. "I doubt that he'd even answer."

"You never know until you try. Here." She handed me another shot. "Liquid courage."

I gulped it down, as I'd done with all the other ones I'd taken since she arrived. At this point, the liquor didn't even burn as it went down my throat. I grabbed my phone off the coffee table and instructed Siri to call Taurus. The phone rang once, and when his voicemail picked up, I hung up.

"I told you." I slumped back on the sofa.

"Text him," she told me.

I picked the phone back up and sent him a quick text asking if he was okay. "Done. But what if he doesn't respond? What if he never wants to talk to me again?"

Emory looked me in the eye and said, "Let me ask you something. Are you really feeling him like that? I mean, clearly, you are, because you let his ass spend the night. But do you really like him?" She paused for a moment. "And I need you to think about it before you answer, because you have to consider whether or not these past few weeks have been worth jeopardizing your relationship with your sister. That's essentially what you've done, real talk."

I thought about the questions and how I really felt about Taurus. Then said, "I do."

"And deep down, do you believe he's feeling you?"

"Yeah," I said.

"Then he will talk to you again," she said. "It may take a while, but he will. You are going to have to give him the same thing your mom told you to give Brittany. Some space and time."

For the next few days, I waited on a call or text from Taurus but didn't get either one. I missed him terribly and wanted to talk everything out: from me not telling him I had a twin sister, whom he'd met first, to explaining my sister's verbal dissertation about my sexual partners, including Brandon. I kept repeating the same two words that Emory and my mother had said to me: *time* and *space*. After a week, I couldn't take it any longer, and I reached out to him again. This time when I called, the phone didn't even ring. The call went directly to voice-mail. Later that evening, I tried again, and the same thing happened. I took another chance the next night, right before going to bed, and got the same results. I realized that the tables had turned, and now I was the one who'd been blocked.

Chapter Sixteen

Brittany

"Well, that's everything," I said, taking a final look around my now-empty house. I'd expected it to be on the market for a few months, but it had sold in a matter of weeks. The buyers were a really nice couple who had just celebrated their first-year wedding anniversary and were expecting their first child. When they'd come to do a tour, they had reminded me of what I'd hoped for in my own life not so long ago: love, marriage, and a family. Now the only thing I wanted was a new job.

"I'm sure gonna miss this place," Duane told me.

When I accepted the offer from the couple, I'd finally called him and asked him to come and get his things, unless he wanted them donated to the Goodwill. He had agreed and had come over the next night. As we went through our things, we began doing something we hadn't done in a long time: we talked. The conversation was both heated and heartfelt, and I realized why we'd grown apart over the past year. We were no longer the same two people we'd been when we met five years ago. Our relationship needs had changed, but we'd become so comfortable with each other that we didn't recognize that we both were unhappy until it was too late. I didn't express my desire to go out and be more social, and he didn't tell me he was just as bored as I was in our relationship, but even more so with our sex life. There were a couple of times when he'd suggest we try something totally out of my comfort zone, and I'd balked and refused, but I hadn't thought it was that serious. It was clear that our final breakup was sad but necessary, because although we loved one another, we weren't in love and never had been. Once the air was cleared, we both felt better, and he happily helped me pack the entire house up and move my furnishings into storage.

"So, are you still moving out of the area?" he asked as we walked out the front door for the last time.

"Yeah, I am. Kyra says I can stay with her as long as I need to, so I'll be with her for the next month, until school lets out. Then who knows?" I told him.

"You still wanna move near Brooke?" he asked.

Ironically, while we were packing up, I'd shared with him what my sister had done. His reaction had been mixed, which was understandable, considering our beef was about a man that I'd planned to have a one-night stand with. He'd agreed that she was wrong for not telling me, but he'd felt that we needed to talk. I hadn't spoken with her since the day I walked out of her apartment, and I had no desire to do so anytime soon. I was still hurt by her actions and felt like she'd betrayed me.

"I honestly don't know where I wanna go. I suppose time will tell, though."

"Well, you know I'm gonna miss you no matter where you go, right?" He smiled. "You and I will always be cool."

"Yes, we will," I said and hugged him. He walked me to my car, which was packed with a few more items that I needed to drop off for charity. "Thanks again, Duane."

"No thanks needed. Oh, and tell your mom, don't be a stranger. She can still check on me every now and then, so she can fuss." He laughed.

I waved at him as I backed out, and then I took off down the street and drove to the same restaurant that I'd seen Duane at with the woman. I walked inside and looked around until I spotted my mother sitting at a table.

"You get everything finished?" she asked as she stood and hugged me. It had been only a month since her birthday, the last time we'd seen one another. I had cried the entire time we drove back to her house, then had cried some more.

"Yes, Ma. The house is officially sold and empty. Thank God. Duane and I just left," I told her.

"That was so nice of him to help you pack up," she said. "I don't know why—"

"Uh-uh. No, Ma. Don't start," I warned her. "We're not getting back together. Period."

"Well, I was just going to say I don't know why you didn't invite him to eat with us, that's all." She sighed. "So, have you heard anything about any of the jobs you applied for?"

"Nope. Not yet. But I've applied only to a few."

"Any of them happen to be near me? You know I got plenty of room in this house, Brittany, and I can help you get a job."

"I'm not moving back home, Ma," I told her for the umpteenth time. I loved my mother and appreciated her offer. And although I wasn't sure in which direction life was going to take me at this moment, I was certain it would not be back to her house.

"Well, if you change your mind, you know you're always welcome," she told me.

We ordered our food, and while we waited, she made small talk about any and everything, from the weather to what she'd found on sale at Target the previous week. I knew she was avoiding the elephant in the room, and it was obvious.

"Mom, why are you here?" I sighed.

"To celebrate the sale of your house." She said it as if I'd just asked her the dumbest question she'd ever heard, then added, "Oh, and you're treating, since you got that fat equity check."

"I'm serious," I said.

Her eyes softened, and I could tell she was searching for the right words before she spoke, instead of blurting out what was on her mind, like she normally did. I prepared myself for whatever it was she was about to say.

"Because I'm worried, and I wanted to check on you," she told me.

"Ma, we talk every single day. What are you worried about?"

"We have conversations every day, Brittany. But we haven't really talked in a while, and you know what I'm referring to," she said. "You can't keep avoiding this."

I became uncomfortably hot and took a sip of my ice water. "There's nothing we need to talk about, Ma."

"We do. Now, I know you've had a lot going on with packing up your house and the end of the school year coming up, so I've kinda left it alone. But it's time to deal with it."

"Deal with what, Ma?"

"Deal with this situation between you and your sister. Now, you want me to be more specific? I can." She sat back in her chair.

"No," I said. "And there's nothing for us to deal with. She did what she did, and that's it. Nothing more, nothing less. And to be honest, it's what she always does."

"What do you mean?"

"She always has to have whatever she wants, no matter what. It doesn't matter what it is. If she wants it, she goes after it and takes it. She's reckless, and she doesn't care who she hurts, including me," I told her.

"Are you jealous of her?" Mama peered at me.

"No. I'm not," I snapped and raised my arms, almost bumping the waitress, who was bringing our food. She put the plates down and hurried off without even asking if we needed anything. I waited until Mama blessed the food before I asked, "Why would you even ask me that?"

"Because you're so angry," Mama said, picking up her fork.

"I'm angry because of what she did," I reminded her. "Not only did she sleep with a guy she knew I liked, but she damn near started a relationship with him too. She betrayed me. Don't you think I have a right to be angry?"

"I believe you have a right to be disappointed in her and maybe even disgusted. But, Brittany, let me ask you a question," she said between bites of food.

"Mama, you can't be serious. Please don't sit here and try to defend Brooke's actions and act like what she did wasn't wrong. You can't expect me to sit here and listen to you do that," I said, now feeling as if my mother had somehow chosen sides, and the one she had picked wasn't mine. She had always been closer to me than to my sister, and I expected her to be a lot more understanding than she was being right now.

"I'm not defending anything. You know I love you, and because of that, I'm just trying to help you process all of this, that's all."

"Fine. What's the question?" I shrugged.

"Why did you like him?"

I was confused. I'd expected her question to be long and difficult and yet easy to answer. Instead, these five simple words had me nearly stumped. "Huh?"

"You said she knew how much you really liked him. So why?" She shrugged. "What was it about him that led you to become so emphatic about how you felt?"

She had now rephrased her simple question, and I paused before answering. "Because the night we met, it was like magic. The way he looked at me and spoke to me. The way he danced up on me. And it was like he couldn't get enough of me. It was chemistry between us. And real talk, Ma. You saw him when he walked out of that bedroom. T is fine."

"Taurus," she said.

"Huh?" I blinked.

"Taurus," she repeated.

"What about a Taurus? What does that mean?" I asked.

"Taurus. That's his name. You keep calling him T."

"His name is Taurus? Well, he told me his name was T."

"So, you loved the way he looked at you? And you're right. He is fine." She nodded.

"Yes, it was as if I was the most beautiful woman in the world. I've never had a man look at me like that. He wanted me." I finally began eating my untouched food.

"Wanted to get to know you or wanted to sleep with you?" she asked.

"Both," I answered. "It's not like he walked up to me and said, 'Come on. Let's go have sex.' We did talk for a little while. And he was charming. He was really into me. We were into each other."

"Okay. I get that. Now, that night, what were you wearing? Were you looking like your normal self or maybe a little different? I'm sure you were all dolled up if you were with Brooke and Emory." She laughed.

"Of course. Emory did my hair, and Brooke did my makeup and gave me this outfit that was a little revealing and these boots that I almost couldn't walk in." I giggled. "I was looking fierce. I definitely didn't look like I normally look."

Then it hit me, and I realized what my mother was getting at.

"Brittany, your sister was wrong for not telling you she'd run into Taurus. She's acknowledged that and wants to apologize. But you're saying he was into you when, in fact, did he even know the real you? The two of you didn't even give each other your real names. There may have been a fleeting moment of attraction between you, but that's what happens at the club. Who's to say you would've even liked one another after the romp in the sack you were hoping for?" She reached across the table and touched my hand.

I thought about the way Taurus had looked at me that morning at Brooke's condo, as I stood outside my car, crying and dressed in my weekend attire. It wasn't the same way the guy I knew as T had. Taurus had looked like he was just as hurt and confused as I was, and even after learning that I was the woman he'd met first, he hadn't seemed very interested. After a brief hug and another apology, Taurus had walked off without even asking me for my phone number. All this time I'd blamed Brooke for his reaction. Thought that she had forced him into this situation of being torn between two women and that he didn't want to have to choose. But as I thought about it now, that no longer seemed to be the case.

"Either way, she should've told us," I whispered. "Like I said, she sees what she likes, and she takes it."

"He wasn't yours to take, Brittany. But, yes, she does like him. She told me that."

"She likes a whole lot of men," I said sarcastically. "She likes men, period."

"Not this time." Mama shook her head. "This time it's different."

"So, you two have discussed this in detail?" I shook my head. "Nice to know the two of you are buddy-buddy all of a sudden. Did you ask her why she likes him?"

"I did."

"And what did she say? Oh, let me guess. Because he's tall and handsome and can dress and is great in bed."

My mother's cackling laughter took me by surprise. I wasn't trying to be funny, but clearly, she was amused. She composed herself enough to say, "She didn't say any of that, but if she had, I wouldn't have been surprised. Your sister is shallow and has a tendency to be a little self-centered at times, but she actually had some valid and heartfelt reasons why she liked him. She enjoys spending time with him, and they enjoy one another. But none of that even matters now, because they don't see each other anymore."

I looked up. "They don't?"

"Nope, they don't. She hasn't seen or spoken to him at all. She's sorry about all of this and really wants to talk. Can you at least hear her out?" Mama said.

The truth was that I did miss my sister. She'd tried to reach out, but I'd been too angry and hurt to respond. I was also embarrassed about the things that I'd said about her in front of my mother and Taurus. I nodded and said, "Yes, Ma. I'll talk to her."

"Thank you." She grinned and began waving toward the door.

I turned around and saw Brooke walking over to us, looking fashionable, as always, in a cute peplum shirt, formfitting jeans, and boots. Her hair was in braids, and her makeup was perfect.

"What? How?" I asked.

"Hey," Brooke said when she reached the table. Her voice was light and timid. I could tell she was trying to read my reaction.

"Hey," I said and looked back at my mother, who was looking as pleased as a mother duck watching her babies take their first swim.

"Hey, Brooke. You can sit here," Mama said, and she slid over so Brooke could sit down. "I'm so proud of both of you. Britt, you sold your house. Brooke got a big promotion. Both of my girls are doing it. Let me go and ask them if they have some kind of cake we can order. I'll be right back."

When she was gone, Brooke looked at me and said, "You know this whole thing was planned, including that little escape moment."

"Of course." I smirked. We both remained quiet until I said, "You got the management job you've been waiting on? Congratulations."

"Thanks, and congrats on selling your house," she said. "I'm happy for you. You know, if you want to come and stay with me while you find a place, it's cool. I don't mind."

I knew she was extending an olive branch, which I appreciated. "Thanks, but I'm good for right now, until I figure out my next move."

"Okay. Let me know if you need anything. I'm not going to be traveling as much anymore, so you know . . . ," she said.

"Thanks." I nodded.

Again, the table became quiet, but it was Brooke who broke the silence this time by saying, "Britt, I'm sorry. I wish I had handled things a lot differently. But I was wrong, and I was selfish. I never meant to hurt you. You are my sister, and I love you. You have to know that I never meant any malice toward you, or anyone else."

"I know, Brooke. I mean, I'm hurt, but I realize I may have been looking at this the wrong way. Ma kinda pointed out some things to me today, and I'm not saying it's gonna be easy, but I'm saying I believe we can get past this," I told her.

"I love you, BB." She got up and reached out to hug me.

"Please, don't ever call me that again," I said as I stood.

"Deal," she said as we embraced.

Mama rushed over. "Look at the two of you. I'm such a great mother," she said as she wrapped her arms around both of us.

Epilogue

Brooke

"Congratulations, Brooke!"

I stared at the silver banner hanging on the wall and smiled. My best friend had outdone herself. The tables were decked out with centerpieces and linen napkins, and there was a huge cake located in the back corner. Everything was silver and black, my favorite colors. I couldn't believe she'd gone all out like this for what was supposed to be a small get-together in the private dining room of Jose's, one of my favorite soul-food spots, to celebrate my promotion, which was finally official.

My coworkers seemed happy for me, including members of upper management, who'd all emailed me. I was grateful for their well wishes and votes of confidence. It made the office a pleasant place to be, which was a good thing, because it was now where I spent nearly all my time. I had become a workaholic. I would come in early in the morning and leave when I could barely keep my eyes open at night. It wasn't because I had to. Brandon had made my transition into management easy, and I was pretty much familiar with my new roles and responsibilities. But working nonstop was a much-needed distraction from my personal life. I no longer enjoyed going out to the clubs or bars. I hardly ever partied with

Emory these days. The only two things that brought me pleasure were working and shopping. And the more I worked, the more I was able to shop. And both working and shopping helped me not to think about him.

"How does it look?" Emory's voice came from behind me.

I turned around and admired the adorable black cocktail dress she wore, along with a beautiful silver necklace, which was quite a statement piece, and gorgeous silver heels.

"Everything looks amazing. I'm wowed by it all," I said. "I can't believe you did all of this. It's really too much, Em."

"It's not. And you are the one who looks damn amazing. That dress is everything," she said.

"She ain't lying," Brandon said as he walked over to us.

"You don't look so bad yourself," I told him. He was looking dapper, as usual, in a black suit, which I knew had to be custom made.

"You know I had to look presentable at the turnup." He popped his collar and raised an eyebrow.

"Technically, this should be a celebration for you too," I said. "You're the one with the big title now."

"True, but nah, tonight is all about you. And this is for you." He handed me the gift bag that he was carrying.

"A gift? Wow. Thanks, Brandon." I gave him a quick hug.

"I'll take that," Emory said as she reached for the bag. "We do have a gift table."

"You've thought of everything." I laughed.

"So, I guess you didn't tell her the news yet, huh?" Brandon whispered after Emory walked away.

"No, I haven't said anything to her. I figured you wanted to tell her," I said.

He shrugged. "Well, I guess we can tell her together."

I looked over at the doorway and saw Miss Helen and a few more people from the office coming in. I gave them a quick wave. "Should we tell her now or wait until later?"

"I think we should just tell her, so she'll know." He paused. "Unless you want to make a big announcement in front of everybody."

"No." I shook my head. "Let's just tell her."

He grinned at me and said, "Yeah."

When Emory came back, I said, "Hey, Em. We need to tell you something."

She looked at us and said, "Okay. What is it? Did someone bring an uninvited guest, because I can't change the head count."

"No, that's not it," Brandon said. "This is something else."

"What?" she asked, her eyes widening. "Oh my God. Are you about to tell me what I think you're gonna tell me?"

"I don't know," Brandon said. "Is that a rhetorical question?"

"Are you guys about to tell me you're a couple now? Y'all are dating?" Emory looked over at me.

"What? No, Em. What the hell?" I hissed.

"Oh, I mean, y'all have been spending a lot of time together, and he's not your boss anymore, so I mean, maybe . . ." Emory shrugged.

"I shot my shot and missed." Brandon sighed.

"Brandon, shut up," I told him.

"Hey, that's no way to talk to an associate vice president of the company you work for." He laughed.

Emory went back to the subject at hand. "So, if y'all aren't together, then what is it you have to tell me?"

"Well," I said, "we have been talking to Gregg, and I told him that you should be the one to replace me in the training department."

"And I agreed with her," Brandon said.

Emory's eyes went from me to Brandon, then back to me. "Wait, I'm being offered a training position?"

"Yep," Brandon answered.

Emory began screaming and jumping up and down. Everyone looked over to see what was happening.

"Is she all right?" Miss Helen called over to us.

"She's just a little excited about some good news she just got," I told her. Then I turned to Emory. "I know you're happy, but I'm going to need for you to act a little more professional."

"I can't believe this. Thank you so much. But I didn't even apply. I didn't even think about applying, for real. How? I don't even have a—" She grabbed one of the napkins off a table and dabbed at the tears of happiness she now had in her eyes.

"You're qualified, Emory. It's not about a degree all the time. It's about experience and knowledge, not formal education. You got this, and we'll make sure you get what you need to be successful. Besides, you'll have a great boss." Brandon motioned toward me.

"True," I said. "Let me go and say hi to everyone else before they think I'm being rude. Congrats again, bestie."

"Thanks, Brooke." Emory hugged me. Then she said, "Who the hell is that with Miss Helen? Lord, I told her she couldn't have a damn plus one. I knew somebody was gonna mess up my head count."

I looked over and saw the unfamiliar man standing beside Miss Helen. "I don't know. But don't trip. It'll be fine."

"A'ight. I mean, it's your party, so I guess it's whatever." Emory shook her head, and I laughed.

I made my way over to Miss Helen and her guest.

"Brooke, you look beautiful. All of this is beautiful," she told me.

"Thanks, Miss Helen." I smiled. "I appreciate you coming."

"You know I wouldn't miss this for the world. And this is my nephew Reginald, the one I've been telling you about. *The doctor.* I brought him so he could meet you." She grabbed the guy standing beside her by the arm and thrust him in front of me. "Reginald, this is Brooke."

"Aunt Helen, chill please," he said, clearly embarrassed. Then he said, "Nice to meet you, Brooke."

"Nice to meet you too," I told him. I had to give it to Miss Helen; she wasn't lying when she said he was handsome. He definitely was. Six feet tall, a slim frame, bald head. And behind the glasses he wore were the kindest eyes I'd ever seen. I wasn't sure if he was shy, but he looked uncomfortable as hell as he rubbed the back of his neck, and his caramel-toned face was turning a little red.

"Let me go say hello to Emory. I'll be right back. You two get to talking," Miss Helen told us. I almost wanted to tell her Emory was the last person she probably wanted to speak to, but I decided to let her go on her merry way.

"I'm sorry," he said when she was gone. "My aunt told me her car was in the shop and she needed a ride. I thought I was dropping her off. Then, when we got here, she insisted I come inside for a quick second. I didn't know this was a party thing. And I didn't know she was gonna do this."

"It's okay. I've known Miss Helen for a long time, so this doesn't surprise me." I laughed. "I love her."

"She's my aunt. So I gotta love her, I guess." He relaxed a little and pointed to the banner. "But congratulations for whatever you did. Aunt Helen has been talking about you for years, and the pictures she's shown me were nice."

"Oh God, she showed you my picture?" I gasped.

"Yeah, and I have to admit, she was right. You're beautiful," he said. "I mean no disrespect of any kind by saying that."

"Thank you. That's so sweet," I told him. "She didn't lie when she said you were handsome, and she also lets the world know that you're a doctor."

"I'm a chiropractor. She acts like I'm a neurosurgeon." He shook his head.

"That's still a doctor." I shrugged.

"Well, I'm sure you have to get back to your guests. But I would love to maybe get your information, and maybe we can meet up and have coffee one day. Aunt Helen seems to think we'd get along, and after meeting you, I'm thinking she may be right."

I gave him an appreciative smile, knowing he wasn't right for me, which was sad, because he seemed like a really nice guy. I was about to respectfully decline flat out his invitation, and then I had an epiphany. "Can you wait right here for one sec? I'll be right back."

"Uh, sure," he said, giving me a confused look.

I rushed over to the table Emory had designated as mine, and grabbed my purse, which I'd placed in a chair. I reached inside and took out my phone, then rushed back over to Reginald.

"Come outside with me for a sec," I told him. He followed me as I headed toward the restaurant's lobby, and I quickly FaceTimed a number and then pulled him to sit beside me on a leather bench.

Brittany laughed when she answered the call. "What's up?" I could barely hear her over the music in the background. "Stop pulling me, crazy."

"Britt, where are you? What are you doing?" I asked.

"I'm hanging out with my favorite client, Marlena, and we're at the skating rink," she yelled.

"Go where you can talk for a second. Hurry up," I told her. Reginald was sitting beside me, looking confused, and I said, "Humor me for a moment. You'll be okay, I promise."

"Okay." He nodded.

"All right. I stepped out," Brittany said. It was now easier to hear her.

"I have someone for you to meet. This is Reginald. He's cute, super nice, and he's a doctor. Reginald, this is my twin sister, Brittany. She's an amazing licensed clinical social worker who just opened her own agency, and she's even more beautiful than I am. Oh, and she's a Starbucks fiend. Here you go." I handed Reginald the phone.

"Um, this is even more awkward than what Aunt Helen just pulled," he whispered as he nervously reached for my phone. "Hello."

"Um, hello," Brittany said.

"I'll leave you two to chat," I told him. Feeling like I had accomplished something, I headed back into my party.

"Where did you go?" Emory asked when I walked back in the private dining room.

"I had to see Miss Helen for a sec," I said. She looked at me like I was crazy, but I promised to explain later.

I continued mingling with the other guests and enjoying the party. Soon Emory announced that dinner would be served, and instructed everyone to take their seats.

Miss Helen walked over to me. "Where did Reginald go?" she asked, looking panicked. "He didn't leave, did he? You didn't like him?"

"He didn't leave, Miss Helen. He just stepped out for a sec," I told her, ignoring her last question.

Luckily, he walked in at that moment and smiled as he gave me my phone. "Thank you."

"I take it the phone call went well?" I asked.

"Very." He beamed. "I'll be having coffee this weekend."

"I'm glad to hear that." I winked.

I was about to go and take my seat, but Emory stopped me and pulled me to the side. "Brooke, wait a sec. I got something to show you."

"What? Now? You just told us to sit down." I frowned. "People are hungry, and so am I."

"They'll be okay, and so will you," she said, taking me by the arm and leading me out the door. Once we were outside the room, she turned me so I was facing her. "Look at me. I have a surprise for you."

"What is it?" I asked.

"I love you, and I'm proud of you. You are my best friend, and so I did something for you."

"What the hell did you do?" I was becoming more and more anxious by the second.

She turned my body slowly around, and suddenly I was standing face-to-face with Taurus. I simply stared at him. I sucked air slowly, as seeing him nearly took my breath away. I couldn't speak or move and was relieved when he spoke first.

"Hey, Brooke." His voice sounded like music to my ears. I'd been longing to hear it for so long.

"Taurus," I said, resisting the urge to rush over and hug him.

"I'll leave you two alone to catch up," Emory blurted, then rushed off and back through the door to the private dining room.

"It's great to see you. These are for you." He held out the dozen roses I hadn't even noticed he had been holding.

"Thank you. How?" I said. "I mean, how did she . . . ?"

"She literally showed up at my door a couple of nights ago." He shook his head as he shrugged. "She's a good friend."

"She is." I smiled at him. "The best."

"Anyway, after forcing herself into my crib, which, by the way she thought looked amazing, she kinda talked to me for a while, then demanded that I come tonight. I was too afraid to decline the invitation. She's kind of aggressive to be as short as she is." He smiled.

"She is," I agreed. "But how the hell did she know where you lived?"

"Apparently, you sent her your location the night you came home with me from the Sky Bar. She used it to find me."

"Damn, I love my bestie." I sighed. "Well, I'm glad she invited you."

"I am too." He nodded. "So, how've you been?"

"You don't want to know." I shook my head, then looked up at him. "I tried calling you a couple of times but couldn't get through."

"I figured you did. I kinda needed a moment to process," he explained.

"I understand. And I apologize for what I did. I put you in a situation that you didn't have to be in, and it all could've been avoided if I had just said something the moment I knew." I finally gave him the apology I'd been holding on to for over a month.

"I'm glad you recognize that, and I accept your apology. And I've really missed you."

Hearing him say that made my heart swell with happiness. "I've definitely missed you too."

"How are things between you and your sister?"

"They're actually good. She needed some time, just like you did. But we're good now."

"And your mom? I was so embarrassed to meet her like that." He exhaled and rubbed the back of his head.

"She's fine." I laughed. "And there was no need to be embarrassed. I think all the other stuff that went on that day kinda overshadowed the fact that you were in my bedroom."

"That makes sense." He smirked. "Well, should we go inside? I'm sure your guests are wondering where you are."

"We can, but, Taurus, I do wanna say one more thing before we go in," I said.

"What's that?"

"Brittany kind of said some stuff about my private life, and I just want you to know that she kinda wasn't lying, but none of that happened after I met you." I swallowed the lump in my throat and continued. "Even the whole Brandon thing. And he's inside the dining room too."

"Brooke, everybody has a past, and I'm not concerned with any of what she said. None of that matters, for real."

He gave me a look that let me know that he still felt like I was the most beautiful woman in the world.

"So, we're good?" I whispered.

He stepped closer, cupped my face with his hands, and the slow kiss he gave me let me know that we were better than good. I wrapped my arms around his neck, nearly dropping the flowers, and became lost in the moment.

Emory opened the dining-room door and peeked out. "Oh God. Can you two please take a breather and get in here?"

Taurus smiled as he took me by the hand. Then he led me back to the party. And I embraced the same feeling of complete happiness that I had had the night he slept beside me in my bed. Finally, I was excited about being attached.

Illusions of Love

by

Latoya Chandler

CHAPTER ONE

Can you imagine seeing a child being pulled into a car by a stranger in the middle of the day? It would probably take you a moment to realize what you were actually witnessing. Many of us have played over and over in our minds how we'd react and what we would do if we were to witness such a horrific and gut-wrenching crime. Disbelief, along with a sense of devastating failure, would fill us. Especially if it was our own child, our only child, that was abducted. Now imagine if it happened on your wedding day.

The moment she learned of the abductions that had been taking place in her neighborhood of Williamsburg, Brooklyn, Eboneé had begun replaying in her mind the actions she'd take if she witnessed such horror. Since she was a mom, she was especially tormented by the fact that child abductors had struck so close to home. Emani was her heartbeat in human form, and that fact alone forced Eboneé to stay on alert. Eboneé had obsessed so much about the kidnappings that she and her fiancé, Kasim, had implemented precautionary measures to try to ease her mind. Such as being sure to avoid taking the same route to and from home. They'd even gone as far as explaining to little Emani the difference between family and strangers. They'd told her that any and everyone outside of their immediate circle was a stranger, and they'd drilled into her the importance of staying close to her parents and never talking to strangers.

Despite all the measures that had been put in place to protect her child, fear immobilized Eboneé when she graced the steps of St. Mary's Cathedral on her wedding day. What was supposed to be the happiest day of her life was about to turn into her worst living nightmare. Emani, who had been glued to Eboneé's side the entire morning, while she and her wedding party scurried around in anticipation of the ceremony, suddenly wasn't anywhere in sight. Eboneé felt panic rush her and swallow her whole as she whipped her head from left to right, in search of Emani. Though she had not uttered a word, members of Eboneé's bridal party picked up on her fear, and when they realized one by one that Emani was no longer standing with the other two flower girls, they all became alarmed. They all began scampering about, searching for the little girl. And the more everyone raced around frantically, the higher Eboneé's pulse went.

Eboneé turned around to try to retrace her steps and couldn't believe her eyes. She saw something her mind would never be able to erase: Emani was standing alone by the curb, and within the blink of an eye, she was snatched from where she stood and shoved into a black truck. Adrenaline shot through Eboneé's veins. Nonetheless, she was stuck in place; she couldn't move a single muscle. All her breath had been snatched from her lungs. Her heart pounded inside her chest. A choked cry forced itself up her throat when Kasim came running to her side after deserting his post at the altar upon being alerted about Emani's absence.

"Eb-Eboneé, wh-what happened to Emani?" he asked, his words colliding. His face showed his distress.

"Some . . . abla . . . tr-tru . . . ," she stammered, making no sense at all.

"Eboneé, snap out of it. Where is my daughter? Where is Emani?" Kasim's words were shrill and deafening. His eyebrows curled inward as his eyes widened with grief. When his eyes closed, teardrops slowly ran down his face.

More fear rose in Eboneé's eyes as the realization that her daughter had been abducted seeped in deeper. A chill shot down her spine, causing her to shudder, and she stood there helplessly, not knowing what to do and feeling too scared to think.

"Someone, please call—" Kasim swallowed the rest of his words when he heard the sound of approaching sirens.

"They're en route. I—I called them on my way to get you out of the church," announced Parish, Eboneé's longtime friend and her maid of honor.

When the patrol cars pulled up, a wave of nausea hit Eboneé. Police officers made the kidnapping real, and that terrorized her. She couldn't deny what had taken place. She hadn't been dreaming. Her baby girl was gone. The more this reality became undeniable, the more her stomach contracted violently, forcing everything up and out. The world around Eboneé spun out of control.

She seesawed, pitched forward, sank to her knees, and wailed, "Please, God. Please bring our baby back to us!"

At the close of the two-and-a-half-hour-long interrogation conducted by the detectives covering Emani's case, Kasim and Eboneé were at odds with one another. Eboneé was both distraught and boiling on the inside. It was difficult for her to understand why the detectives weren't out looking for Emani instead of grilling her, Kasim, and their wedding party. Kasim disagreed with the line of questioning and also felt the detectives weren't doing their jobs. He didn't want to think the worst and told himself Emani would be returned to them safe and sound. On the other hand, he just couldn't banish the numb and empty feeling that had overtaken him. It was the same as one felt following the death of a loved one. And the more Kasim thought about the situation, the more his anger intensified. He felt a vexation that he'd never thought he'd feel, especially toward Eboneé. Even the sound of her voice infuriated him. The woman he'd worshiped the instant he laid eyes on her was no longer perfect or desirable. Each time she spoke, Kasim snapped at her.

"Why would God do this to us, Kasim? We're good people. Why would He let this happen to our baby?" Eboneé cried as they stood in the living room of their house after the interrogation. She dropped to her knees and sobbed, unable to control her pain and fear.

Tears burned Kasim's eyes, and his lip trembled. "God, Eboneé? God? How dare you blame Him! This is your fault. Instead of being happy with the way He made you, you went and lost weight. Lean women aren't strong enough to take care of children."

"My fault? You're not making any sense, Kasim. I know you're upset, but you cannot blame me. Losing a few pounds has nothing to do with what happened to our child."

"It has everything to do with it. You were worried about all the wrong things, and because of it, our child is God knows where." Raw anger shot through him.

The rage in Kasim's voice said more than the words that spewed out of his mouth. Eboneé understood that he was hurt and that he was scared for Emani. He wasn't alone. She was there with him, suffering from the same pain. However, the fact that he had placed the blame on her severed the remaining piece of her heart that she had left. She couldn't understand any of it. His accusations and his vexation frightened her. That wasn't her Kasim. Her fiancé, the man she had taken the time to know and love, wasn't standing in front of her. In the past, no matter the situation or problem that presented itself, the Kasim she knew had always been by her side and *on* her side, and they'd fumbled through whatever it was together. This person before her now was unfamiliar to her. Her Kasim, the man she loved and adored, had stressed time and time again that the blame game was nothing more than verbal vomit, and that individuals who played that game were narcissistic. They got off on engaging in a lot of all-or-nothing thinking and pointing finger at others.

Their daughter, Emani, whom they'd had difficulty conceiving, was gone, and Kasim, in turn, was blaming Eboneé for her disappearance. It pained Eboneé deeply. The two people that she couldn't live without had been taken from her on the very same day. Her wedding day. Emani was gone physically; Kasim had left her emotionally and mentally. From those thoughts alone, Eboneé felt sharp pains pierce her head. Images of Emani flashed in front of her eyes, and she felt like her whole body was being beaten.

"God, please bring our baby back safe and sound. If this is a dream, please deliver us from this nightmare," she cried, feeling as if her brain was being ground from the inside out. Heartache gushed out of her every pore.

"And if she doesn't return, neither will I," Kasim stormed. Then he stalked out of the living room and slammed the door behind him.

Eboneé shuddered as the door slammed shut. The sound echoed through their home, as loud as the cracking of a whip, stinging her insides. She hadn't ever seen Kasim in this state. She chalked it up to the tragic circumstances they found themselves in, and she tried to persuade herself that he had no control over his state of mind, that he was powerless. However, his actions directed at her made it difficult for her to sympathize with him. His eyes were narrowed and cold when he looked at her, and when she gazed in them, she saw a deadness and a stillness, which made her teeth chatter. He no longer sounded like her husband-to-be. Each word he uttered cut her like a razor blade, sharp and cold.

Kasim's voice was one of the attributes that she had always loved about him and that had made him irresistible to her. When they first met, his words, spoken softly, had reached her heart and had stopped her in her tracks. But the man who had just stomped out of the room was unattractive, and she despised the sound of his voice in that moment. Her Kasim would have stayed. He would have wept with her. He would not have raised his voice or walked out in the middle of it all.

Kasim and Eboneé first met during the speed networking event she held for her fledgling fashion business. At the very beginning of her career, Eboneé was a BBW Christian stylist, and after taking a few career detours, she pursued her dream and launched her own fashion business, B&S Styles, which stood for Bold and Sexy Styles. B&S Styles was an expression of Eboneé's love for fashion. The seed for the business was planted during a simple conversation that Eboneé had with a coworker at her job. That coworker would be her first client.

Eboneé had grown up with extra weight on her frame, and then she'd become chubby, according to society's standards. The older she'd got, the more overweight she'd become. No matter what size she was, she'd make sure to keep herself up and live her life, ignoring the saying "She's pretty for a big girl." That saying had always nauseated her. Despite the standards set by society, Eboneé had known from a young age that she was worth being seen, heard, and appreciated just as much as any other person. No matter how much thinner he or she might be. Her nana Mae had raised her and had drilled into her head that beauty didn't have a size. Beauty came in all sizes. Race was a nonfactor when it came to beauty, as was nationality. Eboneé had fashioned her life around Nana Mae's beliefs about beauty. Hence, she'd been drawn to fashion early on.

Eboneé felt women should dress according to their body type, and she did just that. No matter the occasion, whether it was her morning stroll, a girls' night, or a gala, she dressed her best, and she frequently received compliments as well as double takes.

At five foot six and about 250 pounds, Eboneé always presented herself in all her full-figured glory. People noticed her beautiful skin as much as her frame, for she looked as if she had been dipped in freshly made deep brown caramel. Her skin tone accentuated her straight nose, her slightly flared nostrils, and her rather full lips, which were quick to turn into a smile. In terms of her height and weight, she was pretty much identical to her best friend, Parish. Their looks diverged when it came to skin tone: Parish was a darker version of Eboneé.

However, they were opposite in terms of their beliefs and their self-esteem, or at least they were when they first met while working at the local children's hospital. Parish had always been uncomfortable in her skin. But meeting Eboneé in the workplace changed her entire perception of herself. On day one, they didn't gravitate toward one another. However, after some time, they befriended one another, and Eboneé gave Parish encouragement, which enabled Parish to see a side of herself that she'd never seen before. Parish found her own beauty, which had been hidden for most of her adult life. Eboneé convinced Parish to attend counseling in order for her to love everything about herself, no matter her size. To fall in love with the woman that God had created her to be.

Parish was the wife of a local preacher. And she had an amazing voice. Soon after she met Eboneé, she was asked to sing as a guest soloist on a gospel album, and Eboneé encouraged her to pursue it. The album was a success, and soon multiple record labels were seeking out her angelic voice. After careful consideration, she and Kwame decided on the direction in which to take Parish's singing career, and she signed a contract with a prestigious record label. Realizing that she'd now have to spend a lot of time in the public eye, Parish consulted with Eboneé and hired her as her personal stylist and assistant.

Eboneé transformed Parish into a whole new woman. Under Eboneé's direction, Parish went from wearing cardigans paired with denim skirts that hung past her ankles and ballerina flats to donning pencil and A-line skirts, wraparound dresses, tunic tops, blazers, jeans, slacks, and heels. And that transformation was the beginning of what Eboneé then called the Pastors' Wives Club. Because of Parish's 180-degree fashion turnaround, pastors' wives from churches with which Parish and her husband fellowshipped inquired about her makeover. She told them all about Eboneé, and they sought her out.

Eboneé's clientele instantly quadrupled, affording her the opportunity to resign from her job as a verification coordinator at the children's hospital. Parish tendered her resignation too. It was a huge hit for the department to lose both of them at the same time. However, their new ventures were a dream come true for both of them. Without question, all new ventures were accompanied by a backlash, and it manifested the moment the public and church folk got a glimpse of Parish's promotional photo for the record label's promo ad.

Parish's off-the-shoulder, above-the-knee, body-con black dress sent the internet into an uproar. The sanctified side of social media deemed her dress as being too-sexy and distracting and implied that the message that God wanted to get across had somehow been lost and that it was no longer about God. Faced with such condemnation, Parish's husband chimed in, penning an open apology letter to the National Pastors site, a website designed for men and women of the cloth nationwide. In the letter, he had blamed Eboneé for her deleterious influence on his wife. He also publicly fired Eboneé and promised that the promo pictures would be taken down, to be replaced with modest photographs.

Eboneé first got wind of the uproar when Parish called her one afternoon.

"Eboneé, I am sure you've seen the feedback and the comments about me and the promo photo that have been circulating on social media," Parish said after a quick hello.

"N-no, I haven't," Eboneé stammered, having heard the dismay in Parish's voice.

"I'm going to send some of the comments to your phone. Call me when you get them," Parish said, then disconnected the call.

After the call ended, a notification from Parish alerted Eboneé that she had text messages. Eboneé opened some of the messages, read the comments, and felt mortified. She couldn't believe what she read. Frozen to the spot where she stood, her anger rose, and she felt like someone had suddenly turned on a heater inside her body.

"I am not a bad influence. How could they say those things about me? And how could Parish's husband, Kwame, fire me?" she muttered.

The more she scrolled through the comments, the more her stomach churned. She'd already left her job, and negative publicity of this magnitude could ruin her fledgling business.

Why would Parish's husband cosign any of this? she wondered, feeling traumatized.

Ding dong!

The sudden tinny, grating sound of the doorbell startled her. She ran to the front door and looked through the peephole.

"It's me, Eboneé! Please open the door," Parish shouted from the other side of the door.

Eboneé's hand found the doorknob and turned it. She opened the door and stared at Parish without saying a word. Then she motioned for her to come inside.

"I am so sorry, Eboneé. I phoned you from the car. You are not fired. I need you. I am not replacing the pictures. It's a done deal, anyway," Parish blurted upon entering the house.

"How? Your husband said—"

"I have to live my life the way I want. I love God, and I will continue to sing for His glory. And I can look amazing doing it. I am saved and sexy. And guess what? God still loves me. I spoke to my agent. He said we can use this publicity to our benefit. At this point we need to capitalize on all the attention from the press that we get. All publicity is good publicity. We just have to decide how we are going to use it."

Eboneé couldn't believe what she had just heard. Minutes ago, she had thought she'd ruined Parish's marriage and she'd lose all her clientele. However, the opposite was true. Parish had stood her ground, and Kwame had respected her wishes when it came to her career. But he had prohibited her from serving in the church from here on in. He felt Parish had publicly humiliated him, and not allowing her to carry out her role as the first lady of the church was his form of punishment for her transgression. Eboneé could not understand how Parish allowed herself to be treated in this manner. But Parish spent so much time on the road, touring, that none of this bothered her.

Thanks to all the publicity surrounding Parish's promotional photo, pastors' wives from around the world took notice, and Eboneé's clientele doubled virtually overnight. With all the work pouring in, Eboneé realized she needed a staff. And so her one-person fashion enterprise, the Pastors' Wives Club, became a full-fledged company, B&S Styles.

In order to staff her newfound business, Eboneé opted to host a speed networking event in the event room at the Hilton Hotel in Upper Manhattan rather than conduct traditional interviews. Like-minded entrepreneurs, such as stylists and up-and-coming fashion designers, would attend the event, and she would have the opportunity to pursue partnerships with those she liked. Unlike at traditional speed networking events where only entrepreneurs and businesses were in attendance, Eboneé involved Parish and ten of her other clients. She gave Parish and these clients name tags and scorecards and instructed them to sit in designated spots while the stylists and fashion designers rotated around the room every five minutes, when a little bell rang. Each of her clients was asked to mark on the scorecard the stylists and designers whom they'd hire. Those attendees who got the most yeses would be sent an email inviting them for a formal interview.

While wrapping things up at the event, exhaustion consumed Eboneé's entire being. She had had a great turnout and considered the event a great success, as everything had turned out according to plan, but she was overjoyed that the attendees had left. Oddly enough, babysitting had added more stress to the event. The sitter for one of her clients had cancelled at the last minute, and the client had brought her infant son inside with her to inform Eboneé that she'd have to bow out of the event. Eboneé had insisted that the infant wouldn't be a problem and had assured the client that she'd look after him for her. Although she'd enjoyed tending to the infant, she had been so relieved to turn him over to his mother at the end of the event.

After giving a sigh of relief, Eboneé pulled an additional chair in front of the one she had been sitting on, removed her shoes, and then propped her feet up on the makeshift footrest and made herself comfortable.

"Excuse me, ma'am," said a warm baritone voice.

Startled, her heart fluttering, Eboneé jumped to her feet and turned around to put a face to the voice. There was something electric when her eyes met his, and she found herself blushing. At six feet two, he hovered over her. He was handsome, with dark hair and brown eyes that became lighter when the sunlight hit them. The thick, defined eyebrows that he'd been blessed with would have made most females jealous. His beauty took Eboneé's breath away.

"C-Can I help you?" she stammered.

"I was hoping I could assist you."

"I'm sorry . . ." Her eyes widened. "I don't recall requesting assistance, sir . . ."

"Kasim. My name is Kasim, and you don't have to request anything. I already know what you're in need of before you can think of it or ask for it."

"I think you have most definitely mistaken me for someone else."

"No, I believe I am right where I am supposed to be, and where you need me to be. You just don't know it yet."

"A bit arrogant, would you say?"

"Not at all. I am sincere and confident."

"Well, thanks but no thanks, Mr. Kasim."

"My apologies." He extended his hand, but she didn't take it. "You're going to leave me hanging and not shake my hand or accept my apology?"

She shrugged. "Okay. Sure." She shook his hand.

"Let me start over. My name is Kasim. I have been watching you on the camera from my office. I apologize if this sounds disturbing. However, I just couldn't take my eyes off the screen. I've missed three hours of work because I couldn't get enough of your beauty. I know this sounds cheesy, but it's the truth. My truth. Would you please grant me the honor of having dinner with me?"

"Yes, she would love to," Parish answered as she walked into the room.

"Parish!"

"Eboneé, let the man take you to dinner. You are sweating and fidgeting over there like a schoolgirl. He clearly has you all worked up." She cut her eye at Eboneé and chuckled before continuing. "And I mean that in a very good way." She winked.

A voice inside Eboneé said absolutely not; however, there was another nagging voice that said yes. She actually formed her lips to decline his invitation, but Eboneé allowed her emotions to get the best of her, and a yes rang out. Though she had agreed to join him for dinner, Kasim sensed her uneasiness and suggested they dine at the hotel in which she'd just hosted her networking event. When they reached the restaurant, the kitchen staff was in the process of shutting down for the evening, but Kasim was able to pull some strings, as being the Hilton's director of operations came with some perks.

Though she knew nothing about him, Eboneé discovered over dinner that there was just something about him that she couldn't get enough of. A soul-mate connection is immediate; it hits you out of nowhere. The moment your paths cross, you both know without a doubt that the other person is yours. As if God Himself had sent you a telegram laying out all the specifics. There is no doubt or fear in your mind. You have never been more certain about anything in your life. There was an instant union of Eboneé's and Kasim's souls. Her entire existence fell prey to that connection. She had read about this phenomenon but had never experienced it with any of the men that she'd come in contact with in the past.

They talked all night at the hotel, as if they'd been best friends and soul mates for years. It was almost awkward for her. She didn't understand why Kasim felt so familiar, though they hadn't known one another but for a minute. No matter how hard she tried to mentally fight what was taking place, something on the inside of her recognized Kasim way before her mind was able to fully comprehend. Kasim felt the same, and they were inseparable from that moment on.

The abduction of their daughter had brought out un-familiar sides of the both of them, and on their wedding day, they viewed each other as strangers for the first time. Although Eboneé felt hurt, afraid, and alone, she was happy to have Kasim out of her sight. She felt that as a couple and, most importantly, as parents, they were supposed to support each other. Even while enduring such a horrific tragedy. No matter the circumstances, they were supposed to crawl, walk, or run through every obstacle course together. No matter what, they had to do it together. Kasim was supposed to be there with her. So how could he have walked out on her like that, as if the abduction of their child was Eboneé's fault? This man just wasn't her Kasim. Her thoughts and emotions collided, causing her to tremble violently.

CHAPTER TWO

Kasim believed that no matter the situation, he'd survive and prevail. Giving up was never an option. He was adamant about always looking for the best in every bad situation, no matter the magnitude of the adversity. Kasim attributed his beliefs to the Nigerian saying, "I no carry last," which meant "I refuse to be the last person in the race or the victim of circumstances." Be that as it may, there had been circumstances in his life beyond his control that had immobilized him to the core. Kasim had first come to the country on a work visa to secure employment and had intended to bring his expecting wife over later. However, shortly after his arrival, his pregnant wife had lost her life in a car crash back home in Nigeria. There wasn't anything that he'd read, seen, or experienced that could have prepared him for that kind of catastrophe.

Kasim's wiring was different when it came to the "manly" role in the family. He placed a huge value on being the man of the house. And all that it entailed. He felt embarrassed when he could not fix or control crises and events that life threw his way. He had grieved the loss of his expecting wife and had also castigated himself for not being with her as the head of his family. Zoya, Kasim's deceased wife, had been in her first trimester at the time of her death. She had been out driv-

ing long after the sun went down and had collided with
another vehicle. The air bag had deployed, but the impact from the collision had caused a placental abruption.
Zoya's blood pressure had spiked, which had caused her
to bleed more, and that had led to hemorrhaging, and as
a result, she had lost her life.

Losing his family had been the toughest pill Kasim
had ever swallowed. He hadn't been back to his home in
Nigeria, because of the shame he felt he had brought on
his family by not being by his wife's side and prevent-
ing the accident. Had he been there, he would have driv-
en the car, and she would not have lost her life. Kasim
also believed that Zoya had had the placental abruption
in part because she'd been losing weight while pregnant. Zoya had been unable to keep anything down. The
smell of food had nauseated her. Kasim felt that had
she been curvier, she would not have lost the child, because curvy women were more fertile. Wide hips, big
boobs, and FUPAs were prime indicators of fertility.
Zoya's morning sickness and weight loss had impact-
ed those parts of her body. Kasim had disliked seeing
Zoya in pictures and during the video calls that they'd
engaged in.

Kasim's mother, who had died before his marriage,
had been a curvy woman. She'd been what society
would refer to as a BBW. Curves were one of the attributes Kasim looked for in a woman. He believed his
mom had been able to handle all that she had because
she had had enough weight on her to cope with anything
that came her way. Of course, she had also had the de-
termination to strive for greatness, no matter the odds.
After all, she had given birth to six children, had worked
a full-time job, and had cared for Kasim, his siblings,

and his dad as if God had granted her extra hours in the day in order for her to be what she needed to be to for herself and her family. Standards that Kasim had judged women by when the time came for him to find a mate.

Finding a woman who he knew, without a shadow of a doubt, his mother would have approved of, or who shared some of her same qualities, had been impossible. Kasim and Zoya had made it down the aisle due to the fact that she had met his dad prior to his passing, and his dad had given her his stamp of approval. When he had brought her to meet his father, Kasim had been unsure about Zoya, because he'd felt something was missing. Kasim had shrugged the feeling off, though he'd been disappointed that Zoya hadn't gotten a chance to meet his mom. Kasim's parents, Adebowale and Ogunya Oringo, had both suffered from HIV/AIDS. Ogunya, Kasim's mom, had contracted the virus when she was raped at the age of twelve. Adebowale, his father, believed he had contracted it from his wife. By the grace of God, the virus hadn't been passed down to Kasim and his siblings.

He hadn't ever met a woman that he felt was truly like his mom until he met Eboneé. Her voluptuousness and stature made him do a double take when he first caught sight of her. That was a dead giveaway. However, Eboneé's attentiveness to each person that attended her networking event caused him to stop what he was doing. Eboneé conducted herself with professionalism and finesse, greeting and showing hospitality to each and every person that had come through the door, all while cradling a seven-month-old infant to her body. She included the child in order to make her attendees feel comfortable. Especially the working parents. This was similar to what Kasim had witnessed his mom do while cooking, cleaning, and entertaining guests.

The icing on the cake for him was the deep indention near the corner of Eboneé's mouth, which was noticeable each and every time she cracked a smile. And the dimple on her right cheek matched his mom's. Kasim was instantly in awe with Eboneé. Her scrumptiousness and beauty caused his heart to skip a few beats. He knew at that moment, she was his, and that the dimple was a sign from his mom that she was the one.

Noticing that Eboneé fingers were clenched, her nails were digging into her palms, and she was rocking on her heels, Kasim knew she was as nervous as he was. He was suffering from his own bout of butterflies in his stomach. Which was a first for him. Kasim hadn't ever had a problem when it came to the ladies. He was what you'd call a lady's man. He knew what to say and when to say it, and he knew how to leave a lasting impression. Eboneé was different. Everything about her epitomized everything he'd envisioned in a woman, and he recognized all those characteristics in her the moment he gazed into her honey-colored eyes. Despite him being on edge, Kasim's head buzzed with possibilities as they left the restaurant and made their way to the secret place where they would have dinner.

"This way, my lady." He held out his hand, and she took it, and then he led her to the elevator. They took it up to rooftop of the hotel.

Eboneé was blown completely away by the view that welcomed them on the rooftop patio. As she stood at the railing and looked out at the cityscape, she admired the shades of pink, orange, blue, and purple that streaked across the sky as the sun descended toward the horizon. The sweeping view of Upper Manhattan took her breath away. Finally, she turned and admired the European-style garden area, a cozy area for two, the walkway to which was adorned with tea-light candles. So too was the stone fireplace. In the middle of the garden was a large burnt-orange sofa covered in oversize throw pillows. It was a scene from the perfect love story, and Eboneé felt swept off her feet in that moment.

"This is absolutely amazing! I would never want to come down from here," Eboneé gushed as she took in everything that was in front of her and around her.

"I spend a lot of time up here. My position at this establishment comes with a few perks. This happens to be one them. Yes, it cost me a pretty penny, but I couldn't resist. A sublime location, a bastion of tranquility to ease my mind. My place of Zen, as some would call it." He picked up a glass of Chardonnay from a tray on the coffee table and took a sip before continuing. You know, you're the first person that's had the pleasure of joining me here."

"The first person? This is a hotel. How is that possible?"

"This area is separated from the area where patrons gather and party. If you look to the left, you'll see the wall separating my area from the rooftop party area."

"That just makes it even better. I think I am in love."

"I didn't think it'd be that easy, but then again, I think I fell in love the moment I laid my eyes on you."

"You're so silly. You know I am talking about being up here." Her brow rose.

"Wishful thinking on my part, but I knew what you were referring to," he said, then chuckled.

"Is this area soundproof?" Eboneé asked, changing the topic. "I can't hear anything coming from the other side of the wall. And if you don't mind me asking, how are you able to have this space all to yourself?"

"Yes, it is soundproof. And let's just say, some perks can be negotiated when you get promotions. Now, take in all the benefits you enjoy for being the exceptionally beautiful woman that caught my eye and made my heart skip a beat."

Their dinner consisted of pounded yam and *egusi* soup, along with *abacha* and *ugba*. The head chef just so happened to be from Kasim's hometown in Nigeria, which made it easy for Kasim to request a couple of his favorite African dishes. Eboneé was the first American woman that Kasim had shown any interest in; he'd almost always gravitated toward African women, primarily Nigerian ones. Eboneé exceeded his expectations of an American woman: She didn't ask questions about the meal, other than wanting to know the name and origin of each dish. She didn't pick at her food or ask for a salad, as most of the American women that he'd had business meetings with in restaurants did. Eboneé did what his mom and all the Nigerian women that Kasim knew did: she fed her curves. And that intrigued him all the more.

The evening could not get any better in Kasim's eyes. It felt as if God had extended the hours for them, because time was moving slowly. His and Eboneé's interaction epitomized everything that he'd thought had been lost in the world of dating. There wasn't an awkward moment of silence, and they laughed and talked for hours. She didn't pick up her phone at all. He didn't bother to check his, either. The two of them just couldn't get enough of one another. They devoured every minute that they shared together. Kasim felt as if he'd known her all his life. He didn't want the night to end.

When the clock struck midnight, he realized that all good things had to end. "The evening has gotten far away from us, so how about I get you a hotel room for the night? I can come and personally serve you breakfast in bed in the morning, or we can come up here and have breakfast and watch the sun rise together. No strings attached."

Without responding, Eboneé sprang from where she sat, and made her way over to the railing and gazed at the skyline. Kasim could feel her nerves and thought perhaps he'd overstepped his boundaries. However, his heart disagreed, cuing him to follow behind her.

"I know this is a lot, and it might appear sudden or too soon. But it feels so right," he said as he gripped her waist from behind.

Eboneé turned to face him, and the instant their eyes met, nervousness ran through her. Kasim moved closer. Her gaze moved from his dark, penetrating eyes to his thick lips, causing her to lick her own. Kasim was drawn to Eboneé's beauty and couldn't stop himself from tasting her. He leaned in and kissed her. The sweetness of the wine she had drunk was on her tongue as he sucked on it. When she whimpered against his mouth, his body reacted. Boldness filled Eboneé, and she pulled him closer. Their bodies molded against each other, but that wasn't enough for Kasim. Desire coursed through him as he pressed Eboneé harder against the railing. With little effort, she positioned herself to accept his weight against her. Unable to resist the burning desire for one another, Kasim and Eboneé surrendered to the flames and became one. Kasim couldn't drink enough of her to quench his thirst. The more of Eboneé that he consumed, the thirstier he became. He took a swim in her until the sun came up.

CHAPTER THREE

Parish Hargrove-Campbell's father, Dennis Hargrove, a Vietnam war hero, had his life taken the day Parish was born. He was a decorated helicopter pilot and lost his life when his aircraft was shot down. Learning of her father's bravery and dedication, Parish had yearned from the age of eight to follow in his footsteps and serve in the Marine Corps. Parish had refused to have a graduation party upon graduating high school. Instead, she had requested that her mom, Phoebe, have a marines recruiter come to their home as a graduation present, and she'd wanted her whole family to be in attendance. It meant the world to Paris to honor her father by becoming a marine. Parish didn't allow her size or her gender to get in the way of making her dream a reality. She knew her father had yearned for a son to follow in his footsteps, and she made it her mission to prove to her deceased father that she could live up to those expectations.

It was difficult for Parish to conceal her excitement throughout the entire process. She sailed through the Armed Services Vocational Aptitude Battery, passing the test with flying colors. The second step was the required physical examination, and for the first time in her life, doubts flashed in her mind. Parish thought her weight might hinder her from becoming a marine. Refusing to allow her nagging thoughts to stand in her way, Parish vanquished her fears by telling herself, *This is a basic medical examination, and I am in good health*. She did in fact ace the physical exam, causing her to become even more ecstatic. Now the third step in the process stared Parish in the face, making it difficult for her to contain the tears that fell when she met with the Service Enlistment Counsel. Everything that happened that day was a blur, and afterward, Parish had trouble recalling the details, including the moment she took the oath of enlistment. The only thing that she'd been able to digest was that she would soon be on her way to South Carolina for boot camp.

The twelve-week basic training, also known as boot camp, started off somewhat challenging for Parish. Although she had received a clean bill of health, she wasn't as physically fit as she should have been for the rigorous training. She fell behind during several of the drills on the first day, thus inciting the drill instructors. In private, fellow trainees taunted her. They'd tell her, "You don't have to be in shape to get in, but you have to get in shape to stay in." Parish wasn't accustomed to the level of ridicule she endured, and it pained her more than the physical activity that she'd been struggling to keep up with.

"This is the marines. It is what you've always wanted. They're just doing their job to toughen you up," she kept saying aloud to herself.

No later than her seventh week of boot camp, Parish's drill instructors began to single her out for additional training. She'd heard about some of the hazing that had taken place in the Marine Corps, and she knew that the policies against it were strictly enforced. However, somehow those policies didn't make her experience as a trainee any better. On the evening of Parish's forty-ninth day of boot camp, her birthday, she was awakened four hours before the usual 5:00 a.m. roll call.

"Up and at 'em, fresh blood," the senior drill instructor and commanding officer demanded.

Dazed by slumber, Parish rose slowly to her feet and saluted her superiors. In acknowledgment, they simultaneously grabbed each of her arms and escorted her from the squad bay, up the ladder well, and into the fitness room. When she motioned toward the footlocker to retrieve her gear, they shoved her through the door. Upon entering the fitness room, they circled her, and that was when she caught sight of those who had been awaiting her arrival. Eight men were lined up in two lines, facing one another, and in that double line were three drill instructors, two recruits, as well as the guide, the squad leader, and the scribe.

"The real D-Day has been set before you, fresh blood," the commanding officer announced, then took a wooden paddle and struck her on her backside. "You are to walk all the way through. Stay on your feet, and your knees better not touch the floor, or your punishment will be more severe," he threatened.

With tears obscuring her vision, Parish did her best and tried to walk the gauntlet. Every step that she took, she was either struck with the wooden paddle or kicked. Each person that Parish walked by used all their might to strike her and send her to her knees. It was hard for her to stay on her feet. She slipped a few times, and even though she tried to prevent any part of her body from hitting the floor, it was impossible. With each fall, she was either kicked in the stomach or the backside. They made it their business to avoid touching her face. By the time she reached the end of the line, all eight men were excused. Parish was left with the two superiors who had chaperoned her to the ordeal.

"On your feet, fresh blood," the commanding officer demanded.

Wobbly, tattered, and bruised, Parish mustered up as much strength as she could and pulled herself to her feet. The instant she was able to catch her balance, her hands were pulled behind her back, while her cheeks were squeezed together, pursing her lips to receive a fifth of Jack Daniel's, which was forced down her throat. At the drop of the empty bottle, the sweatpants and T-shirt that Parish was wearing were stripped from her.

"Please, don't do this to me," she slurred as the senior drill instructor's pants dropped to his feet.

Parish had never had a drink in her life. The alcohol immediately affected her. She became incoherent and then blacked out as her skivvies were pulled off her. By the time she came to, Parish lay soiled on the maple-wood planks where her superiors had left her. Upon opening her eyes, Parish tried to get her bearings, but flashbacks of the gauntlet walk filled her mind.

"Somebody, please help me," she called, straining her voice.

"Hello. Is there someone in there?" a male voice shouted from the doorway.

When he pushed his way through the doors, the chaplain saw Parish lying on the floor.

Kwame Campbell was the newly appointed chaplain for the recruit depot of Dove Island. The former chaplain had resigned without warning. Although Kwame had been raised in a Pentecostal household and had attended church all his twenty years of life, he had chosen to find his own faith. He had refused to piggyback on his grand-parents' religious beliefs. He was their only grandchild. They had stood on the Bible, and when he was in their home, he had had to serve the one and true living God. And God alone. If his parents had been alive, they would have had the same house rule.

After years of trying to conceive, Kwame's parents had found themselves pregnant with their first child at fifty years of age. They had used the Bible story of Abraham and Sarah as a testament of their own miracle child. The word declaring that she'd birth a male child had been given to Kwame's mother, Deborah, in a dream, and she had structured her life around that word. As with Sarah, the word had been fulfilled, and Deborah had given her husband, Anderson, a son in his old age. In an untimely death, Deborah passed away a week after giving birth to Kwame. Because of her prolonged labor, Deborah suffered postpartum hemorrhaging, which proved fatal. Kwame's family's grief intensified a year later, on his birthday. His father had a stroke and joined his wife in heaven.

At the tender age of fourteen, Kwame was able to digest fully the causes of his parents' deaths, and he blamed himself and God. Hence, his desire to change faiths and become a Catholic. Shortly after graduating high school, Kwame went to seminary school and learned that he'd be able to join the Chaplain Candidate Program. All while training in the ministry. He hadn't been certain what he wanted to do, but he'd known he wanted to do the opposite of what his parents had done or would have done.

"Dear God." He turned his head in embarrassment now.

"Please don't come any closer," Parish said, using her hands to try to conceal her bare flesh. Shame and fear consumed her, causing her to beg for help and reject it at the same time.

With the assistance of Chaplain Campbell, Parish was hospitalized at Dove Island's off-site medical facility. She no longer felt safe at the same location as her superiors. Everything that Parish had dreamed of had turned into a living nightmare. All at the hands of men whose core values were supposed to be honor, commitment, and courage. Parish struggled to comprehend how they could have felt courageous when stripping her of the only sacred thing she'd saved to give to her husband on their wedding night. Becoming a marine and getting married were the most important things that Parish had envisioned for her life, and those men had stopped her from accomplishing either.

The morning following Parish's assault, she wasn't in any condition mentally, physically, or emotionally to report for roll call. Although she'd been hospitalized, her superiors determined that she had gone AWOL. Chaplain Campbell had accompanied Parish when she sought medical attention, and while Parish had undergone an examination, he had notified the general officer by phone of what had taken place. He had told the general officer that although it wasn't his place, he felt led to inform him that Parish had been sexually assaulted. After he ended the call, something didn't sat right with him. Chaplain Campbell felt the general officer had been short with him and hadn't sounded as concerned as he should have.

The medical team had informed Parish that she had broken two ribs and had a fractured wrist, and that they'd have to keep her for seventy-two hours due to her unrelenting headaches. During her hospital stay, Parish received a letter of reprimand from the general officer. He discharged her for going AWOL as well as for having had a blood alcohol level of .08 percent. Parish's medical records were public knowledge, and the general officer had delved into them after her arrival at the hospital.

"How could they do this to me? I was raped. They poured the alcohol down my throat, and I'm the one being punished," Parish choked out as she wept.

"I am here with you. I will help you every step of the way. They will not get away with this," Chaplain Campbell told her.

"They already did." She tossed the letter from the general officer in his direction.

"We will talk to someone about this and pray. There's nothing that's too hard for God—" He stopped speaking, attempting to swallow back his words, when he realized what he was spewing out of his mouth.

"*Pray*? You don't even believe in God anymore." Her lip trembled.

Chaplain Campbell had never openly discussed his conflicting beliefs with anyone, because that would have given them life. But there was something about Parish that made him feel comfortable, and he had felt compelled to open up to her. He had confessed everything that he'd gone through with losing his parents. Although she was sound asleep when he'd divulged it all, he'd felt relief from getting it off his chest. At least he had thought she was asleep.

"I thought you were—" he began, but she interrupted him.

"I heard every word. But it isn't God's fault or yours. Just like what happened to me isn't God's fault. I just wish God had shielded me and had not allowed them to rape me," she whimpered.

Tears blurred Chaplain Campbell's vision as he spoke in a barely audible and breathy voice. "I'm beginning to believe that. You've been so strong through all of this. Even through your pain, I can see and feel your strength. Something I haven't felt in a very long time. I blamed myself for what happened to me. While talking to you last night—even though I thought you were asleep—I felt a sense of relief, and I realized that I have been running from myself. I've tried to avoid living or being the person that I was meant to be."

"I am far from strong. Things like this happen only to weak people. How could I have allowed this to happen to me?"

"How could you have prevented it? is the question. They abused their authority, just like the man I looked up to abused his." He dropped his head in his hands.

"I refuse to believe God punished you or me. God didn't *abuse* you. He doesn't move like that. I hate everything they did to me. I feel worthless and don't know what to do. The only thing I have right now is God. Please don't say He did this to me. I can't handle that right now."

"I wasn't referencing God this time," he replied. He took a deep breath before he continued. "I've never uttered what I am about to say a single time in my life."

He took another deep breath and exhaled. "But my grand-father sexually abused me for most of my childhood." His eyes were red and glossy as he tried to contain the tears that threatened to fall. Chaplain Campbell failed miserably: the tears ran from his eyes, leaving salty tracks on his cheeks.

Parish tapped the right side of the bed, inviting Chaplain Campbell to sit next to her. Once he was within arm's reach, Parish embraced him as tightly as she could, doing her best to avoid causing herself any additional discomfort. Through a fresh round of tears, she said, "I don't have words to make things better or right for either of us. All I know is I am grateful that you're here with me. I don't think I would have made it off that floor if you hadn't come to my rescue. The marines were really all that I had. Now I have nothing."

"I know we've only just met, but you have me. And you have your family, don't you?"

"I cannot go home. I can't break my mother's heart. She is convinced that the marines took my dad's life. She cannot find out that they killed me too." Her eyes showed her pain.

CHAPTER FOUR

After Kasim and Eboneé's first encounter, their lives became entwined. Aside from their work schedules, they spent every waking moment together. It seemed so surreal for Eboneé because she hadn't ever wanted or craved the presence of a man the way that she did Kasim's. She no longer picked up breakfast on the run, neither did she prepare it at home any longer. Her breakfast was either served in bed by Kasim, or he'd have it prepared and served to her on the rooftop while she took in the city skyline. Because Eboneé was her own boss, she wasn't always pressed for time. She often allowed breakfast to stretch into lunch. Her newly hired staff were to blame, she'd confess. They had been hands on so much so that they'd alleviated a lot of the burden, affording her the convenience of working remotely from Kasim's bed and or from his rooftop sanctuary, which had become her newfound place of tranquility. And Kasim devoured every moment of their time together.

Every date included mouthwatering cuisine at a top-of-the-line restaurant, African cuisine personally made by the chef at the Hilton Hotel Kasim worked for, or several dishes that he'd prepared and served to her in his birthday suit at his cobblestone loft. Eboneé was struck by the way Kasim made a fuss over her eating. Kasim made sure that she ate and that she ate very well. He enjoyed feeding her as if she were a baby. He'd explain to her often that she was his baby and that it was his job to plump her up and keep her that way. His philosophy about food was the complete opposite of that of any of the other men that she'd been with. In all her previous relationships, the men would embrace Eboneé's curves upon meeting her. However, once the "getting to know you" phase had passed, they'd encourage her to attend the gym more often and lose weight. As well as suggest that she'd be mindful of her portion sizes and her carbohydrate intake. Kasim was worlds apart from them. He'd feed her every carb there was, and the only workout he required of her was in the bedroom.

Their relationship soon blossomed into what one would envision as the perfect love connection, if there was one. Horse and carriage rides, candlelit baths in tubs adorned with rose petals, long walks in the park or at the beach, roses, and gifts just because. Weekend getaways as well as extended vacations. None of which Eboneé had ever experienced. It all became overwhelming for her. Eboneé's heart melted with each gesture and gift; however, her mind led her to believe that Kasim was too good to be true. *Kasim cannot be this perfect a man*, she often thought.

About two months after Eboneé and Kasim met, Eboneé's assistant fell ill with the flu, and her clients' needs and demands multiplied at the same time, and so she had to devote more time and attention to the business. And this limited her and Kasim's quality time together. Two weeks went by, and one Friday afternoon, unbeknownst to Eboneé, Kasim contacted Parish to see what she could do to assist him with getting Eboneé to take off the weekend. As if God had heard Kasim's yearnings, everything fell into place, and Parish didn't even have to do too much convincing. It seemed that Eboneé's assistant returned to his duties that very afternoon, and he insisted that Eboneé take the weekend off. Eboneé called Kasim to let him know the good news, and within an hour he walked through the doors of her office space in Upper Manhattan, not too far from the hotel he worked at.

"I have a surprise for you, beautiful," Kasim said, making his presence known. He gave Eboneé a dozen long-stemmed red roses.

Eboneé's skin warmed and took on a crimson hue. "Thank you, baby."

Kasim leaned in closer and used his lips to remove the blush-colored lipstick from her lips. "We don't have much time. The driver is waiting out front for us. Are you ready?"

"Ready? I cannot leave my work. Wait, where are you trying to go, and for how long? I have so much going—"

His yearning to taste her lips engulfed him, and Kasim cut her rant short by aggressively pulling her close to him and then feasting on her bottom lip before sucking and pushing his tongue deep into her mouth. As if everything around her had miraculously changed and become clear, Eboneé pulled herself from Kasim's embrace, turned, reached for her purse, and then looked to Kasim for further direction. He ushered her out to their waiting car.

Once in the car, Eboneé couldn't contain her excitement. She'd had a rough two weeks without her right-hand being attached to her, so whatever it was that Kasim had planned she was beyond grateful for it. Before she could ask another question, despite knowing that Kasim would answer only by flashing his infectious smile, they arrived at their destination.

"Well, my love, we are here," Kasim announced as they pulled up in front of the Hilton Hotel in which Kasim worked.

"Here? The hotel? And what's going on? There are so many people at the entrance," Eboneé observed as Kasim helped her out of the car.

"My impatient love, you will see soon enough." He opened one of the front doors at the entrance and allowed Eboneé to enter the lobby before him.

"Oh, my goodness, Kasim!" she exclaimed. "You know how much I love J. T. Bolden. How? This is an exclusive private event for top industry stylists only."

"You're just as good and better than half of these so-called stylists. They should be excited to have *you* in their presence," he said, praising her.

J. T. Bolden was the go-to stylist to the stars. He had been a celebrity stylist for as long as Eboneé could remember. She had been following his brand forever and had used his styles as a springboard for her own, though she never forgot that her audience was BBW women with a sense of style. J. T. had been on tour for months now, and at each venue he visited, he hosted a fashion master class for all the high-end celebrity designers. Tickets were always sold out within five to ten minutes after they went on sale.

"This is the best gift you could have ever given me. I love you for this," Eboneé told Kasim.

"Oh, so you're telling me this is the only thing that has your heart in a frenzy?" he asked. He nibbled on her ear, causing her to blush.

"You're too good to be true."

"I believe you might be right," Kasim said. Then he nodded, drawing her attention in the opposite direction.

Eboneé's heart dropped when her eyes connected with her favorite novelist's vending table. She'd never been to a book signing or met an author face-to-face. Although it had been on her to-do list, which she'd shared with Kasim, Eboneé just hadn't found the time to pursue that goal. She couldn't believe that the hotel was hosting her favorite novelist and a celebrity stylist at the same time. She was in heaven.

He really listens to my heart's desires. Her stomach flip-flopped, and a nervous shiver went down her spine.

Kasim could tell she was deep in thought. "Where'd you just go, my love? It looks like you've seen a ghost."

"Sometimes, I wonder if you are the ghost of my heart."

"What do you mean?"

"Can we go back outside for a minute? I can't hear my thoughts with all the noise in here."

As they made their way out front and then headed over to a bench, Eboneé's hands trembled.

"What is it? Are you starstruck?" Kasim jested.

"I am overwhelmed, excited, and scared all at the same time. Every time I am with you, these feelings swell up inside me, and I feel like I am going to have a heart attack half the time."

"Why? And what did you mean by 'the ghost of my heart'?"

"I feel like you are really too good to be true. There is something that you're hiding. Like you're going to fill up every area of my heart with love for you, and when I get to that point, you're going to disappear."

Kasim closed his eyes as Eboneé spoke. When she was finished, he remained silent, his eyes still shut.

"You're not going to say anything in response? I hate when you do this, Kasim."

Eboneé almost begged Kasim to respond, but his rigid stance, his closed eyes, his tight shoulders, his clenched jaw, and the scowl on his face let her know her pleas would go unanswered.

"Kasim, how do you expect us to go any further if we don't communicate—" she began, but Kasim pulled her into an embrace and silenced her with a kiss. He gently sucked on her bottom lip, sending chills throughout her entire being.

Because of her doubts about him, Eboneé would try to pick fights to see if the "real" Kasim would come forward. Each fight was always one sided. Kasim refused to take part; he'd instead move into her personal space while she was in mid-sentence. When she'd resist, he'd caress her neck or back her into the wall or whatever was nearby and take advantage of every part of her body. Eboneé was always unable to remain firm. Kasim's touch was hypnotizing, and with each caress, she fell deeper into his trance. She had never been an insecure woman. However, the way that she had fallen for Kasim frightened her.

The events at the hotel made it an evening to re-member, one that Eboneé couldn't make up if she tried to. Not only was she able to have a one-on-one session with J. T. Bolden, but she met her favorite writer, Terry McCallister, and received an autographed copy of her book. Kasim and Eboneé ended the evening in the presidential suite of the hotel, and it was an evening filled with roses, chocolates, and lovemaking, something right out of a storybook.

Later, her mind racing, Eboneé lay awake and watched Kasim as he slumbered. After a while, she eased out of bed, hoping not to wake Kasim, and made her way to the bathroom to phone Parish, as she couldn't contain the flutters in her midsection.

Despite the fact that Parish had her own marital woes to contend with, she always gave Eboneé unbiased opinions about her love life, and now that Kasim was in Eboneé's life, their conversations centered around him. Eboneé had shared with Parish her doubts about the authenticity of Kasim's love for her, and she would talk with Parish about this until the two of them were blue in the face. Each time she'd leave their powwow or end their phone conversation feeling inspired and embarrassed for second-guessing Kasim's love for her. However, when she was back in his presence, doubts would nag her again, and she'd start to second-guess things.

When Eboneé called Parish this time, after leaving bed and slipping into the bathroom, Parish suggested that they meet for dinner for a face-to-face. Parish could hear the agitation in Eboneé's voice the moment she spoke. She told Eboneé that she had sensed earlier in the week that a crisis was brewing and that she was one step ahead of her, as she had already told Eboneé's assistant to clear her schedule so that they could have dinner tomorrow evening. Eboneé appreciated Parish's understanding and offered to treat her to dinner at Amy Ruth's as that was Parish's all-time favorite place to dine.

When Parish arrived at Amy Ruth's on time the next evening, Eboneé was already seated at a table.

"What's going on, Ebb? You seem so upset this time," Parish said as she took a seat across from her friend.

"I feel so crazy. I've been panicking about Kasim. Like, why can't I just enjoy the moment? Is there something wrong with me?"

"Yes, there is. You're in love, and you're fighting it. You've never felt this way for a man, and never has a man displayed this type of love and affection for you, and that has you terrified. So much so that it seems you're willing to hold on to and live with the terror for the rest of your life. Instead of enjoying and loving on that beautiful man that God so graciously blessed you with, you're pushing him away."

"I am not. I—"

Her words were cut short when a waiter carrying glasses of water to their table tripped and spilled water on her lap. She had been so engrossed in her conversation with Parish that she hadn't even seen the waiter.

"What the . . . ?" Eboneé looked up to give the waiter a fraction of her mind, and then she watched the waiter take a knee. Her heart dropped.

"I apologize for spilling water on you, my love," Kasim told her. "I know all of this appears to be a dream to you, but I am here to show you that dreams do in fact come true. I know you're afraid. Hell, I am too. But I wouldn't have it any other way. I've never met a woman like you. You are my dream come true, Eboneé." Kasim paused for a moment. "Would you do me the honor of becoming Mrs. Eboneé Oringo?" he asked, proposing.

Parish had assisted Kasim in planning the proposal. They had been able to work things out with the restaurant so that Kasim could impersonate a waiter at the establishment.

When Eboneé realized what was actually taking place, tears of unexpected joy filled her eyes, then spilled over and ran in rivulets down her chubby cheeks. She assumed a kneeling position in front of Kasim and blubbered a yes. Everything that had weighed heavily on her mind just moments ago no longer existed. Kasim's confession that he was afraid had made her feel more secure. At this moment, she felt a sense of relief and reassurance. Kasim was indeed the man that she needed and wanted in her life. So many thoughts and plans flooded her mind once they both were seated at the table.

"Oh, my goodness, Parish! You kept this from me," she squealed as she squeezed Kasim's hand as tight as she could to insure he and the proposal were real.

"Yes, but only so I could bear witness to the love exchange that I just witnessed. And I would do it again," Parish replied, sniffling.

"Thank you, Parish, for what you did. I was beginning to think I'd never find true love in the States. I thought this was a sign from God that I had to return to Nigeria to find love again," Kasim said. "And then Eboneé filled the screen on my computer monitor and has been proving me wrong ever since," he declared before placing a soft kiss on Eboneé's lips.

After dinner, Kasim and Eboneé headed to Kasim's cobblestone loft in Upper Manhattan, and immediately Eboneé went into high gear with wedding plan ideas.

"I want us to have a huge wedding. I think I know the perfect location. I will show you," she said as she stepped through the front door.

She pulled her laptop from her messenger bag. Then she suddenly stopped in her tracks and gazed around and admired her surroundings. She'd been infatuated with Kasim's home from the very first moment she stepped foot in it. The sight of the beamed ceilings, the large casement windows, and the brick walls struck Eboneé each time, as if it were her first visit all over again. Her admiration would have her looking around each time, smiling from ear to ear. Kasim would gloat in appreciation every single time, saying, "I see I'm always stopping you in your tracks, no matter how many times I touch you or you come over.

But this time Kasim remained quiet, his face expressionless. Eboneé noticed the change in his mood right away.

"Kasim, what's wrong? You look like you've seen a ghost."

"I don't want to rush down the aisle. I want us to continue what we have for a while. We can do the wedding ceremony later on down the line," he replied as he headed in the direction of the sofa. Eboneé trailed after him.

"You're not making any sense to me right now. Why did you propose to me just an hour or so ago if you aren't ready for marriage?"

"I am ready to spend the rest of my life with you, sweetheart. I just realized that I want to work on a family, or at least our first child, before we take those steps down the aisle."

"You're really not making sense, and you sound unsure, Kasim." Eboneé's lower lip trembled.

"My love, I think I need to go about things differently this time around. I don't want anything to go wrong. I am aware you are not my deceased wife, God rest her soul. However, I am fearful of losing you. I am a firm believer that if you want different results, you have to do things differently. With that being said, I'd like for us to get started working on a little girl. Once she's here and she can make her way down the aisle with us, I would like for us to say our 'I do's.'"

"What if we have a son? Are you saying you want to delay the wedding until we're able to conceive a girl?"

"Of course not, beautiful. Losing Zoya pained me severely and left me questioning everything that I do, did, and have done. I am fully responsible for what happened to her. God in heaven knows I wouldn't be able to live with myself if something were to happen to you or, God forbid, our child."

"Nothing is going to happen to me, Kasim. I am right here with you, and you are here with me, baby. I promise to do everything that needs to be done to assure you that nothing is going to take me away from you."

"I have no doubt. I just need this and ask that you trust me in creating our own rules."

Kasim sat down on the sofa and stared into space. Eboneé felt her heart tugging as she struggled with delaying their wedding ceremony and wanting to ease Kasim's pain. The more Kasim drifted off into his thoughts, the more Eboneé's soul ached for him. She saw and felt the uneasiness that tormented Kasim and wanted no parts of it. Though she could hardly wait to plan and experience her childhood dream wedding, Eboneé decided that she had to compromise, to give up the traditional relationship and engagement protocol. She sat down next to Kasim and promised that she would honor his wishes as his wife-to-be, and then they began working on bringing their love child into their world.

CHAPTER FIVE

Peering at the desk calendar in his work space, Kasim noted that it had been twelve months—that is, 365 days or 8,760 hours or 525,600 minutes or 31,536,000 seconds—since he'd asked for Eboneé's hand in marriage. And, most importantly to him, this was the length of time in which they'd been working on conceiving. For the past year, they had made love regularly without using birth control, and yet all the pregnancy tests that Eboneé had taken were negative. Kasim had tried hard not to cast blame on Eboneé for their inability to conceive a child, but in his gut, he was sure that she was the one who suffered from infertility. Regardless of how hard Kasim tried to downplay his gut feelings, he found himself circling back to the same thoughts.

Seeing that a year had passed, Kasim spoke with Eboneé about his concerns that evening, and they both agreed to undergo fertility testing. Two days later, they found themselves in the office of a fertility doctor. After hearing about their problem, the doctor made mention of Eboneé's weight.

"Eboneé, most women with a high BMI lessen their chances of getting pregnant," she said. "I'd like you to see a dietician. He or she will assist you with bringing your weight down some, so we can avoid a continuation of these complications in conceiving."

"Thank you, Dr. Sharma. We will take everything into consideration," Eboneé responded nervously.

"She is perfectly fine," Kasim interjected. "Having a healthy weight has never prevented any of the women where I am from, from conceiving. That's some American brainwashing that's being shoved down everyone's throat."

"Well, give it some thought. And come back to see me in three months," the doctor said, ignoring Kasim's outburst. Then she turned and left the examination room.

Kasim detested the words that had left Dr. Sharma's lips. Her medical advice was not valid in his eyes, and he refused to accept that Eboneé's weight was the cause of their infertility and that weight loss was the solution to the problem. Eboneé, on the other hand, took Dr. Sharma's words to heart. Over the course of the next week, whenever Kasim wasn't around or couldn't catch a glimpse of her computer screen, she researched foods she should avoid in order to shed a few pounds, with the hope that weight loss would enable her to conceive. Eboneé dared not include Kasim in her weight-loss program, because she knew he would not agree with it. And she was right.

Kasim prepared all of Eboneé's meals to ensure that she had a balanced diet and ate enough calories. His dishes were similar to the ones he'd seen his mother prepare for pregnant members of their family and pregnant friends. The spread that he prepared always consisted of three staple items: Nigerian swallows, which were starchy foods, such as semolina; tubers; and rice and beans. As it turned out, these were the key foods that

Eboneé had decided to shy away from in order to lose weight. Kasim noticed this and called her on it one evening.

"Eboneé, baby, you haven't touched your food. Is everything all right?"

"Yes, my love. I am so full. I even had seconds."

"I see that. However, you haven't touched the whole left side of your plate."

"I'm not in the mood for any of that tonight. I hope you don't mind," she told him.

"I wouldn't mind if this wasn't the third night in a row that you have avoided those dishes. You know how important it is for you to gain weight and keep it on, so that you are healthy enough to conceive and carry a child, my love."

"Kasim, now, you know Dr. Sharma suggested I actually lose a little weight so that we can get pregnant."

"Dr. Sharma is a skinny white woman. She has no idea what she's talking about. She is probably barren herself, and her misery has her giving you all the wrong information. I've told you several times how my mother was a little heavier than you are. And guess what? She had no fertility problem whatsoever. A woman with no weight on her isn't fit to have a child. If you had been doing as I say, we probably would have two or three kids by now, but no, you want to take the word of a lady doctor who looks like a boy."

"What are you saying, Kasim? That this is my fault? I really don't understand your thought process at times. Dr. Sharma is a doctor. She has a degree. She knows what she's talking about. It has nothing to do with her race or her size."

"So what? She got a degree from attending school and reading a book. That doesn't mean she knows my woman's body better than me."

"You're insane." She jumped up from the table and ran into the bathroom. Slamming the door behind her and locking it, she screamed, "Maybe I can't get pregnant. It might not be in my cards. All of this is stressing me out."

Kasim rushed over and said through the door, "I apologize if I hurt you, Eboneé. Please open the door and let me make it up to you."

Eboneé unlocked the bathroom door and allowed Kasim in to ease her pain. He embraced her, then sucked on her bottom lip like clockwork. It had become his signature move, and Eboneé's knees buckled each and every time that he did it. Kasim used his left hand to explore Eboneé's breasts while he used his free hand to turn on the shower.

"Do you forgive me?" he asked as he pulled her blouse over her head with two hands.

"Y-Yes," she purred.

Kasim ushered Eboneé into the shower and used his mouth to kiss and suck all her disappointments away. The saying was that makeup sex was the best sex, and that ended up being the case for Eboneé and Kasim. According to their calculations, that night was the night Kasim impregnated Eboneé. At their next appointment, Dr. Sharma did, in fact, confirm that there wasn't anything medically wrong with either Eboneé or Kasim. She said sometimes it was all about timing, and when the time was right, it would just happen, and it had happened. Kasim despised the words that she spoke and insisted they look for a real doctor. He swore Dr. Sharma was a fraud and believed she had received her medical degree out of a Cracker Jack box.

Whenever Kasim experienced something good, trauma seemed never to be too far behind. During Eboneé's ninth week of gestation, she miscarried. Eboneé blamed herself for the miscarriage and slowly slipped into a depression. She and Kasim had become emotionally attached to their unborn child upon learning of their pregnancy. Kasim tried his best to comfort his grieving fiancée. But it was difficult for him to do so because he, too, had lost a part of himself.

He didn't want to think the worst, but it was impossible for him not to. Kasim felt that he might have a black cloud over his head and that he had caused the death of his wife and his unborn child and then Eboneé's miscarriage. He allowed his grief to consume him, causing him to clam up and completely distance himself physically and emotionally from Eboneé. Eboneé, in turn, thought that he blamed her for their loss and that he didn't want her anymore. As a result, one night Eboneé quietly gathered her belongings while Kasim slumbered, then penned a letter to him before departing.

> To my beloved fiancé, Kasim,
> You are and have been the answer to my heart's desires. You are my heartbeat in human form. I am sorry that I was not capable of being what you needed me to be. I apologize for not being able to give you the only thing that you asked of me other than my heart and my hand in marriage. I wish I could turn back the hands of time and become your dream come true. Unfortunately, that appears to be impossible. Honestly, I don't know how I am going

to be able to pick up from here and move on without
you. I guess if I want you to be happy, it is what
needs to be done. I know I am babbling and could
go on, but I won't. Just know you've made me the
happiest woman in the world, and I will always
love you.

Eboneé

As she placed the letter in an envelope and enclosed her engagement ring, Eboneé was so engrossed in what she was doing that she failed to notice that Kasim had awaken from his slumber. He crept up behind her.

"Why do you have your jacket and shoes on? And why is your suitcase packed? Did you really plan on leaving without saying anything to me?"

"I thought it would be easier that way, Kasim. I can't do this face-to-face." She kept her back to him.

"Do what, Eboneé? You are not doing anything alone, Eboneé. We're in this together. The miscarriage is a tough pill for both of us to swallow, but I promise we will get through it."

"What are you saying, Kasim?" She shuddered.

"I am saying, I need my fiancée right now. Would you please tear up whatever you wrote and come back to bed? I don't wish to see that letter. And do me a favor. Put your ring back on and never take it off again. I love you, my sweet Eboneé."

Eboneé burst into tears. It pained Kasim to see Eboneé cry. All he wanted to do was make her happy, and he felt that he'd failed her. When he had realized she was preparing to leave him, his heart had jumped into his stomach. He knew he would not be able to live without Eboneé. The love he had for her was something that he had never had for anyone, and he didn't want to lose that feeling.

That night, after she came back to bed, Kasim bared his soul, revealing everything that he had been feeling to Eboneé. And she assured him that none of what had transpired was his fault. Kasim promised to communicate with Eboneé from that day forward, no matter what he was feeling, because he didn't want to lose her.

CHAPTER SIX

While nursing Parish to a complete recovery the best that he could, Chaplain Campbell was released from his duties as chaplain for Dove Island. It didn't come as a surprise to him or Parish, considering that he had been by her side following the rape and the hazing, and he had refused to turn a blind eye to the physical abuse Parish had suffered at the hands of her superiors. Their actions went against everything that he believed in. Parish and Chaplain Campbell had agreed that his actions would not sit well with the commanding officers, and they had known all along that he would receive a reprimand. The commanding officers had created an alliance, and they always stood together against any and all opposition. Parish and Chaplain Campbell understood that it was impossible to penetrate that alliance. But it didn't matter to him. He'd planned on resigning, and not returning to the armed forces, once Parish was back on her feet.

Parish was extremely ashamed about the rape, and she did not want to bring any further attention to the situation or herself by fighting her discharge from the Marine Corps. She also pointed out to Chaplain Campbell that taking the bull by the horns would result only in a "he said, she said" situation, their word against hers. Actually, that was how her superiors had been able to discharge her in the first place, and since they had gone to such extremes, Parish knew they would do so again if she protested her discharge, and she would be fighting a losing battle. Allowing them to get away with a crime stung like hell, but she refused to allow them to emotionally and verbally rape her all over again during court proceedings. Backing down without a fight in the face of injustice went against Chaplain Campbell's beliefs. He wanted everyone to pay for what they'd done to Parish. However; he respected Parish's wishes and understood where she was coming from.

Through it all, Chaplain Campbell had been joined to Parish's hip. Parish appreciated his unwavering loyalty and recognized that he had become a source of strength to her in her time of need. She felt as if she'd known him all her life. They'd shared every part of their lives with one another while she was on the mend, leaving no stone unturned. In their sharing, they had acquired a love and respect for one another that ran deep. Parish had never met a man that actually sat and listened to her without a hidden agenda. She'd never encountered a man as attentive and empathetic as Chaplain Campbell was. His feelings weren't far off from hers, either. Other women that he'd encountered had told him either what they wanted or what he needed to do. Parish was the first woman who'd allowed him to be a man, while she sat back and remained the lady that she was. Even with all the military training under her belt, Parish remained the lady that she was and revered and respected him as a man. They shared the same pain, and that yoked them together emotionally all the more.

Parish had even convinced Chaplain Campbell, whom she'd begun to call Kwame, to reconsider the calling that God had placed on his life. In listening to everything that he'd shared with her, Parish had recognized his love for God. He'd tried to conceal it, and then it'd oozed out of him without forewarning. Especially during the conversations in which he'd start his sentences by saying, "I know you believe this way . . ." He would then proceed to expound on why she should rely on whomever she believed in, because that was where her strength lay.

Parish had admitted to herself that Kwame's presence and their conversations were what had afforded her peace of mind during the moments when she contemplated taking her life. However, it was his connection to God that had allowed him to be who he was for her. Parish refused to return home after she was released from the hospital. She planned to use her savings to remain at the extended-stay hotel she and Kwame had checked into the day the hospital released her. When she told Kwame this on the second day of their hotel stay, he objected.

"Parish, you aren't making any sense at all. We are here so you can get a little more rest. There is no way you can stay here forever, or much longer, for that matter."

"It makes sense to me, and I have no problem with it."

"You're not staying here. I won't allow it."

"You are in no position to tell me what you will and will not allow. I don't appreciate your tone, either."

"Parish, I apologize if I came off as tyrannous. That was never my intention. I just don't think it'd be a good idea for you to be alone after all that you've gone through."

"Honestly, the last thing that I want to do is be alone. I've become accustomed to having you around. I depend on you just being with me. When you're not around for a while, I get inside my head and I miss you. Nonetheless,

I draw a line at you telling me what you will not allow. That is just not your place to do so."

"You're absolutely right, and I admit that I was out of line. I ask for your forgiveness. I just cannot imagine you not being with me. I know we haven't known one another for a long period of time, but my heart feels as if we have always known one another. So I am offering my spare bedroom to you, if you're comfortable with staying with me. Of course, with no strings attached."

Parish avowed that she would probably end up in a mental institution if she were to stay alone in the hotel while Kwame went back home to New York. His place was located on a quiet street in Massapequa, a hamlet in Nassau County. Parish was born and raised in the Bronx and knew only city life. Long Island would be the change of scenery that she needed, she told herself.

A day later Parish discovered that Kwame's home was a traditional split-level house and was well maintained. He had inherited the house from his grandparents. Parish marveled at the view of the shore from the living-room windows, the hardwood floors, and the granite countertops. Kwame's home was the type of house she had dreamed of purchasing and owning when she retired from the marines. Kwame informed her that God knew she hadn't wanted to wait that long, and so his home had become her home, and it would remain so for as long as she liked.

Parish's days at Kwame's house turned into weeks; the weeks, into months; and the months, into years. At first, she and Kwame considered each other roommates. Things started to become uncomfortable for the two of them when their friendship blossomed into something that entailed more than camaraderie. Particularly since they'd been sleeping alongside one another in the same bed for over six consecutive months. Parish had been suffering from nightmares and would go into a fit of rage during each of her episodes. Kwame had to wrap his arms around her and hold her until she fell asleep. It had gotten to the point that if he wasn't lying next to her, she'd have a nightmare that would evolve into a panic attack.

Now it was impossible for them to contain what they were feeling on the inside. During dinner Parish and Kwame found themselves smiling and gazing into one another's eyes just because. While out in public, they held hands, and it felt right and normal for both of them. They also attended Kwame's home church together, which they had been doing ever since Parish insisted that something was missing in her life, that she felt a void that she was unable to explain. Kwame had been experiencing that same vacancy in his life, and he'd recognized that only God could fill that empty space.

Kwame had thought it would be difficult to return to Living Hope Fellowship Church. He hadn't stepped foot in the church in over a decade, but God had been calling him back home. Given Parish's desire to connect with something larger than herself and the tugging he'd been experiencing, Kwame had ignored his pride and had taken her to the only church that he'd ever known. With the passing of his grandparents and most of the members that had attended the church when he was young, Kwame hadn't recognized any of the members in attendance. That first Sunday, it had felt like a whole new church. However, the same spirit of God that he had always known and met there had been present.

During the last sermon that Kwame and Parish heard, they were convicted by the words that the minister was ministering. Although they hadn't been physically intimate, they had been living the life of a married couple, and that had been troubling them to a great extent. The topic of the sermon that Sunday was "living in victory." Pastor Mobley discussed the trials and tribulations that one encountered in life and explained that some were more devastating than others. He said the only way to be victorious and live in peace was to live according to the will of God. He shared his own unfortunate encounter with sexual abuse. Pastor Mobley explained how putting God and God's will for his life first had given him the strength to talk about it and find peace. A peace that was available only through surrendering to God.

During that sermon, everything changed between Kwame and Parish. That very evening, they gave their lives back to God and to one another.

"Parish, I just need your blessing. Please say that I can have you and that you will have me. I know this is unexpected, but I want to be right in the eyes of my Heavenly Father. And because of you, I am where I am supposed to be. I am no longer running from Him but to Him. However, I don't want to run this race alone. Would you please do me the honor of becoming Mrs. Kwame Campbell?" He knelt before her.

"Yes, I would love to be your wife, Kwame."

Their lips became one.

Three months following their engagement, Parish and Kwame became husband and wife. Toward the end of that same month, Kwame was ordained and appointed assistant pastor of Living Hope Fellowship Church. Unbeknownst to Parish, one of her childhood friends, Cynthia Lattimore, who was now a gospel recording artist, had been invited to sing the sermonic solo at Kwame's ordination. The moment that Cynthia noticed Parish sitting on the front row, she went over to her and persuaded her to join her at the podium. Parish held her own alongside Cynthia, and she swept Kwame off his feet. Cynthia then joined the choir and gave Parish the lead, as she had when they were in their youth. Parish's voice was magical. There wasn't a dry eye left in the sanctuary by the time Parish concluded a song.

Parish and Cynthia had grown up together. They had lived on different streets, but their backyards had abutted one another, separated only by a fence. At the age of ten, while playing a "game" of volleyball by herself, Parish hit the ball really hard, and it sailed over the fence and into Cynthia's backyard. Cynthia, also an only child, retrieved the ball and hit it back over the fence to Parish. And so began a lasting friendship. In fact, they became so close that some mistook them for siblings or cousins.

When Cynthia attended Parish's family barbecue/ reunion that Fourth of July, she and Parish discovered their mutual love for singing. Parish's cousins loved to put on a talent show at the family's Fourth of July barbecue. They'd perform for the adults, and their show was always the highlight of the family reunion. Parish's cousins teamed up, as they always did, and Parish decided to sit on the sidelines, as she normally did. But Cynthia insisted that they perform together. The two of them sang their favorite gospel song, "Precious Lord," which left their families speechless. Without rehearsing or knowing what the other was capable of, Cynthia and Parish sang and were in sync, as if they had been prepared beforehand.

The years passed, and they continued to perform together now and again. During their senior year of high school, Parish and Cynthia were scouted and offered a gospel recording contract opportunity. Parish declined, as her dream was to join the marines. Cynthia parted from her friend and promised she'd reunite with Parish when she got the marines out of her system. Cynthia kept her promise.

Not long after Kwame's ordination, Cynthia introduced Parish to her husband, James. It was right after the church service ended one Sunday.

"Parish, I want you to meet my husband, James. James, this is Parish, the songbird that I've been telling you about."

"Nice to meet you, James. Wait, are you *the* James Lattimore? The record producer James Lattimore?"

"Yes. That's what my driver's license says," he chuckled.

"He is better at all things music than he is at telling jokes," Cynthia said, clowning.

"Well, I've heard so much about you, Parish. I would love for you to join Cynthia in recording her sophomore album. I know she'd be honored to have you featured on it as well."

"Wow. I am honored, and yet I don't know what to say or how to feel."

"Please say yes," Cynthia pleaded.

With nervous breaths, Parish replied, "Y-Yes! I'd love to."

The thought of actually recording a song for public consumption, which meant the public could judge her, frightened Parish. However, despite all the fear that overtook her, Parish was excited to take such a huge step in a direction that she had never thought was open to her.

CHAPTER SEVEN

Eboneé and Kasim were in the midst of renewing their love for one another. The miscarriage and Eboneé's decision to walk away from it all had upended everything that they'd thought they shared with one another. Eboneé had suggested that they try different activities other than sex as a way of reconnecting. None of the other four men that Eboneé had been with in her thirty-five years had had the ability to make her body do and feel the things that Kasim did. When Eboneé had divulged her experiences to Kasim, his manhood had surged. However, when she'd suggested they worked on their communication by refraining from sex for two weeks, he'd rejected Eboneé's proposition immediately. How could he go from schtupping two to three times a day to abstinence?

But Eboneé knew this was necessary. Kasim began to pout. He was sure their fourteen-day flesh-and-bone hunger strike was going to be excruciating.

"How in God's name will holding back your love from me help communication when our bodies have a language of their own and require constant social intercourse?"

As she listened to Kasim's words, a tingle formed at the base of Eboneé's skull and surged through her body. It was as if Kasim had cast a spell on her. Eboneé's luscious parts throbbed. She took a long, deep breath and closed her eyes in an attempt to disengage from the spell that her body had succumbed to. "Kasim, as hard is this going to be for both of us, it is important that we learn to please one another with our mind and soul. Not just with our bodies," she explained. "I love you and want everything that comes with you. Me thinking that you no longer wanted me and that leaving would have made you happy let me know something has been missing, and I want to find everything lost between us and put it in its rightful place."

Despite the fact that they craved lovemaking and suffered from dizziness and headaches seemingly from a lack of it, Eboneé and Kasim engaged in activities that required them to communicate more frequently. They decided to use the cell phone and text messages to check on one another throughout the day only. They'd send "I love you" texts here and there. But other than that, all communication had to be done face-to-face. All their dates had to take place outside the house. They made sure this happened by finding new places to dine and shows to see. They avoid their usual date-night haunts, as they had found a way to explore one another's bodies at all those places.

Although Eboneé was the one to initiate the 336-hour sexacation, she found herself struggling to stay afloat. Everything about Kasim began to turn her on to an alarming degree. The way he chewed his food, the way he walked in the door after work, stood at the toilet while using it, bent down and picked something up, the way his lips moved while he was talking. Kasim had a habit of licking his lips while speaking, and that alone was going to be what would make Eboneé cave. She had come to the point where it didn't matter what he did; she just had to have him. In order for her not to throw in the towel, Eboneé did what she did best during times of need: she invited Parish to lunch so that her friend could talk her off the ledge.

"Hey, Parish. How are you doing?" Eboneé said as she took a seat. They were at Parish's favorite restaurant on the Upper East Side.

"I am great. Can't complain. I see you're still suffering from withdrawals." She snickered.

"Chile, I am a whole mess. Look at me sweating." Eboneé wiped the perspiration from her forehead.

"Let me ask you a question. If your relationship isn't based on sex, why is it so hard to abstain from it for fourteen little days? I don't get it."

"Because I enjoy making love to my man, and I don't think it's a crime. Or is it? Besides, it's easy for you to say that. You're married, and you have already gone through the growing pains of getting to know your husband."

"To answer your question, no, it isn't a crime at all. In fact, the Bible says it's not good for man to be alone."

Eboneé rolled her eyes. "Can you talk to me as your friend and not as the pastor's wife? I thought we passed that stage a long time ago."

Eboneé knew it wasn't good for man to be alone, and she felt that "alone" was the reason why she had been struggling with denying herself a dose of Kasim. But she knew she was doing the right thing. As she mulled this over, she revisited in her mind her first encounter with Parish and her scriptures.

When they were first introduced, she didn't take to Parish at all. Parish came off as a Bible-quoting, judgmental know-it-all. At the time Eboneé was the verification co-

ordinator trainer for the department. She had worked for
the agency for six years and had become the supervisor's
assistant. Eboneé pretty much did all the work, while her
supervisor strolled the carpeted runway. The office was
Kamentha's catwalk. She was a beautiful woman. She was
five feet nine, had full 32 DD breasts and a trained waist
to match. Kamentha's suntanned skin and wardrobe choices turned heads regularly. Eboneé often told Kamentha that
modeling should have been her career of choice. But each
time Kamentha frowned and noted that her fascination
with food conflicted with a model's lifestyle. What blew
Eboneé's mind was Kamentha didn't look like she ate anything, and if she did, she stored the food in her backside.

Parish detested everything about Kamentha and
made it known her first day on the job. During Parish's
three-week training session, she was assigned to work
alongside Eboneé, and she wasted no time apprising
Eboneé of her and God's displeasure in everything
that Kamentha stood for. Despite the fact that Parish
had spent a day in her life with Kamentha, she "knew
Kamentha's kind," or so she said, and she pointed out
how Kamentha wasn't right in God's eyes. Eboneé
refused to look down on anyone. She loved how God
created everyone so that they were unique, and she could
not fathom how Parish could be so into God and church
and have a completely opposite perspective.

"You know, the Bible says women should adorn themselves in respectful attire. Our supervisor would never
make it in heaven dressed like that," Parish told Eboneé
after about a week of training.

"For you to be such a spiritual person, you don't show
much love, do you?"

"I love everyone with the love of the Lord, but as a disciple of God, it is my responsibility to be an example and give correction when necessary."

"Look, this isn't your church home, and Kamentha is our supervisor. The only person that has the right to give correction in this here workplace is her and the other managers. I may not go to church every Sunday, but I will tell you, I have a relationship with God, and I know He accepts us as we are, and His love is what draws us to Him. So instead of looking down on His people, maybe you should try loving them and see how many more bees you can catch with honey than with the vinegar that you've spewed out of your mouth from the first day that we met."

From that day forward, Parish had a different outlook on life and people. That was the the day that the bond between her and Eboneé was cemented. They'd developed a bond by sharing their beliefs, and this had allowed Parish to see that the person she'd become was someone she wasn't too fond of.

"I apologize, Eboneé," Parish said, jerking Eboneé out of her daydreaming. "My intention was not to come across as someone other than a friend. What I will say is, Kwame and I lived together for over a year, and we didn't have sex until our wedding day. So, if we can do it for that long, you most definitely can make it through the rest of this week, or whatever time you have left of the fourteen days."

"If I am not mistaken, you had just experienced something horrific, so sex would have been the furthest thing from you mind, so you can't compare your experience to mine. How often do you two have sex now that you're married, if you don't mind me asking?"

"We've been married for some time now, so sex isn't a necessity. However, we make sure to satisfy one another on special holidays and our birthdays."

"You're not serious, are you?"

"Sex doesn't define us. We know who we are to one another, and we are happy."

"There's no way you're happy penciling in sex."

It dawned on Eboneé that Parish used sex as a controlling mechanism in her relationship with Kwame. Parish's revelation about her sex life, or lack thereof, gave Eboneé all the impetus she needed to put an end to her and Kasim's sexual hiatus. Eboneé refused to use sex to correct or make a change in her and Kasim's relationship. And this made her want Kasim even more.

Eboneé made sure to make it home before Kasim arrived. She had moved in with him permanently and had renovated her own place and turned it into an office space. Eboneé took the roses Kasim had given her a week ago, plucked the petals, and made a trail from the front door to their bedroom with them. She collected all the candles that she had and placed them throughout the bedroom. Night was falling, so she lit a few candles and placed them along the trail of petals, then turned out all the lights. She then hopped in the shower, and after bathing, she used her body oils to lather herself up. Finally, she put on a pair of red pumps.

When Kasim made it through the front door, he followed the petals and found his fiancée lying across the bed, in anticipation of his arrival.

CHAPTER EIGHT

Things between Kasim and Eboneé had been incredible lately. She satisfied every area of his life. When he was ill, she became his doctor; when he was upset, she became his joy. If he had a problem, she'd assist with solving it. Kasim hadn't ever met a woman of Eboneé's caliber. He'd oftentimes envisioned being with a woman who at least had many of his mother's characteristics. But Eboneé surpassed his expectations and then some.

And she'd helped him realize his deceased wife's passing wasn't his fault or even her fault. It was actually God's will for their lives. This revelation had blown Kasim's mind, because he'd undergone thousands of dollars of counseling, and still the guilt had weighed heavily on his heart. Eboneé had pointed out the fact that he'd said he fell in love with and married Zoya primarily because she had met his father. Eboneé had insisted that if Kasim had loved Zoya for herself, he would never have come to the States alone and left her behind in Nigeria, especially when she was expecting. He would have made sure she accompanied him to the United States. When he'd disagreed, she'd asked him if he would be comfortable leaving her for a long period of time in order to build a life for them. That question had scared Kasim; he couldn't imagine his life without Eboneé in it. Waking up to her beautiful face was what made his life complete.

The one and only issue that still troubled Kasim was his and Eboneé's to conceive and sustain a pregnancy. For this reason, he'd planned a perfect romantic getaway for the weekend of Valentine's Day, which was right around the corner. He hoped to spend the weekend making love in a different place, and that place was a resort in the Catskill Mountains. Their new fertility doctor, Dr. Moultrie, had suggested a change of scenery, and Kasim had made it happen.

When Kasim got home from work on the Friday evening right before the Valentine's Day, weekend, he found Eboneé in the living-room area. He couldn't wait to tell her about their getaway. As it turned out, Eboneé had a Valentine's Day surprise of her own.

"Good evening, gorgeous," Kasim breathed as he embraced Eboneé and stared at her full lips.

She blushed. "Hey, baby. How was your day?"

"It just got better. I have a surprise for you."

"And I have one for you," she told him.

"Well, you can give it to me when we get to our destination."

"Our destination?"

"Yes, my love."

"Is that right?"

"Yes. Now, pack light. Matter of fact, just bring a change of clothes. With what I have in mind, you won't need to cover that sexy body." He palmed her bottom.

"Okay, Mr. Nasty. Can I give you my gift before we leave?"

"It can't wait?"

"I don't want it to."

"If you insist." He took a seat in his recliner, and Eboneé ran into the bedroom.

"Okay, close your eyes," she squealed from the bedroom doorway. He obeyed, and Eboneé returned with a gift box in her hand and placed it on the table in front of Kasim. "Okay. Open your eyes."

He grinned from ear to ear when he saw the gift box. Then he removed the red top. Tears threatened his eyes as he removed the picture frame that was inside the box. "Is this what I think it is?" he asked, his voice cracking, as he stared at the image in the frame.

"Yes, it is. We are having a baby. I am five weeks pregnant. That is the gestational and yoke sac that you're looking at." She pointed at the framed sonogram. "I heard our baby's heartbeat," she added.

Kasim had difficulty processing what Eboneé had said. He saw the sonogram and understood what had taken place, but he just couldn't process it. His heart jumped, while his mind raced. And another part of him became riled up because Eboneé had gone to the doctor without telling him anything. She'd heard their unborn child's heartbeat without him, and he had difficulty digesting it all.

"Kasim, baby, it's okay. You can breathe. It's really happening."

"I-I'm breathing. When did you find out we were pregnant?"

"I figured you knew or had suspicions like I did. I had gained so much weight, and I didn't have my period at all last month. So I waited until over a month had passed since my last period, and then I went to see a doctor, because I was afraid."

"You could not have been that afraid if you assumed you were pregnant, went to see a doctor, and selfishly excluded me from experiencing it all with you."

"I would never—"

"But you did, Eboneé. You knew how much this meant to me, and you kept it from me. I thought we were communicating about everything and not holding anything in or back."

"Kasim, do you hear yourself? You are taking this out of context. After the miscarriage that I had, it was difficult for both of us in many ways. I wanted to be sure things were good, and that I was really pregnant, before I got excited or possibly upset either of us. How can you say I was selfish or held anything back?"

Kasim's eyes glazed over as he tuned out the words spilling from Eboneé's lips. And the more Eboneé explained, the more vexed he became. If he heard any more, he thought he might snap. He'd been trying hard not to pressure Eboneé about getting pregnant. He'd actually been following her lead and just allowing it to happen. They had planned to revisit working on things around the holidays, because they didn't want to worry about getting pregnant and putting any more strain on things.

"I'm going to take a shower," he said, then rose from the recliner. He stormed into the bathroom, with Eboneé right on his heels.

"What do you mean? You said we were going away for the weekend, Kasim."

"*Were* going away. You're pregnant, so we cannot go." He then slammed the door behind him.

"Why not? This is supposed to be one of the happiest days of our lives," Eboneé said through the closed door.

"It is, but you cannot go out now. The sun is going down, and darkness isn't good for the baby, Eboneé," he shouted through the door.

Kasim was indeed elated that they were expecting. He just had to shower to wash away the frustration that was consuming him. He didn't want to upset Eboneé any further, especially with her being with child. Kasim's mom used to say that when a mom-to-be was upset, this affected the baby, who would be born fussy. Although he'd been looking forward to their getaway, Kasim had made the decision to put it off until tomorrow afternoon. In Nigeria, expecting mothers were forbidden from walking at sunrise or late at night, as this put them at risk of spirits possessing the babies. Eboneé strongly disagreed with Kasim's superstitions, and this issue had caused one too many disagreements between the two of them.

"Kasim, how in the world will me going out in the morning or the evening bring spirits to our unborn child?"

"Because there aren't many people out in the morning or late in the evening. It is easier for spirits to attach themselves to you when there is no hustle and bustle of people coming and going."

"Don't you think there are spirits everywhere at any given time?"

"You're right. That's something to consider," he said through the door.

"If you think I am going to be cooped up inside this house because of these old tales you've made up and forced yourself to believe, you're sadly mistaken, Kasim."

"I am not saying you cannot go out of the house. You don't need to be running the streets or to be out for long periods of time, either."

"This pregnancy will not force me to be imprisoned by your beliefs, Kasim."

"We will take it one day at a time."

Kasim also preferred that Eboneé work from home during her pregnancy, but she could not abide this, as she had made sure never to work anywhere near the home that they shared. He loathed Eboneé's stubbornness when it came to such matters; however, he knew that the more he told her not to do something, the greater was her desire to do the exact opposite. At the very beginning of their courtship, she had made it clear to him that no matter how their relationship went or what transpired, he must allow her to continue being who she always had been. She had never been one to sit around, no matter what the circumstances were, and he was well aware that if he tried to turn her into a stay-at-home wife, girlfriend, or fiancée, they'd bump heads. Kasim recollected that discussion now and decided to arrange his schedule around Eboneé's work hours so that he could spend more time with her when she wasn't working.

However, Eboneé's company was really blossoming, and so it required more of her. She began putting in even longer hours, and this did not sit well with Kasim. He instructed her to hire more staff, but Eboneé refused. She argued that all she did lately was sit at a computer, eat, and use the bathroom. That her work didn't require any strenuous activity. Kasim disagreed, insisting that the fact that her brain was on overload would cause the baby to be born with a troubled mind.

CHAPTER NINE

Things weren't going the way that Parish had envisioned they would go. She'd thought that when she
was offered the opportunity to join Cynthia in recording
her sophomore album, things between her and Kwame
would turn around. Instead, everything seemed to be
going in reverse. She'd always draped herself in clothes
to camouflage her curves, as Kwame had said that he
found her even more attractive when she didn't show and
tell. He'd argued that her beauty was natural. However,
lately Parish had taken notice of how he'd compliment
some of the women in church, especially when they had
on a new suit or sported a new hairstyle. She'd chalked
it up to him showing the love of the Lord in his Father's
house.

But today he also complimented women on their looks
when he accompanied her to the recording studio for her
very first session. He admired Cynthia's attire several
times, as well as the attire of other women. Parish was
taken aback by this, because he usually turned his head
or frowned when he saw a woman exposing her cleavage or wearing formfitting attire. In fact, there wasn't
anything wrong with what Cynthia had on. She wore a
nude-colored wraparound dress with minimal cleavage
showing. However, Cynthia was well endowed in all the
right places, and Parish swore that Kwame took note of

this, despite the fact that he'd sworn that he preferred it when all women, not Parish, left much to the imagination.

On the ride home, Kwame noticed right away that Parish was peeved about something.

"What seems to be the problem, my angel?" he asked her.

"Maybe I am making something out of nothing, but you paid extra attention to Cynthia today. To her dress in particular."

"You're right. You are turning something into a problem that isn't there. You are acting insecure, and that it was not of God. I complimented her out of respect. I was just making small talk."

"You could have just asked how she was doing or inquired about her kids. Kwame, you told her how nice she looked twice in the same sentence."

"Trust me, Parish, my heart and my eyes belong only to you. I was not disrespecting you, and I would never disrespect you or what we have like that."

"Well, make sure you keep your eyes on me from now on."

However, a week later, at the final recording of Parish's song for Cynthia's sophomore album, Kwame again fawned over Cynthia and her background singers. Again, Parish thought his behavior was not befitting a pastor or a husband. But this time, rather than planning to confront Kwame, she made up her mind that she would work on herself so that she regained her husband's attention. Parish was also relieved that her work on Cynthia's album had been completed. She didn't think she'd be able to remain cordial to Kwame at another recording session if he carried on the way he had been doing.

Despite Kwame's behavior, Parish was thrilled with Cynthia's album and her own singing on it. Parish's song on the album was such a hit, she soon received recording contract offers from three different record labels. One of those offers, of course, came from Cynthia's husband, but Parish also attracted the attention of two other prestigious, well-known record labels. It all happened so fast that Parish had difficulty deciding which label to go with. She actually had a falling-out over it with Cynthia, who conveyed that the whole thing was a no-brainer and that Parish should not have to think it over. She should sign with her and her husband, James Lattimore, since, after all, the possibility of a future contract was the reason why they had given Parish the opportunity to contribute to Cynthia's album in the first place. And it was Cynthia's album that Parish was featured on, not some other singer's. Parish became outraged by Cynthia's egotistical expectations. And she told her so during a phone call one afternoon.

"Are you kidding me, Cynthia? So, what you're saying is that the only reason I have any offers is that I was featured on your album? That my *gift* for singing has nothing to do with it at all?"

"That is not what I said, Parish. You're twisting my words around. James and I pulled some strings to get you on the album at the last minute, and we had the label draft up a contract for you that is essentially better than what I was offered."

"I appreciate you having me on your album. It brought back old times and memories from our youth. However, I am going to decline your offer. I appreciate what you and James have done, but I'd rather not mix business with pleasure."

"What you need to worry about mixing in is a new wardrobe. Your album is going to flop once the world catches a glimpse of the old handmaiden you've become. And you cannot forget about Kwame. He's already *gone*." With that, Cynthia disconnected the call.

It had been a little over a year since Parish had had that conversation with Cynthia, and Parish had recently completed her first album. While at work on the album, she'd carefully observed all the women that she encountered at the studio, and she'd noted that none of them dressed like she did. And so she had often recalled Cynthia's last words, about her looking like a handmaiden. One of her label mates must have noticed Parish's lackluster wardrobe, too, as she'd offered Parish her stylist. She'd told Parish, "Don't get ready when you're onstage. Be ready beforehand, and I am not just talking about your voice." She'd eyeballed her from head to toe.

That advice caused Parish to turn her thoughts to Eboneé. She'd always admired Eboneé's fashion sense, especially since they had the same frame. Eboneé's style was impeccable, and Parish knew she needed that type of fashion in her life. She also thought that revamping her wardrobe and developing some fashion sense would aid her in her efforts to regain Kwame's attention. During the first six months of their marriage, he had struggled to keep his hands off of her. He'd pick her up from work at lunchtime just to indulge in his wife. He would yearn for her so much that he couldn't wait for the close of her workday. The sparkle that he'd once had in his eyes when he looked at her had disappeared, and this had been troubling Parish.

With the advance that the record label had given Parish, she was able to hire Eboneé as her personal stylist and assistant and purchase all the staple items that Eboneé recommended she keep in her closet. While shopping and trying on clothes, Parish actually began to fall in love with herself all over again. Parish didn't recognize herself when she tried on the first formfitting dress that Eboneé recommended. The dress wasn't tight, but it also wasn't baggy and oversize, like the clothes that Parish was used to wearing. When she took her first glance in the dressing-room mirror, tears stung Parish's eyes because she'd thought she lost the person that she was looking at in the mirror.

"You *should* cry. You look beautiful," Eboneé said, praising her.

"I—I haven't seen this woman in a very long time. I almost didn't recognize myself."

"After all that you've been through, Parish, I can understand how you got lost underneath all those garments."

Parish tilted her head as she looked at Eboneé. "What do you mean?"

"Well, you know . . . what happened to you in the marines. You are a brave woman to have made it as far as you have. Had it been someone else, they might have lost their mind or, God forbid, taken their life. But not you. And here you are now, embarking on the next chapter of your life with grace and now some style."

"You know what? I was so consumed with being the best wife and the best Christian that I could be that I forgot about myself. You're right. I have been hiding in my clothes. I hated my body for a long time because of that wardrobe, but right now, I am loving everything that I see in this mirror."

"As you should. Now, come on and take that dress off. We have a ton more items that you have to try on."

Parish adored everything that Eboneé had her try on. However, she became particularly fond of the first dress that she tried on, and selected it as the perfect garment for her upcoming photo shoot for her album cover. The off-the-shoulder, above-the-knee, body-con black dress hugged Parish's curves in a tasteful yet seductive way, and she wanted the world to see the beauty she had rediscovered in herself. And she also wanted to refresh Kwame's memory of what he'd forgotten he had. Little did Parish know that not only was her new ensemble going to change her husband, but it was also going to cause hysteria within the house of the Lord.

Excited about the proofs from the photo shoot she'd received in the mail, Parish went straight to the church to show Kwame. He'd noticed a change in her, especially in the way she dressed. Parish had been wearing blazers, pumps, and slacks a lot lately, whereas in the past she'd worn skirts and dresses with flats most of the time. She'd rarely wore pumps. Kwame enjoyed the change in his wife, especially since she always dressed so tastefully.

She found him sitting on the first row in the sanctuary, killing time before Bible study. She walked over to him and took the seat next to him.

"Hey there, handsome," she whispered in his ear.

"Aren't you beautiful!" he complimented.

"Thank you, baby." She flushed. "I came early to show you these." She displayed her promotional photo proofs.

Kwame frowned. "Parish, what are these? What are you wearing? Where are your clothes? You cannot let anyone see these."

"Kwame, you're overreacting. These are pictures of me, all of me. I am no longer hiding in oversize garments. There's nothing wrong with these pictures."

"I beg to differ. It's too much. You need to have them redone."

"It's funny how you compliment everyone else's wife when they wear the right-size clothes, but when I do, it's a crime."

"I give compliments, that's it. As a man of God, I show love to everyone. That does not mean you had to go out and become someone you're not."

"Yeah, you've shown everyone love and admiration except for me. And I did not become someone else. This *is* me. I became who I thought you wanted me to be, and it felt good, because I was mad at myself and hated my body because of what happened. But God erased all that pain and shame. I thought you'd be happy. I guess I have to be everyone else in order for you to appreciate me and show me love."

"That is false, and this is the wrong time for us to be having this discussion. We can talk later, after Bible study."

"It's always the wrong time with you," she snapped, then stood and charged off.

For the first time since giving her life to God, Parish skipped out on Bible study. She knew that her love for God hadn't changed and that she hadn't done anything wrong. Instead of going to Bible study, Parish decided to pick up some candles and bath beads. She wanted to enjoy some one-on-one time with herself. She hadn't sat in the tub in forever and realized it was what she needed.

Kwame became incensed when he noticed Parish hadn't returned for Bible study. His mind was so preoccupied with the exchange of words that they'd had, as well as the photo proofs, that he had trouble concentrating. So much so that he asked one of the deacons to officiate over the Bible study. Then he left the church and headed home to confront Parish.

"Parish, where are you? I don't know what has come over you, but it has to stop now. We need to pray," he shouted when he graced the threshold of their home.

Parish had her earbuds plugged into her ear and her eyes closed as she enjoyed the soothing bubble bath.

"Parish, are you ignoring me?" he said as he barged into the bathroom.

She didn't see or hear Kwame come in. But Parish felt someone standing over her, and when she opened her eyes, she almost jumped out of her skin. Kwame had frightened her by catching her off guard.

"Are you trying to scare me to death?" She stood from her bath.

The sudsy water trickled down her body as the light from the candles flickered over her coffee-colored skin. Kwame's manliness sprang to attention at the sight before him.

"I see someone remembers what they've been neglecting." She licked her lips as she stepped out of the bathtub.

"How could I for—" he began, but she placed her pointer finger against his lips to silence him.

Kwame closed his eyes and nursed on her finger before he made his way to her breast. Parish used her free hand and found her way to all of Kwame's goodness and mercy. She unbuckled his pants and threw her tongue down his throat. Panting and moaning, Kwame grabbed Parish and bent her over the bathroom sink. For the first time since they'd been married, Kwame took his wife in an unconventional manner, and both of them shared an orgasmic experience that was greater than they'd ever imagined.

From that day forward, Kwame couldn't resist loving and taking advantage of his wife. Parish devoured every moment of it. At some point, Parish assumed he'd forgotten about the photo proofs, being that he hadn't mentioned them or anything else that had transpired before Bible study that day. That was until Parish's promotional photos were shared with the world. Kwame had been scrolling Facebook while in his study, and a notification from RCA about their new gospel recording artist Parish Campbell flashed across his screen. His heart leaped into the tips of his toes and a lump lodged in his throat as he stared at the picture of his wife. He had been so sure that she'd have the pictures redone, which was why he hadn't brought the topic up again. As he read over the comments about Parish, Kwame felt extreme anger and embarrassment. A few of the pastors that he'd fellowshipped with had rebuked his wife openly in the comments section, and this was a comedown that Kwame was not prepared for.

"Parish, please come here now!" Kwame yelled, his voice cracking from the strain.

"What is it? Why do you sound like that?" she asked as she entered his study.

"I thought we agreed you'd have your promotional photos retaken. What happened?"

"We agreed to that? I recall you getting upset over nothing. Then me leaving the church and us making love that evening. Nowhere in any of that had an agreement been reached."

"This is no time to be sassy, Parish. Do you understand what you've done? The Pastors' Association has circulated your pictures and has rebuked you openly. I've responded to the comments that I could and informed them that the photos would be replaced and that we're firing your stylist. I've also penned a letter to the pastors. The devil used Eboneé, and we will not allow the enemy to have a field day in our lives."

"I read all the comments, and the last time I checked, none of those men have the right to judge me," Parish retorted. "God is in everything that I've done, that I do, and that I did. I will not fire anyone, nor will I change anything because of man's opinion. The only 'person' you or I have to answer to is God."

Kwame didn't approve of Parish's decision and felt disrespected by his wife. However, he knew she was still the same woman. Parish hadn't changed at all. In fact, she'd been more loving and humbler recently. The more Kwame looked at the photos, the more he realized that there really wasn't anything wrong with them. He recognized that no matter what Parish wore, her curves would show in some way or the other. The only way that she could conceal them was by wearing clothes two or three sizes too big, which was exactly what she had done for so long. He actually liked Parish's new choices in fashion. And he acknowledged that his attraction to his wife had increased with her newfound confidence, and he didn't want to put a damper on what they'd been experiencing with one another.

The downside of accepting Parish's decision was that the pastors of their church didn't approve when the photos were not replaced, and they suggested that Kwame divest Parish of all her duties in the church indefinitely. She was also prohibited from sitting in the section of the church in which all the other first ladies had sat. The pastors' actions did not sit well with Kwame. He thought their response was a little extreme, and he didn't appreciate that his wife was being ostracized in the church and even criticized openly, albeit subtly. It seemed that the sermons were loaded with subliminal messages about sinning that were targeted at Parish. Kwame was unable to stomach any of it. He requested a sit-down with the senior pastors, and in doing so, they felt he was challenging their authority. Parish and Kwame were asked to leave the church. It troubled them to the core. Neither of them could understand how pictures that someone didn't approve of could get them kicked out of a church.

The God that Parish and Kwame served was a God of love and kindness. He would not have turned His people away. Instead of allowing their faith to be altered, Kwame suggested they start their own fellowship. Parish thought it was a great idea and was elated that they were able to find solace in something that had been designed to cause them skepticism. In turn, they pledged to serve God's people with love and kindness.

CHAPTER TEN

Eboneé spent the remaining five months of her pregnancy sick, puffed up, and on bed rest. She threw up the majority of the time on any given day and suffered from headaches, body aches, and nosebleeds. The extreme nausea and vomiting, a condition known as hyperemesis gravidarum, was serious enough for her to be hospitalized on three separate occasions due to dehydration. It was during the third hospitalization that she was placed on bed rest for the remainder of her pregnancy.

While at work one day before the bed rest commenced, Eboneé fainted because of the dehydration. Kasim had been working at her office to keep a close eye on her, but he'd stepped out minutes before she fainted to get her some ginger ale and Gatorade at the store. When he returned, he found her lying on the bathroom floor, unconscious. Fear and panic swallowed him whole. Kasim didn't know what to do; he thought he'd lost Eboneé. Flashbacks of what he'd long imagined Zoya endured the day of her death played in his head, causing him to wail in agony.

"Someone please help!" he screamed from the bathroom.

Eboneé's assistant, Patrick, rushed to the bathroom and then phoned 911. The paramedics revived Eboneé and transported her to the emergency room. After being hospitalized for four days, Eboneé was discharged with a peripherally inserted central catheter, also known as a PICC. It'd been placed in a vein in her upper right arm so that she could receive a continuous infusion of liquid, to fend off dehydration, as well as the antinausea medication Zofran. Kasim hired a nursing service so that Eboneé had a nurse available at any given moment.

He feared the worst, and it showed. If Eboneé sneezed, he'd jump out of bed and run to her side. She no longer slept in their bed, as it had become uncomfortable for her. Eboneé longed for her husband's touch and intimacy. However, Kasim forbade it. He said that sex would harm the baby and that Eboneé had enough medical things going on. They didn't need to give birth to a baby with its own set of medical problems because they couldn't refrain from sex until after he or she was born. Eboneé knew Kasim meant well, but she found all his superstitions intolerable. Still, she stopped trying to explain to Kasim that the things he believed weren't true. She knew she had been fighting a losing battle the entire time. Instead, she started yessing him to death . . . except on one occasion.

"Eboneé, be sure to turn the television off if you feel yourself falling asleep."

"I sleep better with it on, Kasim. I need *some* sort of entertainment to hold me at night," she told him in jest.

"It's not about you or *that* right now. It is about our unborn child. Leaving the television on will cause the baby to be confused all his or her life."

"Kasim, you cannot really believe that. Do you?"

"I wouldn't say it if I didn't believe it, Eboneé. I am not sitting over here making things up, you know."

Eboneé didn't think Kasim was making up the things that he had been saying. She did know that someone had invented these superstitions that he'd been sharing, and she hated that these outlandish notions had been drilled into her husband's head. She assumed it was the result of his Nigerian upbringing, because she hadn't ever heard anything remotely like some of his pronouncements. Despite it all, Eboneé loved Kasim all the more.

A month after Eboneé was placed on bed rest, Parish and Kwame invited themselves over to Eboneé and Kasim's house for dinner. Eboneé hadn't been out of the house other than to doctors' appointments in an entire month, and Parish thought she was slipping into a depression. Eboneé's staff had stepped up and had been handling everything for her, and that meant that she had had too much time on her hands. She was so excited to have company that she had a cleaning service come and tidy up their already immaculate home. Eboneé had flowers and desserts delivered the day of the dinner, as well as bottles of Château Montrose. It had been Parish's and Kwame's favorite wine ever since she became a celebrity. They'd previously opted for a $10.99 bottle of wine, but now they indulged in their guilty pleasure, as they called it, every once in a while.

While shifting in her seat during dinner, Eboneé felt a slight crack in her stomach. She laughed it off and said to everyone, "This little one is doing gymnastics today. It felt like the baby just jumped and landed in a split or something. Something cracked."

Everyone, with the exception of Kasim, erupted in laughter.

"What do you mean, something cracked? That doesn't sound normal. Have you felt anything like that before?" he quizzed, worry lines creasing his forehead.

"I am fine, Kasim. Please relax," Eboneé replied.

He called for Eboneé's nurse. When she appeared, he said, "Rebecca, can you check my wife out? She's talking about things cracking and splitting inside of her."

As Rebecca assisted Eboneé to her feet, she totally soaked the pants she was wearing.

"You're water just broke, ma'am. We need to get you to the hospital," Rebecca told her.

Kasim could feel his heart racing through his ears. With every beat, it felt as if his chest was going to burst. He'd waited for this moment for so long, and now it was scaring the life out of him, making him speechless. Throughout his wife's entire pregnancy, he'd told her what she should or could not do. He had been her doctor, chef, nurse, and whatever else Eboneé needed. He felt sweat drench his skin when he caught a glimpse of Eboneé's saturated maternity pants. His hand trembled from his extreme trepidation as he hastily grabbed Eboneé's overnight bag. Rebecca took it upon herself to phone Eboneé's doctor, as it appeared to her that Kasim might be on the way to a panic attack.

During the ride to the hospital, Kasim didn't speak. He merely smiled and nodded his head, sweating profusely, as Eboneé gripped his hand. Parish and Kwame, who were also in the vehicle, were overjoyed that they'd be present at the hospital for the arrival of their godchild.

Parish and Kasim had decided to wait until the birth to learn the sex of their baby. By the time Eboneé reached labor and delivery, she was already dilated to ten centimeters. Her contractions weren't as bad as she had envisioned they would be. With four hard thrusts, Eboneé gave birth to a seven-pound, nine-ounce baby girl. Emani Nicole Gringo came into the world kicking and screaming. Eboneé wept at the sight of her baby girl. Kasim, on the other hand, had to be wheeled out of the delivery room due to delivery-room anxiety. Witnessing the birth of his daughter had terrified Kasim. He couldn't believe Eboneé's body was able to stretch the way that it had in order for her to push Emani out. And when he'd seen that, he'd become dizzy and light headed. As Emani had made her entrance, along with the blood Eboneé lost while delivering her, Kasim had fainted. Although blood was common with any delivery, Kasim hadn't been able to handle it.

CHAPTER ELEVEN

Three years later . . .

Emani's third birthday was three weeks away. Kasim and Eboneé's impromptu wedding day was scheduled to follow fourteen days thereafter. Everyone thought they had lost their mind; however, Kasim and Eboneé saw things differently. Kasim hadn't seen and had barely kept in touch with his siblings back home in Nigeria. They'd phone on birthdays and holidays, but that had been it. Eboneé was an only child, so she didn't know what it was like to have siblings. And she had only had one aunt and an uncle. Kasim, on the other hand, had five siblings, and he didn't want Emani to grow up not knowing her family. It meant a lot to Eboneé for Emani to get to know Kasim's side of the family and develop relationships with those extended family members.

Since Eboneé's mom had passed away from natural causes, Kasim and Emani, along with Parish and Kwame, were the only family that she really had left. As a result of a falling-out between Eboneé's mom and her aunt years ago, Eboneé's extended family had become estranged. Everyone had gone their separate ways and had gone on with their lives as if the others didn't exist. And when Eboneé had reached out to members of her extended family, no one had wanted to discuss what had taken place. They'd wished her well instead of revealing to her the truth behind their family's disfunction.

Her dad's side of the family had always blamed Eboneé's mom for her dad's passing. He had been his sisters' only brother, and his passing had caused them enormous heartache. Everyone blamed Eboneé's mom for causing him too much stress, which they felt had led to his early demise. After his passing, they had dissociated themselves from Eboneé and her mom.

Eboneé had made a vow after Emani's birth to break the generational curse that had plagued her family. She refused to allow Emani to grow up without a structured family life enriched by those relatives who desired always to be a part of their lives. Over the years Eboneé had developed a strong bond with Kasim's sister Adaeze. Following Emani's birth, they had talked on the phone weekly and had been sending photos of their families to one another. Their bond had been instant, as if they'd been old friends catching up on lost time. Adaeze and Eboneé were the same age, and both of them were professional stylists.

Adaeze was a stylist for several aspiring and well-known African actresses. Her international clientele had been growing rapidly in recent years, which meant that she and her family would be traveling back and forth to the States frequently. Eboneé offered her apartment, which she no longer used as an office space, to Adaeze and her family while she was in town for work.

Kasim was not aware of these arrangements, nor was he apprised of his sister's secret upcoming travel plans. Eboneé and Adaeze organized everything without Kasim knowing so that they would be able to surprise him during Emani's birthday celebration. However, Eboneé was spending an enormous amount of time away from home during the three weeks leading up to Emani's celebration. Kasim started to get suspicious, but he chalked up her long absences to her being engrossed in both her work and the party planning. However, when she began returning home past Emani's bedtime, he became quite concerned. Eboneé kept Emani with her as she and Kasim didn't trust a sitter to keep their daughter safe, especially since there had been a recent rise in kidnappings in their neighborhood. But when Eboneé arrived home one night with the stench of alcohol on her breath, Kasim had enough. His suspicions grew wild.

"Eboneé, this is the third night in a row that you've either dropped Emani off and left immediately after or phoned and said you'd be home late because of work. What I am struggling with is this. Since when did your work involve you reeking of alcohol and returning home during hours when a woman has no business being outside of her home alone? Especially my woman and the mother of my child."

"Kasim, you're exaggerating. You know I meet with clients throughout the day and my schedule doesn't have set hours. As well as the fact that I meet with clients over a drink or two occasionally."

"This is too much, Eboneé! I will not sit around and have my woman, the mother of my child, returning to our home at these hours, smelling like she was doing everything except her job."

The evening before the party, Kasim was overcome with uncertainty, and he decided he needed to follow Eboneé to ease his racing mind. Eboneé had informed Kasim that morning that she'd probably return home later than usual that evening, and this news didn't settle well in the pit of his stomach. He knew he had been the lover, protector, and companion that Eboneé needed him to be and a wonderful father to their child. He had trouble understanding what Eboneé was up to.

He knew Eboneé would be picking up a birthday cake at their favorite bakery at around 6:00 p.m., so he drove his car there and waited across the street. Eboneé emerged with Emani and the birthday cake, and after buckling their daughter in her car seat and putting the cake on the passenger seat, she got behind the wheel and drove off, Kasim trailing behind. Eboneé stopped at the Wine & Spirits a few blocks away from her old apartment. Kasim became enraged as he shadowed her two to three cars behind. He watched Eboneé park and take Emani inside the apartment building, even though she'd informed him that she had rented out her apartment when he suggested having the party there.

He allowed Eboneé a few moments to get inside the apartment, and then Kasim made his way inside the building. In no time, he was outside the apartment and kicking the door. "Eboneé! What the fuck is wrong with you?" he barked. His chest heaved up and down.

"It's not what you think. Please calm down," she begged as she opened the door a crack.

Kasim barged through the door. "How coul—" he began, but the rest of his words got lodged in his throat when he caught sight of Adaeze leaving the bathroom.

Kasim felt an electrical charge surge through his veins, and everything around him slowed down. Adaeze leaped from the high-gloss floor into Kasim's arms. He felt as if he was having an out-of-body experience and dreaming at the same time. Seeing Adaeze seemed unreal and too good to be true. Kasim stood seemingly lifeless, glued to the spot that he'd been standing in. Everything around him was still moving slowly, and yet he wasn't able to catch up with it.

"Breathe, baby. Adaeze is my surprise for you, but you . . . ," Eboneé told him, her voice breaking.

Nothing else mattered, though. Seeing her husband's wish to be reunited with his sister fulfilled was worth all the secrets, the heated words they'd exchanged, and the suspicions. Kasim traded places with Eboneé that evening. He didn't return home until it was way past his and Emani's bedtime. Eboneé put Emani to bed that night and then cried herself to sleep. But they were tears of joys. Today had been one of the happiest days of her life.

While visiting with Adaeze that evening, Kasim had the opportunity to reconnect with Mitaire, an old childhood friend. Mitaire was now Adaeze's husband and thus Kasim's brother-in-law. Kasim also met his niece, Naija, for the first time. Then Adaeze presented him with a gift, something for both him and Eboneé.

"What do you have there, Adaeze?" Kasim asked as he stared at the garment bag.

"Before you open it, I want to tell you something," she said.

"I'm listening."

"Ma would have been so proud of you and would have loved Eboneé. She is a keeper."

"Are you about to give me bad news? Are you all right?"

"I am fine, and the happiest that I have been in a long time. Remember when I said that if I were to ever get married, I was going to wear Ma's dress?"

"Yes, I do recall. When we were knee high, you used to put it on and pretend it was your wedding day."

"I remember that as if it were yesterday. You know, I had the opportunity to wear it on my wedding day. It made the day even more special. It felt like Mom was there with me. I know you would love for her to be there when you make your way down the aisle, which is why I had some alterations done and a few things added, in hopes that Eboneé would wear Mom's dress." Adaeze unzipped the garment bag.

"This is unbelievable. I don't know what to say . . . Thank you." Kasim ran his hand over the dress as a lone tear fell from his right eye. So many emotions were running rampant throughout his entire being. He felt like he was dreaming, and he didn't want to be awakened.

"You're welcome. I know this is what Mom would have wanted." She folded herself into his arms. "I just hope I will be able to be here for your big day."

"How long will you here?"

"Another two weeks. Then I'll be back in three to six months possibly."

"That means we will get married in two weeks. I need you here with me, Adaeze. There's no way we're going to wait any longer. This dress, you being here right now—these are signs from God. We cannot wait any longer."

When Kasim returned home to his wife late that night, he awakened her to share in his excitement. And it was contagious; Eboneé became as excited as he was.

"Eboneé, I have something for you." His hands trembled as he gripped tighter the garment bag that he had been holding.

"I can see that. What it is?" She sprang to her feet out of excitement.

"This . . ." He took in the air around him before continuing. "This is my mom's wedding dress. I would love for you to wear it on our special day. Adaeze had some things done to it for you. I hope you—"

Eboneé snatched the garment bag from him. Tears stung her eyes as she unzipped the garment bag and then took in every inch of the off-the-shoulder ivory ball gown with a plunging V-neck.

"From the looks of it, I can see that you approve. I was thinking maybe we should—" Kasim began, but Eboneé interrupted.

"I—I am sorry for cutting you off, my love. This is the perfect dress, for the perfect man. I know we haven't talked about it in some time now, but I don't want to wait any longer. Can we get married after the party?"

"I wouldn't have it any other way. Maybe not the same day, but a week or two after would be perfect."

Time had gotten away from them after the birth of Emani. But now they refused to waste another minute or another year. It was all a dream come true for the two of them.

CHAPTER TWELVE

Emani's birthday party turned out to be especially fun for the adults, maybe more than it was for the children. Although the kids had an amazing time at the fairy-themed celebration, the mothers of the kids in attendance expressed that they were in awe and loved the opportunity to indulge in lots of activities. All the girls and women arrived at the party dressed in tutus, fairy wings, and flower crowns. And everyone admired the butterfly balloons, the crystallized flowers, and the fairy dust, and enjoyed the games and refreshments. It was a special day for Kasim and Eboneé's baby girl, Emani. And by the end of the party, Kasim and Eboneé agreed that bachelor's or bachelorette's parties weren't necessary. Nothing could top the birthday party and creating special memories for their princess.

Planning the wedding began immediately after the party. Eboneé, Parish, and Adaeze went into full gear, doing whatever it took to pull together the wedding of Eboneé's dreams. Eboneé had had her sights set on St. Mary's Cathedral ever since Kasim proposed to her. She'd visited the church on numerous occasions, and with each visit, she'd felt as if she was returning home. The church had felt welcoming the moment she stepped through the doors during each visit. It was a feeling akin to what she'd experienced before and during the family

barbecues that her family had when she was younger.
The church was perfect; the problem she faced was the
two-week window, since St. Mary's was a popular venue
for weddings.

Two days after the birthday party, Eboneé was still
waiting to hear if the church would have an opening for
her wedding ceremony. This uncertainty distracted her
as she worked in her office, to the point where it was
difficult for her to really focus on all the other things that
had to be done. Eboneé was excited, but not as excited as
she wanted to be, because of the unknown. As she was
considering whether to contact the church again, Parish
burst through the door.

"Eboneé, is it all right if I give you your wedding
present early?" Parish asked.

"Parish, having you, my singing maid of honor, is gift
enough."

"I had this whole speech prepared, but I can't hold it in
any longer. I was able to pull some strings, with the help
of Kwame, and guess who will be getting married at St.
Mary's Cathedral?"

"Oh my God, Parish! Are you serious?" Eboneé
squealed.

"Very much so. All you have to do is show up. We took
care of everything else."

Tears ran down Eboneé's face as she hugged Parish.
Everything was coming along perfectly now. Parish had
put the icing on the cake for her.

The big day was approaching, and for the past week,
Eboneé hadn't been able to keep anything down. She
figured it had to be the wedding day jitters getting the

best of her. As a result, she had shed some weight, and because of it, she had been bumping heads with Kasim. It was as if Kasim had a built-in weight-loss detector, and it had been going off nonstop for days. He kept complaining about how much thinner Eboneé looked and airing his distaste for fragile women. Especially his woman.

The evening before they would be joined in matrimony, Kasim became a little unhinged when he walked into the master bath following Eboneé's shower.

"Hey, baby. I am just finishing up," she said. "Did you want to join me one last time in the bedroom as my fiancé?"

"No. That's fine."

She abandoned the bath towel that had been draped around her. "Are you sure? It would be your last chance to take advantage of an unwed woman," she said, trying to entice him.

"If the woman that I fell in love with was standing before me, that suggestion would be a no-brainer."

"What are you trying to say, Kasim?" She snatched her robe off the sink and put it on.

"You're not the same person. You've been brainwashed by society to think that a bride must look thin. Instead of remaining the woman that the man you're marrying fell in love with, you've starved yourself into looking like someone that won't be able to keep me aroused. Your voice alone used to turn me on. During these past few weeks, your voice has been strained, and half the time, if you hadn't been right in front of me, I wouldn't have recognized who I was speaking too. Nothing about an unhealthy woman is sweet or stimulating."

"Sometimes you can be so cruel and insensitive. How can you say something like that to me the night before we're to marry? How do you think that makes me feel, Kasim?" she barked.

"When you gain weight and have weight on you, it arouses me. I am in love with a heavier you. That's who I have been attracted to from day one. You know all of this already, and you and I both know who the real selfish and insensitive person in here is," he retorted. With that, he turned on his heels and stormed out of the house.

Eboneé stood there, her heart heavy, as tears streamed down her face. She and Kasim only ever disagreed when the topic was her losing weight. Eboneé had always been comfortable with her thickness. She'd never been one to follow the latest weight-loss fads. Bold and beautiful was who she was, and she loved everything about herself. She could not help that the wedding jitters had caused her to lose weight, and she knew she would put it back on after the wedding. And one of the advantages of having lost the weight was that her wedding dress, which had been a little snug, fit perfectly now. Eboneé didn't want to have Kasim's mother's wedding dress altered any more than what Adaeze had done already. She'd fallen in love with the dress the moment that she'd laid eyes on it. So the weight loss had happened at the perfect time.

Parish and Adaeze arrived at Kasim and Parish's place to do the final preparations for the wedding ceremony and spend the night shortly after Kasim stormed out of the house. Eboneé spirits were down, and both women noticed right away.

"What's bothering you, Ebb?" Parish asked as they sat in the living-room area.

Tears poured from Eboneé's eyes like water through a levee. She was too choked up to speak.

"She's crying! What's wrong, Eboneé?" Adaeze re-marked.

"I have lost weight from wedding nerves, and Kasim is no longer attracted to me. He doesn't want me any longer," Eboneé explained, then sobbed even harder.

You're beautiful no matter what," Parish insisted.

"This is not true. My brother loves you. I've never seen him this happy before," Adaeze interjected.

"Why did you say, 'No matter what,' Parish?" Eboneé asked, ignoring Adaeze's comment. It was hard for her to wrap her mind around Adaeze's words, as she had been tripped up by Parish's statement.

"You lost some weight. I know you love all your curves and wouldn't have it any other way. Your self-acceptance is one of the things that has given me the confidence that I needed to love my roundness. And whether you're really curvy or not, you're still beautiful," Parish explained.

"She's right, Eboneé. You're still beautiful, and you probably really are suffering from wedding day nerves. It's normal. My emotions were all over the place when I got married," Adaeze chimed in.

"It's a few pounds. How is that even noticeable? Especially to the point where Kasim is disgusted by the sight of me and the sound of my voice," Eboneé mused.

"I am sure he didn't mean anything that he might have said. He is nervous, just like you are. You'll see. He will be apologizing when he sees you in that beautiful dress," Adaeze said, coming to her brother's defense.

"Eboneé, she's right. Those were male nerves speaking. He didn't mean any of it. And I think you lost a little more than a few pounds. I thought you were starving yourself or were pregnant, with morning sickness. Remember how much weight you'd lost when you realized you were pregnant with Emani?"

Sirens went off in Eboneé's head as Parish spoke. She knew she hadn't been adhering to a strict diet or an exercise regime. And she wondered if wedding jitters really could cause the severe nausea she'd been experiencing. After Parish and Adaeze reassured her that she was, in fact, the most beautiful bride-to-be in the world, they both turned in for the night. Eboneé wasted no time locating a pregnancy test that she had tucked away under the sink in their master bath. As she took the test, Parish's words stayed in the front of her mind. If she'd omitted carbs for a long period of time, she would understand her weight loss. But the weight had started dropping less than three weeks ago. And why was she so nauseous?

I am sure I am overreacting, Eboneé thought as she paced back and forth, waiting for the test to reveal to her whether she was going to be blessed.

Minutes later, she looked down at the pregnancy-test stick. *A line.*

"Oh my goodness! It cannot be, can it? I am marrying the man of my dreams while carrying our second child," she said aloud. She lowered herself into a kneeling position and thanked God for continuously blessing her and her family.

CHAPTER THIRTEEN

Kasim had never been a huge drinker, but a drink was all that he needed and wanted. He was upset with himself for speaking the way that he had to Eboneé. However, he was really disappointed with Eboneé. One of the attributes that she possessed that he'd fallen in love with was her confidence and her willingness to break the norms that society set. Eboneé reminded Kasim of being back home in Nigeria. He belonged with her. She could be related to him by blood, given how connected he felt to her. Her size wasn't the only attribute that had won him. It was her desire to maintain it and not be afraid if she tipped the scale occasionally. For Eboneé to willingly change into someone else right before his eyes outraged Kasim. And because of it, he longed for a stiff drink with his cigar.

Kwame had pulled together a man-themed gathering for Kasim and his groomsmen, and they were all enjoying themselves. Although he had been against having a bachelor party, Kasim had allowed Mitaire and Kwame to convince him to have a man-themed gathering. They had pointed out that the get-together wouldn't be anything like a traditional bachelor party. It would be just a few of the fellas seeing him through his transition to marriage.

Even though Kasim had asked Mitaire to be his best man, Kwame had been pulling things together for the wedding, as he was the most familiar with the man Kasim had become. Mitaire knew the youthful Kasim, and so Kasim felt it was only right that he be by his side during the wedding ceremony. Kwame had agreed and was perfectly content with his role as one of the master planners of Kasim's big day. Over the years, Kasim and Kwame had become like brothers, thanks to their wives' sisterhood. While their initial introduction had been rather rocky, they'd come a long way. Kwame hadn't been particularly fond of Eboneé at the beginning, as he'd felt she was responsible for the backlash that his wife received after her promotional photo was made public. Although Kwame and Parish had reached a mutual understanding about that photo, so to speak, he had still struggled not to place the blame solely on Eboneé. When Eboneé would come around or they'd run into each other, Kwame had made sure not to go out of his way to speak to Eboneé. Although he'd known his actions were not of God, he'd struggled with being cordial to her.

For instance, when Eboneé had organized a birthday celebration for Parish at her favorite restaurant last year, Kwame had been in attendance, but when Eboneé had kept going out of her way to make conversation with him, he'd given her the cold shoulder. Kasim watched Eboneé's facial expression change each time Kwame spoke to her, and he knew Kwame was giving her a hard time. Kasim became defensive and asked if he could have a moment to speak with Kwame outside the restaurant.

"Hey, man, is everything all right?" Kwame inquired once they were standing on the sidewalk.

"I am not sure. You tell me. I am not one to beat around the bush or make waves. However, I would be lying if I said I didn't pick up on your interaction with my wife. I also wouldn't be a man if I sat by and allowed it to happen. Is there a problem that I need to be made aware of?"

"Not at all, brother. If you think there is something going on with us, you can relax," Kwame said and chuckled.

"That is by far the least of my worries. I am aware of the public humiliation that you caused my wife. She let it go and asked that I do the same. It's just that I can see that you're still carrying and holding on to something. And because of that, I asked you to come outside so we can clear things up. I will not allow my wife to be made uncomfortable, especially in my presence and at the hands of another man. So, what do we need to do to fix this?"

"You know what? You're right, and I am wrong. I owe you and Eboneé an apology. None of what transpired is or was her fault. In fact, it all worked together for my wife's and my good. I was wrong, brother." He extended his hand.

They dapped it up, and from that day forward, they had been the best of friends. Kasim and Eboneé had even become members of Kwame's church. Although Kwame was a man of the cloth, he was also human, Kasim would often say. He felt Kwame was as real as a man could be, and he respected him. Kasim had never been a spiritual man; however, his brotherhood with Kwame had allowed him to see things differently.

Being that Kwame had come to know Kasim quite well, he was certain something wasn't right when he watched Kasim throw back four shots of Hennessy back-to-back at the man-themed get-together. In all the time that he'd known Kasim, Kwame had never seen him drink anything but a glass or two of wine, and so the heavy drinking alarmed him.

"Hey, brother, you want to slow down and tell me what's going on?" Kwame asked when he joined Kasim at the bar. Kwame had rented out a suite at the hotel Kasim worked at, as it was a few blocks away from the church.

"Yes! Hey, man. Are you ready for tomorrow?" Kasim slurred.

"The question is, Are you ready? But I have another question. What's with this?" He pointed at the empty shot glasses.

"Eboneé is allowing the women she works for on television to brainwash her. She's lost so much weight that she's unrecognizable, Kwame. I didn't even recognize her body when I saw it today. It was like I was in the bathroom, looking at a naked stranger. Almost as if I was cheating on my woman, but she was the one standing there."

"Maybe you have had a little too much to drink, because I saw Eboneé yesterday, and she looked the same, minus a few pounds."

"That's my point. The minus the few pounds. She has no reason to lose anything."

"Knowing Eboneé, she's not trying to lose weight, the way that your mind is telling you she is. You have to remember, you two went from planning a sweet sixteen–type celebration for your three-year-old to planning a royal wedding. Now, I am no mathematician, but it seems to me that you two, primarily Eboneé, have pulled this off in a really short amount of time. So, yeah, it would be abnormal if she didn't drop a few pounds. Your nerves have allowed your mind to create something that isn't there, man. Trust me, your wife is the poster child for all full-figured women. I know, because my wife is her protégée."

They erupted in laughter.

Kasim allowed what Kwame had said to him to settle, and then he slept on it. He didn't want anything to interfere with yet another day he had designated as the happiest day of the life that he'd shared with Eboneé. Emani was the daughter he'd dreamed of, and his baby sister was in the States to celebrate his daughter's birthday as well as his new beginning with Eboneé as his wife. Kasim had trouble concealing his emotions. At the thought of the upcoming wedding, tears slipped from his eyes.

When he entered the church the next morning, Kasim was grinning from ear to ear. He was ready to receive his bride. As he stood in anticipation at the altar, awaiting his bride, he felt his heart skip several beats. The doors opened, and his stomach fell to his feet. It was happening, and he couldn't contain his emotions. Tears of joy ran down his face as he anticipated that first glimpse of Eboneé. But it was a frantic Parish who entered the church. She ran toward her husband.

"Kwame," she croaked when she was several feet from him.

Kwame ran to her, as the fear in his wife's voice frightened him. When he turned to retrace his steps back to the altar, where Kasim and Mitaire still stood,

Kwame's look of horror made it down the aisle before he did. Kasim's heart hammered in his chest as he counted the steps Kwame took to return to the front of the church.

"Kasim, Eboneé needs you. Something happened to Emani—" Kwame began.

"What do you mean, something happened?" He charged toward the door and ran into Parish.

"Someone took her, Kasim. Hurry! Eboneé needs you," Parish said frantically.

Kasim instantly felt life leave his frame. His worst nightmare had materialized before him. The recent abductions in the neighborhood had alarmed him, but he hadn't been fearful. He and Eboneé made sure to have Emani with them at all times. If she wasn't with one of them, she was with Nurse Rebecca, who had remained in their employ and had turned into everything that they needed her to be for Eboneé and Emani. He'd thought Eboneé had been overreacting when she insisted she carry Mace and a pocketknife when she wasn't with him. All these details rushed through his mind as he made his way outside.

CHAPTER FOURTEEN

Six months later . . .

Eboneé's life had been stripped down. She'd been left alone and pregnant. Kasim hadn't returned home since Emani's abduction. He had cut off all communication and had gone home to Nigeria with Adaeze and Mitaire. Snot ran from her nostrils and tears streamed down Eboneé's cheeks, leaving tracks on her glowing umber skin, as she turned the pages of memories in the discolored album as she sat alone on the sofa in the home she'd once shared with Kasim and Emani. Then her hand stopped, and Eboneé stared, captivated, at image before her. It was the picture Parish had taken of her the day Kasim proposed to her. She refused to look away. She shuddered with grief.

Eboneé tried to force herself to reflect on the unforgettable moments leading up to the day her life did a complete U-turn, stripping her source of happiness from her. But her hands clenched and became shaking fists as she fought a desperate battle against sorrow. Today was the anniversary of Kasim's wedding proposal. Although she'd been trying to repair the pieces of her life as best she could, when she cried, there was a rawness to it, indicating that the past was still an open wound.

After Emani's abduction, Eboneé and Kasim had been interviewed by detectives for what felt like a thousand times. When forty-eight hours had passed since the abduction, Eboneé and Kasim had been informed that the chances of finding her were slim. That the first twenty-four hours were crucial, and that they didn't have any leads. When the words left Detective Simmons lips, Kasim lost it. He assured Eboneé that the chances of her ever seeing him again weren't even slim. They were zero. He promised that he would never step foot in the same space she inhabited ever again. Kasim blamed Eboneé for Emani's disappearance, and he wanted nothing else to do with her from that day forward.

After Kasim left home, he stayed with Adaeze and Mitaire for two weeks at Eboneé's old place. Adaeze helped ease Eboneé's racing heart the best that she could, but her loyalty remained with Kasim. She started off as the mediator between the two of them, as she recognized that they needed one another during the horrific time. But Kasim refused to take his sister's advice and encouraged her to do as he had done and sever all communication with Eboneé. She wasn't family, and blood was thicker than water, he reminded her. Although it broke Adaeze's heart, as she had grown fond of Eboneé, she granted Kasim his wish. All communication was terminated. When Kasim, Adaeze, and Mitaire left Eboneé's apartment to return to Nigeria, they left their cell phones behind. Eboneé had no way of communicating with them thereafter. They left no forwarding address, too.

When her calls to Adaeze's phone kept going straight to voicemail, Eboneé feared that she and Mitaire had left the country. She talked Parish into accompanying her to the apartment to check. When they walked inside the apartment and found three phones and a note attached, Eboneé picked up the note and saw that Adaeze had penned it. But she couldn't get past the first line, which said that returning home to Nigeria was the only thing that would make this situation somewhat bearable for Kasim. Eboneé was devastated. Her entire world had been stripped from her, and there wasn't anything that she could do to fix it. And she was pregnant.

"This can't be happening, Parish. How could he leave me like this?" She eyeballed the note.

"I am so sorry, Ebb. I don't understand any of it at all. But I need you to try to calm down. You're pregnant," Parish told her friend.

"How can I, Parish? Seriously, how can I calm down?" She tore the note into tiny pieces. "I can't read this."

A tear escaped from the corner of Parish's eye. She hated to see her friend suffer.

"I thought he loved me, Parish. This isn't love. We lost our little girl, I am pregnant, and to add insult to injury, he abandoned me. Do you know how I feel right now?"

"You're pregnant? When did you find out? Never mind all of that. If it'll make you feel better at this moment, we can tear this whole place up." She knocked a lamp from the coffee table.

They completely destroyed everything that was sitting or standing in the living room. As Eboneé threw, tossed, and broke things, she was overcome by a sense of relief. As she headed to the kitchen, Eboneé's phone rang, startling her.

"H-Hello?" she panted into the phone.

"Hello? Mrs. Oringo?"

"This is Eboneé." She cut her eye at Parish.

"We are at your home. I have some news, but I must wait until I see you to share it. How soon can you get here?" Detective Simmons said.

"N-Now. I will be there in ten minutes," she said, then disconnected the call.

"Who was that? Is it about Emani?" Parish quizzed. "Dear God, we need you now."

"It was Detective Simmons. He told me nothing. I assume what we've feared the most has been confirmed. Unless it is about Kasim. I really don't know, Parish. I don't think I can take much more. It feels like my heart is being cut piece by piece with a knife. That's how bad my chest is hurting."

"'God won't give you more than you can bear,' is what I am supposed to say, and believe, but right now I don't know what to say or think. I will call Kwame and have him meet us at your place. We need his help right now."

Eboneé wasn't in any condition to drive, and neither was Parish. Both of their emotions had been in overdrive for so long. When Parish phoned Kwame, he wasn't too far from where they were, and offered to drive them over to what had been Eboneé and Kasim's home.

When they arrived at the house, Detective Simmons greeted Eboneé before she got out of the car. "I have some great news for you, Mrs. Oringo."

"We are not married. He left me. Please stop calling me that. My name is Eboneé," she growled.

"My apologies, ma'am. But as I was saying, I have some great news. We found Emani."

Eboneé was unable to make it very far from Kwame's car. When she took a step, her legs gave way, and she passed out. The detective could not revive her, so he called for an ambulance, and she was rushed to the hospital.

The moment Eboneé came to in a hospital bed, she had trouble processing where she had been and what had happened.

"Hey, there. Glad to see you're back with us." Parish stroked her face.

"What happened? I had a nightmare that Emani was kidnapped on my wedding day and Kasim left me. It felt so real, Parish. My heart is racing just thinking about it."

"I-It wasn't a dream, Eboneé," Parish replied, her voice dropping.

"So, what you're saying is I am alone and I have no one? Oh, correction. I am pregnant and alone? Is that what you're saying, Parish?"

"No, that that's not what—"

"Mommy!" Emani shouted as Detective Simmons carried her into the room.

Eboneé couldn't believe her eyes. She thought she was hallucinating. "Parish, am I dreaming? Is that really her?" Overcome with emotion, she trembled uncontrollably.

"Yes, this is really your baby girl," Detective Simmons confirmed as Emani leaped from his arms onto the bed and hugged Eboneé.

During an attempted kidnapping of twin ten-year-old girls, Shelby Garrett, a thirty-two-year-old custodian for the local library, was arrested. Shelby was trying to muscle the girls, named Tatiana and Taylah, into his car as they made their way home from basketball tryouts at school. A Good Samaritan intervened, wrestled Garrett to the ground, and held him down until police arrived. After seven hours of interrogation and a little roughing up, Garrett admitted that he was responsible for a number of kidnappings that had taken place over the years, but he insisted that he'd never hurt any of the girls and that it had been just to make his grieving mother, Cicely, happy.

Cicely's two-year-old daughter, Ramani, had been abducted and murdered five years prior. Each year, on the eve or anniversary of Ramani's passing, Shelby would kidnap little girls that were the same age that Ramani would be if she were alive. He began to get sloppy and thought the police were on to him, so he began kidnapping little girls that he thought were the same age as Ramani was when she was kidnapped.

During their investigations, the NYPD Special Victims Unit was able to narrow down Garrett's place of residence, as he refused to give it up. He said he was protecting his mom and little sisters. When the officers arrived on the scene, they found six girls, including Emani, that had gone missing over a period of four years. All were between the ages of two and seven. Three of the girls had been there for four years. They were two and three when they were abducted, and so they considered Cicely their mom. All the girls appeared to be well cared for. When they were found, their hair was in pigtails, with huge pink bows attached. They were all dressed in ballerina slippers and tutus. Each of the bedrooms looked fit for a princess: pink walls, lots of glitter, and dolls and toys galore. When the officers arrived, the girls were having a tea party with Cicely. She and her son were arrested and were being held without bail. After a full examination of all the girls, they were returned to their families.

CHAPTER FIFTEEN

Parish and Kwame were totally unnerved by everything that had transpired during and after "the wedding that didn't happen." After Emani's abduction, they had been as strong as they could be for Eboneé and had even moved her into their home with them so that she wouldn't be alone. Parish couldn't imagine not being by Eboneé's side. She carried her friend's pain in her own heart and unloaded it all on Kwame behind closed doors. While in the presence of Eboneé, Parish did her best to be strong and to conceal her pain and sometimes her tears. Kwame would pray with her every morning and anytime she left their bedroom so that God granted her the strength she needed to help Eboneé.

Kwame spent a lot of time at his blossoming church, but he made sure to be available if and when Parish called. Eboneé had been attending services on Sundays. She said only God, alongside Parish and Kwame, would be able to get her through it all. Eboneé's pain had brought Parish and Kwame closer. They couldn't imagine losing or walking away from each other. They'd been through a lot together from the day they met. Kwame said their heartaches had prepared them to be a source of strength for Eboneé and everyone else that God sent their way. Before the abduction Parish hadn't been as committed to the ministry as Kwame, but Eboneé recent trials drew her closer to the ministry. She decided to work with Kwame full-time in ministry once Eboneé was back on her feet.

Parish's music career hadn't taken off the way that she'd envisioned it would. It had all started out with a bang, but her unwillingness to spend days away from Kwame had taken a toll on her career. Parish hadn't been fully healed from the rape, and this had affected all areas of her life, including her singing career. For instance, she was still afraid to be alone with more than one male at a time. She would never forget one particular incident. It was when she was working on a song as a featured soloist for one of the top gospel artists. She was at the recording studio, and Kwame was supposed to pick her up, but he was running late. A few of the engineers were there, wrapping up. When they saw that Parish was still there, they asked if she wanted to work on a song that they'd been working on until Kwame came. She agreed to do it, but then she found herself in the booth with the recording engineer and the producer. Parish had a panic attack.

"What are you doing? Get away from me!" She swung her headphones.

"Parish, we are not going to hurt you. Are you on something? Please calm down," the recording engineer told her.

"No! I am perfectly fine. Get away from me." She swung the headphones again as if her life depended on it.

As Kwame entered the studio, he heard his wife shouting and ran to her aid. When he entered the booth, the recording engineer and the producer both had their hands in the air, as if surrendering, and were pleading with his screaming wife.

"Parish, it's me, baby. I am here. Everything is all right. They're not trying to hurt you," Kwame told her

She ran into his open arms.

Following that incident, word got around, and no one felt comfortable working with Parish. She became the talk of the gospel world and was pretty much blackballed, as everyone saw her as a lawsuit waiting to happen. No one wanted to sing with her, and her album wasn't selling. Kwame insisted she seek counseling. He said that God gave therapists gifts to help hurting people and that she needed to take advantage of it.

Parish was embarrassed by her actions and hurt that she had been ostracized. She wanted to be free of the hold that the marines had on her. If she continued to allow what they had done to her to make her fearful, it meant that they'd won, and Parish refused to be their hostage any longer. Seeing what Eboneé was dealing with made Parish do an internal checkup, and she agreed she needed help. Parish sought counseling, and Kwame followed suit. They wanted to be deal with all the things that had been haunting them. Kwame said in order for them to be great friends, leaders, and lovers, they had to get the junk of their past out of the way.

Therapy was just what Kwame and Parish had needed. They could feel the impact that it had on them. A huge weight that they hadn't realized they were carrying was lifted. Life looked better from the new vantage point. No matter what was going on, they found the good in it. So much so that they made love at any given moment. Even on the days when life seemed to suck them dry. They found something good in it and celebrated in their birthday suits.

After two and a half months of therapy, Parish had never felt happier. However, she had been so caught up in rediscovering herself and healing that she hadn't realized she hadn't had her period in nine and a half weeks. By then Eboneé had moved back into the home that she'd once shared with Kasim. Rebecca was there, which made life much easier for Eboneé, who was hugely pregnant and was now a single parent to Emani.

In an effort to pick up the pieces of her life, Eboneé hosted a dinner party in honor of her guardian angels, Kwame and Parish. Parish put up a fight and declared that a party in their honor was unnecessary, but Eboneé insisted.

During dinner, Parish suddenly felt quite nauseated.

"Parish, do you need some water?" Rebecca questioned, noticing that the color had left Parish's face.

"I think I am fine—" Parish began, but then remnants of her lunch made their way into her lap.

"Dear God, we are having a baby," Eboneé announced.

"I think you might be right," Rebecca agreed.

"She's ill, not pregnant, ladies," Kwame said, correcting them.

"How about someone get me a towel or something?" Parish demanded. "Keep your theories to yourself."

"Let me help you into the bathroom to get cleaned up," Rebecca volunteered.

"I should have a pregnancy test in the drawer by the shower," Eboneé announced.

While she was changing into the dress Eboneé insisted she borrow, Parish decided to take Eboneé's advice. She went into the bathroom and took the pregnancy test.

"Kwame, please come here," she shouted from the bathroom ten minutes later.

"Yes, baby?" he called as he ran into the bathroom.

"God answered our prayers." She placed the test in his hands.

Although they'd say they hadn't been trying to get pregnant, they had prayed and asked God to bless them with a child.

"I guess practice made perfect, because you're going to be a father, Kwame."

They embraced one another and cried tears of joy.

CHAPTER SIXTEEN

Returning home to Nigeria had been an impulsive act, and it had been eating away at Kasim ever since his arrival. But he had refused to be with Eboneé for another minute. Kasim hadn't been back home in Nigeria since he left decades ago. The same regret and failure that he'd been adamant about avoiding in the States had greeted him with a vengeance in Nigeria. The deaths of his wife and unborn child had occupied all his waking hours since the instant he stepped off the airplane after a thirteen-hour flight. The tragedy of their deaths wouldn't leave him, and he was filled with guilt and regret. Anger began to strangle him as his thoughts moved to the moment he decided it was time to leave America for good.

The last thing Kasim had envisioned after he moved to the States was losing another child, as well as a fiancée. In his mind, Eboneé had been kidnapped and murdered along with Emani. He couldn't face her; she was dead to him now. Adaeze had tried her best to reason with him before they left New York, but he'd refused to hear anything that she had to say. He remembered one conversation in particular.

"Kasim, you cannot really believe what happened is Eboneé's fault," Adaeze said.

"Was she not responsible for keeping watch over my daughter?"

"Yes, but we were all there, and it happened under all our noses."

"Where is Naija?"Kasim asked.

"She's in the bed. Why do you ask?"

"Because you have never been so caught up or so malnourished that you were prevented from keeping an eye on and protecting your daughter. So yes, all of this is her fault."

"Kasim, I cannot even imagine or begin to feel what you're possibly going through right now. But what I do know without a shadow of a doubt is that this woman loves you and Emani. She'd give her life before she'd allow something to happen to you or your daughter."

"You have a point there. She gave up her life, all right. All the weight loss caused her to selfishly lose herself, and she lost the nurturing abilities that a healthy woman possesses."

"You're not making sense, Kasim. Her losing a few pounds had nothing to do with what happened. Some monster is responsible for kidnapping that child. You cannot punish Eboneé."

"Whose side are you on? You're my flesh and blood, not her. I am the one that has been punished and is suffering because of her selfish actions."

"Two wrongs don't make a right, Kasim."

"We're done discussing this, Adaeze. I have to think about what I am going to do. I don't ever want to see that murderer's face."

"Kasim, do you hear yourself? Eboneé is not a murderer. Please stop saying that. You're scaring me right now. I am afraid to return home right now. I don't know what you're capable of doing."

"You don't have to worry about that. I am going home with you. This isn't where I want or need to be anymore."

"You cannot walk away from your life here, from everything like this, Kasim."

"I have nothing left here. My fiancée and my child are gone."

No matter what Adaeze said back in New York, Kasim wouldn't budge. Emani's abduction was all over the news, and that made him look weak. As if he wasn't man enough to protect his family. He refused to walk around in humiliation. He cursed Eboneé for making him look like a disgrace. She had murdered what they had, and Kasim could never forgive her. Which was why he was determined to leave America.

Being back in Nigeria was bittersweet for Kasim. He had to face the fact that he'd run away from his problems; however, that reckoning, he believed, was easier to withstand than dealing every moment with the reality that his daughter had been kidnapped and murdered. Since his return, he'd occupied his time by visiting family and old friends. As well as cozying up to his newfound companion, cognac. Since his return, Kasim had spent countless hours in the local shebeen, drinking his troubles away. Adaeze had become so worried about her brother's dependency on alcohol that she'd asked Mitaire to keep an eye on Kasim. Mitaire had never been a drinker, either, but on several occasions when he joined Kasim at the shebeen to watch out for him, he found himself heavily intoxicated too.

One evening, during their drunken stupor, Kasim admitted to Mitaire why he had left his home in Nigeria in the first place.

"You know a man's responsibility is to be a provider and a protector to his family, and I've failed. Had I been here, Zoya and my unborn child would still be here. I cannot believe it took losing another child to send me back to what I've been running from. I feel helpless and less than a man. I let this happen twice because I trusted a woman." Kasim's eyes watered.

"You cannot take blame for anything that has happened. None of this is or was scripted. Life has a way of handing us things beyond our control or imagination. I can't imagine what you're going through, and I understand your pain, but I do know none of this is your or Zoya's or Eboneé's fault."

Kasim had never confessed his guilt and remorse over leaving Zoya behind to anyone other than Eboneé, although Mitaire and the rest of Kasim's family had already guessed his feelings on the matter. Mitaire was a mortician, and so he explained to Kasim how some grieving families would come to the morgue and ask to speak with their deceased family member. The request always sounded strange to Mitaire, but then he'd see the relief on the family members' faces after they'd said their piece to the deceased. It was as if a burden had been lifted. With that, he stopped drinking and sat a while to sober up, telling Kasim that he would drive him to the location where Zoya had lost her life. Kasim knew the location, but he had vowed he would never travel on or near that road, but this time he agreed.

They set off two hours later. When arrived at the site of a memorial that had been erected for Zoya, Mitaire got out of the car, went around to the passenger side, and opened the car door for Kasim. They headed up a path together. When they reached the memorial, Kasim felt his heart stop. He thought he had died and was having an out-of-body experience. A lump formed in Kasim's throat.

"Take your time. You'll feel so much better when you're done, trust me," Mitaire told him before he turned and headed back down the path.

Kasim sat before the wooden cross, around which were stuffed animals, pictures of Zoya when she was younger and when she was pregnant, and her last sonogram. Every emotion, from anger, sadness, and frustration to guilt and shame, that Kasim had been squelching resurfaced in that moment, and he cried and moaned as if he were an infant in need of a feeding.

"This is so wrong. It was not supposed to happen like this. Why did you allow this to happen? I did everything that a man was supposed to do. You knew you should not have been out after the sun went down, Zoya. Because you disobeyed everything that I taught you, you're no longer here. Our child had to suffer because of your disobedience. You were fine just the way you were, but you allowed other people's opinions to cause you to not take care of yourself the right way. Had you been healthy, you and our child would still be here. I thought I had found the woman of my dreams in America, but she is just like you, a selfish murderer. Now I must mourn the deaths of two children. I will never forgive you, Zoya. I will never forgive a murderer."

He stood up and kicked and threw the items that surrounded the wooden cross.

CHAPTER SEVENTEEN

Eboneé could not believe her life had got out of control the way that it had and that she was still alive to talk
about it. Never in a million years would she have guessed
that she'd soon be a single mother of two. Even with
all that she'd been through, she would not change any of
it, because if she did, she would not have Emani and she
would not be expecting her second child. Since Kasim's
departure, her nights had been lonely and full of regrets.
However, when she put everything in perspective, the
good outweighed the bad. Her story could have ended
tragically, and she was grateful that it hadn't. It was difficult for her to let go of her thoughts of Kasim, because
the love that she had for him was real. Eboneé had never
felt the love that she had for Kasim with anyone else, and
she had promised herself to redirect that love and pour
every ounce of it into her children.

With everything that had transpired, Eboneé had
taken a leave of absence from B&S Styles. Patrick, her
assistant, was virtually her clone now, and he had been
making it easy for her to take some much-needed time off.
He had shadowed Eboneé's every move when he joined
her company, and in no time, Patrick knew what Eboneé
would think about something before she even thought
it. In the beginning, his ability to read her mind and be
on point had creeped Eboneé out. For instance, when

Eboneé had first met Kasim and had started clocking in during the latter part of the day, Patrick had taken it upon himself to reschedule Eboneé's entire calendar. He had moved every appointment to the late afternoon or early evening and had even sent a bouquet of flowers to each client, confirming the appointment and apologizing for the inconvenience the rescheduling might have caused.

Eboneé prided herself on developing a personal connection with all her clients, and because she loved flowers, she always made sure to find out her clients' favorite variety. She had never shared any of that with anyone, so she was thrown for a loop when Patrick did exactly as she as she would have, though he'd been her employee for only three weeks at that time. To some, Patrick's actions showed he was proactive. But when he shared what he'd done, Eboneé considered letting him go. Eboneé recalled the conversation they'd had that day like it was yesterday.

"Patrick, can I see you for a minute?" Eboneé called, inviting him into her office.

"Sure thing. Did you want to touch base on next week's schedule?"

"No. I think it's fine the way that it is. I wanted to ask you a question."

"This sounds serious. Is everything all right?"

"I am not sure. How did you know to order flowers or, better yet, the type of flowers to send each client? Did you go through my purse and search through my journal?"

Eboneé kept a journal in her purse, and in it, she wrote letters to herself, described her feelings, secrets, and kept track of personal details about her clients.

"First, I want to say that I would never search any of your personal belongings. Secondly, your purse was with you when I ordered the flowers. I would never overstep my boundaries, violate your personal space or trust. You have to believe that," he told her, his voice cracking.

"Then please explain to me how you knew to send flowers and how you knew the type of flowers to send. And how you knew I had planned to do the same."

"Wow. I *am* good. But when I started, and you and I would talk, you shared with me how you wanted to be a florist when you were a child. You loved how flowers always brought a smile to a person's face, and you wanted to be responsible for spontaneously putting smiles on your clients' faces. You also stated you want to have a unique touch with everything that you do, so your clients always remember you. With that in mind, I called each of them to ascertain their availability, as well as their favorite flowers. I thought I'd be leaving your signature, expressing your unique style and grace, and most importantly, I hoped the gesture would leave a smile on the clients' faces."

Eboneé was blown away by Patrick's way of thinking that day, and he had never ceased to amaze her from that day forward. Patrick was always twelve steps ahead of Eboneé, and she cherished him as if he were her child. Patrick was the twenty-year-old son Eboneé had never had. He respected and looked up to Eboneé like a child honored and revered a parent. Patrick had been raised by foster parents. His birth parents had had him when they were just fourteen. They had agreed with their parents that they were too young to raise a child and that putting their child up for adoption following his birth was the best course of action. His foster parents had loved him as their own, but Patrick had always felt something was missing. He said he'd found what had been missing in his life when he met Eboneé.

Eboneé kept herself busy during the day with caring for Emani, going to doctors' appointments, attending counseling, and doing whatever else she could to help keep her mind occupied. She wanted to hate Kasim for abandoning her, but the love she had for him wouldn't allow her to. Getting through the days was easy: Emani gave her joy. Expecting another child excited her as well. But when the sun set, and she was alone in her bedroom, her heart ached. It had been eight months since he left, and still she rocked herself to sleep every night, tears running down her cheeks.

She'd hoped counseling would help her erase him from her mind, fill the gaping hole he'd left inside her, except she'd learned that avoiding her feelings or erasing the past would cause more harm than good. During her counseling sessions, Eboneé had learned that not dealing with things, pushing them out of her mind, was similar to loading a plastic bag with canned goods. After a while, the bag would break from the weight of the cans. And that was what would happen with her if she ran from the issues that had been circling her.

Eboneé tried her best to deal with her feelings and fought through the pain and the embarrassment that Kasim had left her with. While Eboneé was growing up, her cousin had become a teen mom and a single mother. Eboneé had sworn then that she would not become a statistic and follow in her cousin's footsteps. In fact, she hadn't even been sure back then, and later, if she wanted kids. But Kasim had changed her mind, and kids had been all that she wanted and dreamed of. With him, of course. His leaving her alone with one child and one on the way had hurt Eboneé to the core, and she was so ashamed to be a single parent, the very thing she used to judge her cousin for. After sharing her criticism of her cousin with her therapist, Eboneé had been given an exercise that she was now struggling to complete. Two months had passed, and she had come to realize that the only way to complete that exercise was to face her shame head-on.

So she picked up the phone and dialed a number.

"Hello?"

"Hey, Jazzy! How are you doing? How are those babies doing?" Eboneé said into the phone.

Jasmine was Eboneé's older cousin, the one who had gotten pregnant at fourteen and had been on her second child by the age of nineteen.

"How are you doing, Ebb? I've been meaning to give you a call, I am sorry to hear about your daughter, but I'm glad she's home safe and sound? But yeah, girl, their grown now, and I have another on the way."

"Congratulations. And thank you."

"Girl, this is it. I have five kids already. Six is more than enough."

"I agree. And I wanted to call you to apologize to you—"

"Apologize for what?" Jasmine interrupted. "Girl, life distracts all of us. We just have to make an effort to stay in touch from now on."

"You're absolutely right, but that's not what I was talking about." Eboneé took a deep breath before continuing. "When we were younger, I used to judge you. In fact, I thought I was better than you because you had a child at a young age. You became a mother when you were a child yourself. I want to apologize for my ignorance. I was wrong. In actuality, at this moment I can say I admire you for your resilience and perseverance. You didn't allow anything to stop you from going to college and working while you raised your children. I am pregnant and have a three-year-old, and my husband left me. Everything I criticized you about is happening to me, and I deserve it."

"Wow, Ebb. That was huge. I saw how you used to look at me, and yes, it hurt like hell, but we were young and dumb. Just like I was and am, you are a strong woman and can handle everything life is throwing your way. It is not happening because you deserve anything. God is making a warrior out of you. I love you, Ebb, and will make sure to keep in touch and, if you don't mind, visit you sometime."

"I would love that," Eboneé cried into the receiver.

After she hung the phone up, she sat on her bed and sobbed uncontrollably. Eboneé cried so hard after she spoke to Jasmine that her water broke. Her breathing became labored as she continued sobbing. Rebecca overheard her weeping and ran to her aid. When she got to the bedroom and helped Eboneé up from the bed so she could get some air, Eboneé's contractions intensified. She took a step and stopped her in her tracks.

"I don't think I can do this, Rebecca. I can feel the baby between my legs."

Rebecca sat Eboneé back down on the bed, pulled down her pajama pants, and conducted an internal exam. After determining that Eboneé was nine and a half centimeters dilated, Rebecca texted Parish and phoned the ambulance, as well as Eboneé's doctor, who coached her until the ambulance arrived. Rebecca hurriedly washed her hands, grabbed a bucket of warm water and some bath towels from the linen closet. She rushed back into the bedroom and wiped Eboneé's vaginal area, and while doing so, she saw the baby's head crowning.

"Dr. Simpson, I can see the head," she shouted into the phone.

"Okay. Tell Eboneé to breathe. And then tell her to push."

"Okay." Rebecca threw the phone down. "Eboneé, I need you to breathe. And when I tell you to push, I need you to push with all your might, okay?" Rebecca said.

"I'm breathing," Eboneé gasped.

"I don't know what I am doing, but I think you should push now. Push, Eboneé. On the count of three, push as hard as you can. One . . . two . . . three, pushhh."

Eboneé grunted and pushed with everything that she had in her, and ten minutes later, as Parish and the paramedics raced through the front door, she gave birth to a baby boy. Then and there she named him Kasim Kwame Oringo. She had had a feeling all along that she was carrying a boy. Although she had struggled with naming her son after the man who had broken her heart, her first glimpse of the baby had revealed that he was a newborn version of his father, and she knew that there wasn't any other name that would fit him. Her decision to give her son the middle name Kwame had to do with the fact that Parish and Kwame were her children's godparents, and with the fact that Kwame had become the brother, father figure, and protector that Eboneé needed for herself and her children.

CHAPTER EIGHTEEN

After three days in the hospital, Eboneé and Kasim Jr. returned home. Emani couldn't get enough of her little brother. He was like a doll baby to her, and she was very protective of her toys, so now she was protective of little Kasim. Eboneé adored Emani's love for her brother. She was also excited about being the mom of a newborn for the first time in a long time. Even though she knew she'd be doing it alone for a long time, she was all right with that. It had gotten to the point where Eboneé knew for sure she would not be able to be what she needed to be to her kids if she held on to the hurt and pain that Kasim had left her with. She had chosen to enjoy her kids and all that motherhood had to offer.

Eboneé had been communicating regularly with her cousin Jasmine. As it turned out, Jasmine had given birth to her son Jamal the day after Eboneé had Kasim. Since the babies were too young for a playdate, the two cousins agreed to schedule doctor's visits on the same day for their babies and then have brunch together to catch up. While on her way to brunch, Eboneé's phone rang.

"It's a private number," Rebecca informed her from the passenger seat. She had come along to care for the children.

"They can leave a message. I don't do 'private' and need to see his or her number before I answer the phone."

A minute later, the phone rang again.

"It's ringing again. Do you want me to answer it?"

"Sure. Go ahead, since they're so persistent," Eboneé seethed.

"Hello," Rebecca greeted before pulling the phone from her ear.

"Who is it? Is it Parish? Is everything okay?" Eboneé quizzed, noticing the fear on Rebecca's face.

"No, it's Adaeze."

Eboneé's world spun before her eyes. She felt herself becoming light-headed and nauseous, and so she pulled the car over and parked alongside the road. Taking the phone from Rebecca's hand, Eboneé hung up immediately.

"Are you okay?" Rebecca inquired.

"Why would she call now, Rebecca? It has been eight months or so, and she remembered my number all of a sudden? I can't do this. I won't allow them to put me through anymore. I just cannot."

"You don't have—" Rebecca began, but the ringing of the phone interrupted her.

Eboneé answered the call. "What do you want?" she roared into the phone.

"I—I went through my old phone records and found your number. I am here in the States. We need to talk. It's extremely important."

"*Important*? More important than me and my children? There is nothing that you can say that is more important than my children and that will make me come anywhere near you. They are what's important to me, so if it isn't about them, I don't want to hear it," Eboneé snarled. Then she disconnected the call.

Eboneé fumed and had trouble regaining her composure. She had been parked across the street from a park. Rebecca took advantage of the fact that Kasim was sleeping in his car seat, and took Emani to the park to play while Eboneé pulled herself together. As soon as they stepped out of the car, the phone rang once more. Eboneé closed her eyes, hoping it would stop ringing. Adaeze just wouldn't give up. It angered Eboneé even more.

Eboneé picked up. "What do you want? Leave us alone!" she screamed into the phone.

"Please, Eboneé. Please see me. I am so sorry," Adaeze blubbered.

"I don't want to see you. I don't want to hear from you. Lose my number."

"It's Kasim. He's in trouble. He needs you."

Eboneé's stomach curdled as if it were spoiled milk. She couldn't believe what she'd heard. How could he need her? How could Kasim expect her to be there for him when he'd abandoned her and their children? But her heart wouldn't allow her to let go.

"You have five minutes. Talk, or I am hanging up and changing my number," she threatened.

"His anger has gotten him into a lot of trouble. I think he's going to be arrested and sent away for a long time, Eboneé. He brought my husband into this mess, and there's nothing I can do to fix it."

Eboneé couldn't believe what she was hearing, and couldn't picture Kasim getting into something that would bring harm to himself or to anyone around him. Despite her nagging mind telling her to hang up the phone, Eboneé allowed her heart to intervene, and she agreed to meet Adaeze at her place right away. On her way back home, Eboneé rescheduled with Jasmine and asked Parish and Kwame to meet her at the house, as well. She knew Parish would be excited to get out of the house, since she'd been stuck at home for a while now, eating and waiting out the last three months of her pregnancy. When Eboneé, Rebecca, and the kids pulled up to the house, Parish, Kwame, and Adaeze had beaten them there.

"I'll get the kids taken care of," Rebecca volunteered as she and Eboneé got out of the car.

"Thank you," Eboneé told her as Adaeze approached her and caught sight of her children.

"Is that Emani? Oh my God, she's alive?" Adaeze exclaimed.

"You would have known that had you not fled the country with your brother," Eboneé snapped.

"I tried to talk him out of it. I am so sorry. I should have never listened to him. Is the baby yours as well? You've moved on already?"

"What kind of woman do you take me for? And never mind worrying about my children. What is so important that you needed to harass me into meeting with you?"

Before Adaeze answered, Eboneé ushered her, Parish, and Kwame inside, and they all gathered in the living-room area. Adaeze explained that Kasim had been taking his pain out on women in Nigeria. He had been working alongside Mitaire at the mortuary and had been drinking from sunup to sundown. Kasim had used his charm to console grieving women who had lost a loved one. Primarily, widowers, and they had to meet a certain requirement. The women had to be healthy and had to favor Eboneé or Zoya. He'd get to know them, and then he'd kill them. In the eight months that he'd been back home, he had strangled four different grieving women.

Eboneé felt the air evaporating around her as Adaeze spoke. "This isn't making sense, Adaeze. Kasim isn't capable of hurting anyone."

"He hurt you, Eboneé. He hurt you bad when he left," Parish interjected, correcting her.

Eboneé shook her head. "Yeah, but to strangle women? That is insane."

"I thought the same thing until the detectives broke everything down for me. The pieces added up, and it was Kasim that they were looking for. He was living a double life, and Mitaire got caught in the middle of it all."

Adaeze went on to explain to Eboneé that each of the women had the word *murderer* carved into her forehead. And they were raped, urinated on, strangled with a belt, and left for dead. While preparing one of the dead women at the mortuary, Kasim blacked out and began choking the corpse, screaming profanities, and shouting, "Murderer." Mitaire walked in on the frightening scene and wrestled Kasim to the floor. When Mitaire questioned Kasim about his actions, Kasim confessed what he had been doing and begged Mitaire not to tell anyone. And he didn't, until police officers questioned Mitaire as a person of interest in the case. The belts that Kasim had been using to strangle the women belonged to Mitaire.

After an investigation of the items found with each of the bodies, the police officers had been able to trace the belts back to Mitaire. He'd had his initial engraved in all his belts. When Mitaire was a kid, he had had to share everything with his four brothers and had never had anything to himself. Once he was able to acquire things of his own, Mitaire had put his initials on everything that he owned. Especially his belts, because that was one of the main things that his brothers would take from him, and his pants would fall from his waist. As a result, his parents would chastise him for wearing loose pants.

In the end, Mitaire hadn't been charged with anything, but psychologically, he had fallen apart. He had been placed in a mental institution because of it all. Kasim had been arrested and was now awaiting sentencing. He had threatened to take his own life if he didn't see Eboneé one last time.

"The man that you're describing isn't the man that I fell in love with. This has to be a mistake. There's no way he could have done all those things," Eboneé declared. Her lip quivered.

"I wish none of it was true, but it is, Eboneé," Adaeze insisted. "I never could have imagined hearing anyone say those things about my brother. But he's not in a good place. He hasn't been for quite some time. He fell in love with you with a broken heart."

Adaeze's words caused Eboneé's head to spin.

"I think I am going to throw up, Adaeze. How could this happen? All I wanted was to live happily ever after after I met and fell in love with Kasim. I actually fell in love with the fairy tale of love, because he showed me that it was possible. Sometimes I wonder if it was all a lie, but when I look at Emani and Kasim, I know they were meant to give me abundant joy and happiness, so he and I were supposed to happen."

"Don't think like that. He loves you. He's just broken in some areas of his life, and because of this, he's done things that will make it impossible for him ever to come home to any of us."

"What do you mean? Do you really think he'll take his own life?"

"Well, they have him on watch, but they're saying he will more than likely spend the rest of his life behind bars."

Eboneé felt the room circling around her as those words floated from Adaeze's lips. Deep down inside she'd hoped that one day, somewhere down the line, Kasim would come around and would want to be a part of his children's lives. She'd already made up her mind that Kasim was sent by God to show her that love was possible, as well as to bless her with two beautiful children. However, hearing Kasim had been considering taking his life and, if he didn't, would likely spend the rest of his days in jail caused her to experience again the deep pain she'd felt when he abandoned her.

No matter how much love she still felt for Kasim, and no matter how much Adaeze pleaded with her to travel back with her to Nigeria, Eboneé refused to take the trip. The man that had deserted her, and the one who had been thrown behind bars, wasn't the man that she'd fallen in love with. The predicament that Kasim had put himself in wasn't something she wanted to participate in. She didn't want to travel to the other side of the world to see him. She didn't want to talk to him. Adaeze was disappointed by Eboneé's decision, but she promised to stay in touch and to make sure she became a part of Kasim Jr.'s and Emani's lives if Eboneé allowed it.

Eboneé couldn't imagine keeping the kids away from their family, and she planned to share all the good times and the man she'd known Kasim to be with her children. She would continue to pour the love that she had for Kasim into her babies. Especially after learning that Kasim would invariably be spending the rest of his life in prison.

Later, after reflecting on everything that had transpired, Eboneé realized she didn't regret any of it, because she wouldn't have Emani and Kasim if none of it had happened. She found peace with it all. And she knew that one day true love would find her again and would stay forever, and she would experience something similar to the bond that Parish and Kwame had. Eboneé knew it would not be anytime soon, but she told herself that it would happen, that she'd be happily in love forever after, just like her glowing, pregnant best friend, Parish.